Dawn in Catland

Other books by the author:

Bella: An ordinary cat with an extraordinary gift

Stories of Love, Hope and Healing for All Ages

STOP Family Anxiety: A guide for anxiety disorders in parents, grandparents, teenagers and children of all ages

Depression: Light at the End of the Tunnel

The Third Generation

The Elephant's Footprint

The Scent of Oranges

Dawn in Catland

JOAN ZAWATZKY

First published in Australia in 2019 by
VeritaxBooks. Victoria, Australia

Website: www.placeofbooks.com

Cover illustration © Joan Zawatzky
Season illustrations © Joan Zawatzky

Typeset by BookPOD

ISBN: 978-0-9945532-5-6
eISBN: 978-0-9945532-6-3

"I believe cats to be spirits come to earth. A cat, I am sure, could walk on a cloud without coming through."

– Jules Verne

Summer

 # Bella

Water is meant for drinking. Avoid baths,
showers, swimming pools and rain.

Another day of the heatwave in Catland. The cobalt sky is cloudless, dazzling light shimmers and moist air clings to my heavy coat as I lie on the patio floor waiting for a cool breeze. I take a deep breath, sniff the perfumes of flowers and plants lazily and relax. A fly buzzes past, but in this heat. I don't bother to lift my paw to grab it. From the patio, I can keep an eye on events outdoors and in the house.

Handsome Oliver, a Siamese cat who shares the house, sits near me. Our most important Humans are feeling the heat intensely. Karen lies in the shade almost naked sipping a drink from a long glass. Tony wears a tiny piece of material covering his delicate bits. George, the little one, is almost three and scantily dressed too. Tony's grandfather, the oldest Human in the family, affectionately called Pops, is partly covered and sits in the shade. He has wrinkly skin with blotches like a hairless cat.

How ridiculous they look, almost furless. I smile a cat's smile. Humans don't know that we smile inside. They are not meant to be nude and cats aren't meant to wear clothes. Going against nature can cause trouble. How easily their bodies can be burned by the sun or scratched. I have seen them all naked after their showers and on days like today, I almost envy their lack of heavy, body fur. Tony has a strong body with hair on his chest. There is some on his back, arms and legs too. Karen has a curvy shape with little hair except for a bushy patch. The heat intensifies the smell of their bodies. George has a sweet, child's smell. Tony's smell is male and pungent, while Karen's is flowery. I remind myself that Humans are animals who walk on two legs instead of four, but have their own scent.

George moves closer to me. 'Love you beautiful Bell-Bell. It's so...hot.' His small fingers glide over my coat. His touch burns and I flick my tail in annoyance. He moves back. 'Sorry, Bell-Bell...too hot to touch.'

I like George calling me Bell-Bell, his special name for me instead of Bella. Our owner, Karen, has taught him to be gentle with us and not to pull our tails or ears. He is an unusual child who knows if I am angry, sleepy or worried. Sometimes he even senses what I am thinking. I sense his moods too. Our intuitive connection is a joy. The older Humans notice our bond and smile. Oliver plays with George, but finds him a little too talkative. Oliver wants to be heard too in his high-pitched Siamese voice. It's a pity that he is missing out on a closer relationship with George.

'Where are you, George?' Karen calls.

'I'm with the kitties near the big door.'

'I should've known that you'd be in the coolest spot with Bella and Oliver.' She bends to pat our heads and smiles. 'You're turning into a cat, Georgie.'

He grabs his mother's hand.

'Come, my darling, we're all going down to the pool to have a swim. The cats can come too.'

He jumps up to follow his mother.

The Humans are enjoying a holiday at home and spending time at their pool. Tony is taking a break from his job and Karen has time off from her work as a counsellor.

Oliver stretches slowly before following them across the parched grass. I prefer to remain inside to watch them from my cool position.

Karen carries food and flasks of cold water to the pool, while Tony erects umbrellas and places easy chairs under the shade. A small chair under the awning is for George. Tony looks up at the blazing sun and reaches for his hat before relaxing in a chair. The others join him under the shade of the umbrellas. Oliver lies next to Tony. Karen, a true mama, keeps an eye on George whether she's cutting fruit or chatting.

She feels in her bag for her hand phone. 'George, I want to take a picture of you and Oliver with the pool in the background. Stand still and smile.'

So much attention is heaped on this small dark-haired child. She has prepared special food for him as well as a change of clothing in case there's a speck of dirt on him. He is treated like a prince of a Human and he smiles happily. Adoration and care are his parents' gifts.

The house is quiet apart the buzzing of insects. All the fun is happening across the grass at the pool. I am lonely, but anything watery – pools, baths, rain or snow upsets my *catquilibrium*. Other than for drinking, I dislike water. My dislike of water comes from fear, and I know it.

After battling with myself, I leave the safety of the patio and step lightly, alert for danger. I hesitate at the high fence, erected to prevent George and other children from coming to harm by falling into the pool when adults are not about.

Karen spots me. 'There you are Bella. Come to me!'

At my slow pace, I go to her. She strokes my head gently.

'Sit next to me in the shade, Precious. Don't be afraid of the water.'

As Tony lifts George into the water, the small Human squeals with delight and paddles to the edge of the pool.

Pops puts down the book he is reading. 'I can't remember the weather ever as hot as this…and I've been around for a very long time. I'm glad you can all cool down.'

'It's a perfect time to have a swim with us, Pops,' Tony says with a grin. 'The pool has been a wonderful gift from you, but you haven't even swam in it!'

Pops laughs. 'I prefer showers and warm baths these days, but I'm glad you're all having fun. I'm enjoying watching everyone swim especially Georgie doing his paddle.'

Tony laughs too as he watches George play in the water.

'Whooo whooo!' George shouts as he jumps into the pool creating a huge explosion.

I keep my distance from the droplets and sprays. Once George is tired of swimming, it is peaceful under the awning. That is, until Karen produces a fat tube of white stuff that she calls sunscreen. She smears it on her face and body and carefully covers George with it, despite his complaints. Tony spreads some on his body too.

I know what's coming my way. Karen holds me tightly, covers my pink nose and the tips of my ears with the slimy cream. *Meow, meow!* I squirm even more than George did. It feels horrid.

She pats my head. 'Stop being a drama queen, Sweetie! You're a ginger with a pink nose and ears. You'll hate sunburn.'

Lucky Oliver with his dark nose and ears avoids the entire procedure.

A whisper of a cool breeze encourages me into the sunlight closer to Karen. I touch her affectionately with my paw. She is my favourite Human – rare and precious. I owe her more than I can repay her in all my cat lives. I will be devoted to her forever.

At six weeks old I was a helpless, unwanted kitten thrown

near a pile of slimy garbage. It was Karen, who heard my desperate *meows* and rescued me. No one stopped or heard my call, except a dog that sniffed me. As it began to growl, I heard a gentle, human voice – Karen's voice.

'Don't worry little one, I'm here...I'll look after you,' she said softly.

I don't want to think of what the dog would've or could've done to me if she had not been walking past just then and heard my desperate cry. She yelled at the dog until it ran away. Then she scooped me into her arms, wrapped me in her warm jumper and carried me home with her. I knew I could trust her. I was safe. From that day she has understood me, cared for me and shared her life with me. Cat logic tells me that there are no coincidences in cat life. I was intended to survive. Karen and I were meant to be together. It was Karen who gave me my name, "Bella", that means beautiful. Once I had established my territory in the house with my family, my life's path was set and I hoped to find my purpose.

Karen smiles at me and strokes my head tenderly. In the intense heat, tiny drops of water trickle down her face and neck making her aroma more intense than usual. I doubt it's the onions, garlic or spices she likes to eat that have changed her flowery smell. I take a deep breath as I try to remember. Did she smell like this when she was carrying George inside her tummy? I sniff her again and again. Yes, I'm certain of it now. She is carrying one or more kitten babies in her tummy. Isn't nature wonderful! I call Oliver to ask him to confirm my suspicions. He sniffs Karen's body and agrees. She is carrying new life. As hot as I am, I put my ear to her belly to listen. It is very early to tell, but I think she has only one kitten baby inside. My joy for her gathers and it feels as if I will explode. I lick her bare tummy.

'What are you up to Bella? Why are you licking me?'

I look up at her and give her one last lick. How long will it take for her to be aware of the changes in her body?

If only I could give her a present, to show her my affection. I look about. There it is, a large bug. I swipe it with my paw, lift it into my mouth and take it to Karen.

'Something for me, a gift? Thank you, Bella. Put it down, Treasure.'

She strokes me gently. Later, I notice her putting my bug gift into a napkin. Perhaps she is keeping it because it is special. When I think about the new baby, I'm no longer as thrilled. Another tiny Human to deal with like George will be too much to cope with. The endless crying will put an end to my calm. Karen won't have time for me either. I wonder if everyone will make such a fuss over her with a second baby. Will there will be a party and gifts? Tony and Karen adore George, but will they love the new little one as much?

I visit Bastet, the statue of the cat goddess on the dresser in the sitting room, who features powerfully in my life, and dutifully thank her for bringing new life to Karen. Later, when Oliver is asleep, I will visit Bastet for longer.

It is late afternoon. Oliver enjoys swimming and before Tony cleans the pool, Oliver is allowed swim. He has been restless all day anticipating the pleasure of a swim. Perhaps he was a water cat in a past life and liked fishing.

Alert with his eyes fixed on Tony, he waits for the word "swim". As Tony utters the magic word, he runs to the edge of the pool and with a leap he's in the water. After a few initial wriggles, he swims or rather cat paddles. His head with its pointed ears pokes out of the water, his legs move like small motors and his long tail provides balance. Oliver's expression is one of intense pleasure, but I shudder as I watch him. He appears fearless, something I struggle to understand with my terror of water. His athletic body is ideally suited to swimming, and his short coat doesn't drag him down. The Humans are intrigued. They stop whatever they are doing to watch him swim. They find a cat swimming hilarious, but I admire him. Karen laughs holding her tummy and wipes away tears of laughter. Tony's laugh is like a Bengal cat's roar, George jumps up and down giggling and Pops holds his sides as if in pain. When Karen stops laughing, she takes photos of Oliver in the pool.

Tony calls, 'enough!'

Oliver reluctantly stops and climbs out of the pool. Everyone claps, but he dislikes the noise and attention. He shakes himself and dashes away with his wet tail down.

As the sun goes to sleep behind the distant mountains, the Humans collect their belongings as they head for the house. I look back at the dark pool. The glistening water is even scarier now.

Tony is cooking outdoors tonight. The whiff of the meat on the huge, black contraption they call a barbeque makes me hungry. I stand near enough to the sizzling food to be noticed, but avoid flying sparks. My food arrives on a tiny plate – delectable, fragrantly spiced sausage and a small piece of lamb. I lick my lips and luckily more arrives. I look for Oliver who is missing a treat, but I can't see him. He is not in his usual spot under the fan or at the open door. When I find him, he is curled up asleep in the cool wash basin in the bathroom exhausted from his swim. The dripping tap makes the basin even cooler. Karen and Tony follow me into the bathroom and laugh loudly when they see Oliver in the basin. Fortunately for him, they don't disturb him.

Satisfied after their meal, the Humans move to the

television room where they attempt to cool down under the ceiling fan. There is little talk or action as they lounge on the chairs and sofa sipping icy drinks. It is even too hot to sit on or near them, but I lie on the carpet next to Karen's feet and sleep. Huge yawns interrupt my rest.

'Bed calls, but I doubt we'll sleep much in this heat,' Tony complains.

Karen sighs. 'Oh, well, it can't last forever.'

They are asleep at last. Even little George is making soft purring, sounds in his bed. Once the Humans are asleep our secret cat time begins. At night, we are at our most alert, our senses sharp, our vision intense and clear. We perform our final ritual of checking and guarding the house, first our inside territory, then we view our garden through the windows. We delight in the night's intense perfumes wafting through the house and listen to ceilings and walls that creak. Outdoors stray dogs and feral cats hunt for food. Two owls in the high branches of a tree call and frogs add to the orchestra of the night. Mice and cockroaches are on the move in the dark house through the pipes. Oliver has missed his meal and is hungry. He stalks a mouse attracted to a cupboard where food has spilled. He pounces. After enjoying the mouse he catches another. Then he vomits part of their skeletons. Karen will complain about clearing away the remains, but she ought to be pleased that he kills mice.

Our Humans have not noticed the hordes of mice in the roof and in the house searching for food and water. In the heat they double in numbers. I wait near a dripping tap and catch a small mouse. A delicious treat. Oliver is hungry and still hunting.

After a bird's early chirp, I hear a rustle and purr. It is strange that Oliver does not appear to be aware of the sound. I check. His body is relaxed, his ears aren't back or twitching. I follow the source of the sound to the large, comfortable chair. I see nothing, but sense a presence. Slowly I approach the chair. An outline of a fluffy cat with a bushy tail is visible. There is a faint cat scent. I stand before the image respectfully. The ghost cat is Samantha, Karen and Tony's previously beloved cat, who is visiting tonight. In the big bedroom there is a framed photograph of a longhaired, pale cat with a haughty bearing and bushy tail. She must be Samantha. Karen and Tony have created a circle of tiny flowers with a pile of rocks in their garden. Samantha's bones lie there but her spirit is free. They talk of her often. No other cat, no matter how smart or beautiful can take her place. Loyalty to a cat who has passed shows that my owners have character, or Humanness. I met Samantha's spirit previously when I was a kitten, and again later, but I haven't seen or heard her since Oliver arrived. Why has her spirit returned to her former home from her resting place across the Rainbow Bridge? Perhaps she is aware that Karen is carrying new life and has arrived to protect her.

Oliver wakes and follows me to the lounge. He looks at me curiously. He appears to be unaware of Samantha's presence. I must be more sensitive to creatures of the past.

I watch Oliver sleep and remember how tiny he was when he arrived. I heard his frantic kitten calls in our garden. He was barely alive when I found him dumped in a box on the grass. A cruel Human who didn't care about him had tossed him aside. Possibly, he didn't realise that Oliver was a purebred kitten and valuable, or he found his large eyes and huge ears ugly. Instinctively, I carried him into the house in my mouth. Karen kept him warm and fed him. With her constant care, he thrived. After much discussion Karen and Tony decided to keep him.

His arrival changed my comfortable, life completely. At first, I resented him and had nothing to do with him, even though I had saved him. It took me ages to accept him, to allow him to leave his scent near mine, create his own path in the house and have his share of our territory. I watched as he developed from a helpless, frightened kitten and passed through a wild phase of biting to become the proud, magnificent cat he is now. We became close friends and that hasn't changed. Admittedly, he put me through a lot, and being with him required patience. Just as well I am a tolerant cat.

He is a different breed of cat to me. I am an easy going, ginger tabby with green eyes. Other than being feline with a cat's features he is unlike me in many ways. His face and body are leaner, he is more powerful, his ears are larger, his coat finer and his legs longer. His most striking features are his bright, blue eyes like the tiny, blue flowers in the garden. His cream body has tips of dark brown on his ears, face, long tail and delicate paws. While I am clever in many practical ways, he is smarter at solving problems. His meow has a sharper pitch than mine. Sometimes I think he talks a different cat dialect. He is athletic, active, chattier and self-opinionated. I can't remember being anything like him when I was younger. Despite all his positive gifts, he is emotionally sensitive and reacts to the slightest changes in routine. If Tony or Karen are in a hurry or tired, or the tone of their voice alter he runs away, or turns his back on them.

Just when I thought he was maturing, he sprayed his pee indoors for the first time. Apparently, Siamese cats mature early and he was expressing his desire to mate. Karen was horrified at the smell and Tony was upset. They decided to have him neutered immediately and took him to the vet. I have been "fixed" too and can't have the kittens I long for. I was sad for him as he could've helped to make gorgeous kittens, but that's a cat life. Even though Oliver has been fixed, he still has a wild streak.

George is old enough now to sleep in a proper bed that we can jump on easily. Some nights, we sleep snuggled between him and Bonzo, the big bear that his grandmother Liz gave him. She's a cat hater and perhaps her gift of a bear was meant to encourage him to cuddle a soft toy instead of his cats.

Does he realise that we are more than the cuddly bears that lie motionless on his bed - that we have another side to us? He is young and he might find understanding that aspect of cat life too complicated. Soon he will learn that we are predators who have been hunters throughout the centuries. We owe our survival to our *Catness* – our independence, hunting skills, athletic ability and excellent memory, that helps us to adapt to most situations.

Fat Bonzo is George's favourite toy bear. He has four other smaller bears he plays with and talks to. Yesterday, he ignored me and spent the entire afternoon playing with his bears, and it is not the first time. Am I just another plaything he cuddles when he feels like it? I am not at all pleased that he is ignoring me.

After pacing through the house filled with resentment, I decide to act. I wait until he is asleep with Bonzo in his arms and the smaller bears are lying at the bottom of his bed. Onto the bed I jump, grab the smallest bear and carry it in my mouth to my basket. Then I return to collect the other small bears and place them in my basket too. Apart from Bonzo, they are all in my basket. I fall asleep with them around me. They are cuddly, and I sleep well. I am a happy cat.

I wake to Karen's giggles. She calls George, 'Look, Bella has stolen your small bears and slept with them in her basket.'

'But they're *my* bears! Why did she take them?'

'I think she's telling you something.'

George stamps his foot.

'I think you have been playing with Bonzo and ignoring your cat who has always been there for you. You wouldn't like Bella and Oliver playing together and not coming to you when you call them.'

He grabs two of the bears from my basket. 'I'm sorry Bell Bell, you know I love you lots. You can keep the baby bear as a present,' he says, as he pats my head. He runs off to play. Karen sits next to me and strokes me until I'm in cat heaven.

When the sun blazes high in the sky, Karen leaves the pool for her therapy room to work on her computer, tidy, and print papers. I sit at her feet waiting for her to notice me, stroke my head, or give me a cuddle. I claw the carpet and nudge papers that fall on the floor. Apart from a quick pat, she ignores me. I jump up and tap her knee with my paw to remind her I'm here, but dismissively she pats my head again. I expect more, much more. She deserves to be ignored all day. I depart with my tail quivering.

Tony is in his study working on his computer too and Oliver is in our garden. I want some attention and affection and look for Pops. I find him in his room reading a newspaper.

'Hello, Bella.' His hand moves towards me. 'Lovely, you've come to visit me.'

I jump up onto his lap avoiding his scratchy, grey beard.

He is wearing a jumper, as he does even in summer. Sitting on him is soft and comfortable.

'I'm feeling the cold more lately, the price of old age,' he says with a smile and then a shrug. He whispers to me in his gravelly voice and strokes me until we are both asleep. Karen wakes us when she returns.

She smiles with delight. 'I should've guessed you'd both be here. 'We hardly see you during the day Pops, you're hiding away in your room.'

'If you see little of me you'll enjoy my company, but too much of me could be irritating.'

Pops is as wise as an old cat who has lived life to the full.

I am busy with one of my most important cat tasks, grooming myself according to my personal cat ritual. We groom ourselves several times a day and each of us performs the ritual in a unique way. We use our tongues with their rough barbs to lick ourselves. The barbs don't only remove dust, dirt and loose hairs from our coats, they are incredibly useful when eating, making it easier for us to scrape meat from the bones of our prey. We cats are built so efficiently!

I begin my cleaning by licking the underside of my front paws until they are wet with saliva. With my wet paws, I clean my face and whiskers. My ears are hard to reach, but I manage. My tiny front teeth smooth out any matted hairs or food stuck in my coat. Then I pull out each claw and remove any dry husks to ensure that my claws are sharp. My soft, pink bits I clean vigorously. We cats are hygienic creatures and absolute cleanliness is necessary to prevent our enemies from identifying our scent. We do this instinctively, even when we lead comfortable lives. In the wild we have many predators. Dogs, foxes, owls and eagles are our enemies and enjoy the taste of cats.

I am comfortable and clean. A total body tongue lick cools me and spreads the oils that make my coat glossy. Next on my list of cat chores is a territorial inspection, through all the rooms in every corner, along the floor, carpets and furniture. Territory is virtually number one to every cat in the wild or living in domestic bliss. I check my area twice a day and leave my scent. My scent glands along my tail, on each side of my head, the underside of my front paws and my lips call out loudly "this area belongs to me". Once Oliver has marked his own scent channels, we are doubly safe. Since we were recently reprimanded by Karen wielding her torturous water spray, we cannot follow our instinctive desire to leave our scratches of ownership on the furniture. We leave our marks on our scratching posts instead.

In this corner of the house I find a collection of dust and tiny claw marks. I sniff. Rats! In the heat mice and rats search for water. Young mice are tasty, but rats are larger rodents and tougher, a last choice to keep in mind if tinned food and mice are unavailable. So far, I have been fortunate with food. Karen provides an excellent cat menu.

I follow the rat scent along the edge of the floor to the wall. It continues all the way high up into the ceiling. Frustrated, I turn away. When the rats come out in the dark I will return with Oliver to destroy them or frighten them off.

With my chores completed I have nothing to do but sleep. The heat makes me lazy. There must be more to cat life than keeping cool, eating and sleeping.

Tonight, the moon is perfectly round, and the sky dazzles with sparkles. Our Humans are asleep and we sit at the window to watch and listen to the sounds of the night. As branches swish against the window in the breeze, a possum climbs a tree, rats and mice scurry past. A large owl with huge eyes sits on a branch. *Hooo...Hooo...Hoooo... Hooooooooo*, it calls. The large bird makes me nervous. It is a dangerous cat predator with sensitive hearing. Once I watched an owl hunt using its sharp beak and talons to catch and eat its prey. It is a terrifying creature. I cannot understand why Karen likes owls and keeps four small, dead owls on the sitting room table for decoration.

A crunching sound on the path outside the house alerts us. Footsteps. In the moonlight, a large Human wearing black to cover his face, prowls. Only his eyes are visible. He carries a bag, places it on the grass and looks around. He is as cautious as a cat about to pounce on a mouse. The intruder takes a light from his bag and stepping lightly, he approaches the front door. He turns the knob, but it resists his grasp. We see him walk to the back. He cannot open the back door either. His attention turns to the windows. Every night before going to bed Tony checks that all the doors and windows are locked with tiny keys. When the windows refuse the intruder entry, his angry grunts are loud enough for us to hear. Why is he attempting to enter our house?

Now he is outside our window shining his light inside. I am about to run to the big bedroom to wake Karen and Tony, when Oliver acts fast. He stretches his long, pale body against the glass, growling and baring his teeth. Most frightening of all, his blue eyes turn red in the torchlight. When the intruder sees the creature with red shining eyes pressed against the glass, he steps back in fear and drops his torch. He grabs his bag and runs down the driveway. We are safe. Our house and our Humans are safe. We move towards each other. I butt Oliver's head affectionately. He nuzzles against me. He is pleased that he frightened off the intruder with his quick action.

In the morning, Tony notices large muddy footprints on the grass and a torch. When he checks the doors and windows he finds them all locked. He shrugs and looks concerned. Over breakfast he tells Karen about his find. Neither of my Humans have any idea about the drama of the night.

While Oliver is having his morning nap, I visit the small, wooden cat goddess Bastet to thank her for Oliver's quick action and seek her protection for another day. Oliver does not venerate Bastet as I do. He believes in his own ability to survive. I disagree, but cats are entitled to their views. Karen laughed when she told me that Bastet came from a distant land, Egypt, many moon shines ago. I wish Karen wouldn't laugh at Bastet. Each morning, I stand before the small cat goddess, the symbol of *Catness,* and absorb her powerful glow. I know instinctively that she is my shield. She guards me and my Humans who feed me and provide my home and care.

I leave Bastet calm and at peace. Somehow, I sense that she expects more from me this year. Last year I learned much and matured, but this year I will continue along my learning path. But, it is too hot now to think of such serious matters.

Oliver

Humans are easy to control.
Soon we may domesticate them.

We are both in our carry boxes in the back of Karen's car and extremely uncomfortable. Car travel is all very well for Bella accustomed to the constant movement, but it makes me nauseous and dizzy. I hope I won't vomit.

I noticed earlier that Karen did not take suitcases from the top cupboard to pack her clothing, so I assume that the Humans are not going away on holiday and taking us to the cattery. That is a huge relief! As Bella is not wearing her work harness, I deduce that we are our way to the vet. Not a pleasant thought either after everything that was done to both of us in the name of medicine. We have been deprived of essential parts of our being by neutering, or to put it crudely, by being "fixed". We were not fixed at all. I am no longer a proud, fertile male and Bella is not able to fulfil her most important role of motherhood and produce kittens. I am seriously resentful and would like to bite the human hand that performed this cruelty.

As Karen carries us into the building, the smell of many animals is familiar. I meow as loudly as possible and Bella joins me. What a dreadful place! Karen sits in the waiting area with our carry boxes on the floor next to her feet. The glass door bangs open and a Human enters the room carrying a huge basket. There are sounds of scratching and meowing. If I stretch, I can see inside the basket. A mama with her five, tiny kittens clinging to her and each other. The mama moves closer to her kittens to protect them. Bella, sensing the mama cat's fear, purrs loudly to let her know that we will not harm her or her babies. Another Human enters with his dog on a lead. The dog stares in our direction, growls softly and strains on his lead. Karen places her hands protectively over our boxes and draws them closer to her. We are safe, but the presence of the dog is unpleasant.

A voice calls us. I smell the tall Human and recognise his large hands. My body bristles with a mixture of hatred and fear. He is the one who performed my cruel operation. My ears are back, my claws ready to scratch and a low warning sound leaves my body. He ignores my warnings, confidently removes me from my box and places me on a cold table.

'Hush, hush cat. It's only an injection to keep you healthy,' he says softly.

When I snarl and attempt to bite his hand, he shakes his head.

'This won't work. I'll ask Sophia to examine him and give him the injection. Cats have long memories.'

I allow the gentler, sweeter smelling Human to touch me. I feel no pain as a needle is jabbed into my neck fur. Now it's Bella's turn. She is more placid and does not make a fuss. I am not at all pleased with my instinctive behaviour. I'm a cat of course, with instinct that can overpower logic, but I pride myself on being able to control myself. The vet does deserve a scratch or a bite, but such action needs to be decided logically. I am a smart cat and will have to practice more self-discipline.

Once we are home, Bella is tired and dizzy after the injection, and sleeps. It has no effect on me. I run through the cat door into our garden. I must remain fit and exercise by jumping over the rocks and running. Spent, I rest on the grass in the shade of the half tree. As I am about to close my eyes, I see dots moving in the distance. They are not birds or fruit flies. As they fly closer, their tiny, delicate wings flutter in the light. My energy returns in a rush and I chase them. One I catch in my claw and it flutters until it dies. I try to eat it but spit it out in disgust. The tiny creatures fly from flower to flower and then disappear into the sunlight.

Neighbours and their young ones have arrived for a swim - a teenager and young boy and girl who are almost identical. Karen is friendly and invites them to join the family at the pool. The visitors have heard from others that I swim and want to see me perform. News, whether good, interesting or negative, travels fast among Humans.

While the parents chat, the teenager is occupied with his phone, but the girl and boy yell, running wildly around the pool. They call George to play with them, but he is scared of them and clings to Karen. She looks hopefully in their parent's direction, expecting them to say or do something to control their children, but the parents do nothing.

'Scaredy, why won't you play,' the girl shouts.

George begins to cry.

'What a baby,' the boy sneers.

The girl points. 'Look, now he's crying like a baby.'

Karen's jaw tightens. She is as angry as a cat mama whose kittens are threatened. Pops is about to stand and comment when Karen holds up her hand.

'Enough you two! Behave yourselves and stop bullying George,' she says in her sternest voice.

With a smirking glance at each other, they sit on the grass.

The twin's mother flicks her long, gold hair in annoyance. 'Oh, they're just having fun.'

Karen scowls. 'Hmm, bullying is not fun!'

'Well then, is the cat going to swim?' The father asks.

'He had a swim just before you arrived. I don't know if he'll want to swim again,' Tony says.

'Seriously, are you going to ask the cat if he wants to swim?' She sniggers and then laughs.

Tony frowns and looks at me. 'Swim Oliver?'

My answer is a clear. I hide behind Tony's chair and dig my paws into the grass.

'Oliver's answer is a definite "no". He's had enough for today.'

'Oh, the kids will be so disappointed,' she says.

Karen is empathic. 'In our house our much-loved cats have rights and are well-treated.'

'Some people don't know where to draw the line with animals and spoil them,' the mother replies as she gathers towels and her handbag. She motions to her children to follow her, and the unpleasant visitors leave.

'I'm glad they've gone! With any luck they won't be back,' Tony says.

'Those twins are bullies and their parents didn't do a thing to control them, and they are only four! I don't want to think what they will be like at eleven,' Pops says shaking his head.

George has stopped crying, but he is still upset. Karen gives him a kiss.

'I will ask some other children over to swim and play with you, my darling. You need to learn to stand up for yourself and have fun too.' She strokes his head.

Tony bends to pat me. 'All they came for was to see you perform, Oliver.'

'You're a smart cat! You weren't going to entertain them, were you?' Pops adds.

The twins are like the strongest, largest cats of a litter who dominate and bully the others to be first to drink from their mama and be close to her for warmth. They kick and bite the others and drink up all the milk. Human parents ought to teach their children some self-control. Little ones learn by watching their parents. They don't care a cat's paw about George or me. How unfeeling and sad.

 # Bella

Do not put up with bullies, whether they are cats or humans.

Another pleasant day spent at the pool. The sun is dipping in the sky and shadows lengthen. Tony and Karen are about to leave, when Karen's phone rings disturbing the late afternoon quiet. Karen tries to ignore it, but it continues ringing.

'Oh, Dr Drummond gave you my number and told you about Bella, my therapy cat.' She listens and nods. 'Oh, I'm sorry, poor Noah. I am taking a break from work... but I'll do my best to find some time and bring Bella to see him.'

'Come cats,' Karen calls as she walks towards the house. Tony catches up with her and she tells him about the phone call.

He scowls 'You promised to spend a few weeks relaxing. You should've told them to wait.'

During the night, I dream of a water monster devouring me. I meow loudly and Oliver leaves his basket to comfort me.

The bright morning sun wakes me. Karen is up. I listen to the sound of her emptying our litterboxes, refilling them with clean stones and putting water in our bowls. I find a more comfortable spot in my basket and fall back to sleep.

I sense Karen near. 'Wake up, Bella...we're working this morning.'

I roll onto my back, yawn, and ignore her. It's holiday time, after all. When she stretches her arms towards me, I glare at her. She knows I hate her carrying me. I yawn again and slowly follow her.

'Come on Treasure, eat,' she says and points to my food bowl.

I hate being hurried when I eat. Grudgingly, I eat a few pebbles and then lap some water. I like real food and she knows it. This will have to do.

Tony strolls into the kitchen still in his pyjamas and looks at the clock. 'It's early. You must be visiting that sick child.'

'Yes, I promised his mother that I would come and bring Bella. I think she'll help him.'

'Don't be too long.'

She gives him a kiss. 'I'll have the rest of the day free and we can spend it together.'

Oh no! She's is holding my dreaded harness and lead, a Human tool of control and oppression. In this heat wearing it will be extremely uncomfortable. I turn my back on her to let her know that I am not pleased with her.

'Sorry Bella, I know you dislike the harness and lead, but you need to look like the professional therapy cat you are.'

Sissss, I hiss. I don't remember hissing at Karen since I was a kitten.

'I'll ignore your bad behaviour. It's hot, but you'll have to wear the harness.'

As she straps it onto me, she mutters that I have put on weight and it will be tight around my middle. I ignore the discomfort without complaining this time. Once Karen sets her mind to something, trying to shift her is useless. I've tried crying, even wailing or rolling on the floor. She knows me too well, ignores my shows of resistance and pushes me gently into my new carry box. At least the new box is lighter for her to carry and it has some open slots for me to see through. Soon we are in the car and on our way. Thankfully, the journey is short.

A tall, skinny human with yellow hair falling on her shoulders is waiting for us.

She greets Karen and sighs. 'When Noah heard you were coming he hid in his room.'

'You told me he likes cats. I'm sure he'll come out to see Bella.'

Noah must be listening to our conversation. His bedroom door opens and a small child with yellow hair like his mother's runs towards us. I have learned something about age in Humans since working with Karen, and I guess that Noah is about five-years-old.

'Where's the cat? I want to see the cat,' he says excitedly.

Karen opens my carry box and I sit on the carpet and assess the room. It is large with comfortable chairs and a couch. I take a deep breath. It smells cat friendly.

'Oh, she's beautiful.' Noah bends to stroke my head. 'I love cats.'

'Sit with Bella while I chat with your mum,' Karen says.

The mother tells Karen that recently Noah was a passenger in a car crash - unhurt but badly shaken. She explains that she and his father are divorced, and that the accident occurred during Noah's weekend spent with his dad. Noah was in the car with his dad when another car crashed into them from behind. Fortunately, Noah's kiddy seat protected him, but the impact caused his dad to fall forward and hit his head on the wheel. His dad wasn't seriously injured but unconscious and bleeding. Though paramedics tried to reassure Noah that his father wasn't in danger, it didn't help. When he saw the blood on his dad's head, he panicked and feared he was dead.

'Since the accident, he is terrified of going in the car. Before the accident, he was an active, happy boy. Now he cries for no reason and wakes up with nightmares about his dad dying. I don't know what to do to help him,' she says tearfully. 'He has seen doctors, but they haven't been able to help him. Dr Drummond knows about you and Bella, and he suggested I contact you.'

As Noah sits on the carpet next to me, I watch him carefully to ensure that he doesn't pull my tail or attempt to hurt me. I do not bite small Humans who are rough with me. Instead I hide or run away for safety. His little hands are still clumsy as he tries to touch me.

'Pretty, ginger cat I'm glad you came to visit,' he says, as tears dribble down his cheeks.

Karen smiles at Noah reassuringly. 'Talk to Bella, Noah. She understands everything.'

Karen says that to all the children who come to see her, to encourage them to relax and tell me their troubles. I don't always listen to what Humans say while I am with them, but I do my job of purring and cuddling them. It seems to help.

I understand this child's fears. The image of my own Water Monster and fear of anything wet flashes past, and I snuggle closer. This time I want to listen, but the child's voice is soft, and I struggle to hear what he says. Karen has stopped talking to the mother and is listening too.

'I'm scared that more bad things will happen.' His voice is almost a whisper.

'Noah thinks the accident was his fault. Before it happened, his father took him to a toyshop to buy him a present. Noah saw an expensive toy car and wanted it, but his dad refused to buy it for him. His dad explained that it would break soon and was a waste of money. Noah wanted the toy and began to cry. He was still crying when the accident occurred. Somehow he believes he caused it.'

There is a lot I don't understand about this accident. I am sure that Karen will have a huge job helping this sad, little Human to recover.

Noah strokes me while Karen talks to the mother. I purr for Noah and then drift into sleep. My eyes open again when Karen asks Noah how his father is now.

At first, tears fill Noah's eyes again and he doesn't reply. After stroking me a few times, he tells Karen that his dad has recovered and that he visited him a few days ago.

'They had a good time together,' his mother says hugging and kissing him.

Karen takes Noah's hand. 'Bella is a very smart cat. She knows the accident wasn't your fault.'

He stares at her and nods slowly.

I know exactly what to do. I shift closer, place my head on his leg and cuddle him. He whispers to me, burrows into my fur and kisses my head. Though I dislike the feel of him so near and the kiss is an invasion of my cat privacy, I don't move away. He needs me in the way that I need Oliver when I am scared.

At last, thank cats, he moves back.

'Lovely Bella, I know you understand.'

Karen smiles her warm smile. 'I told you she would.'

Noah looks at his mother pleadingly. 'Please, please, can I have my own cat, one just like Bella?'

'Perhaps when you feel better you can help to look after a cat.'

I am relieved to leave Noah and his mother. I am tired now and feel drained after giving him so many cuddles.

Tony has been away all day and hasn't returned. Karen has been out too. She is singing to herself, and when she sings, I know she is happy.

As soon as the front door opens, she runs to greet Tony with a hug and kiss. 'I have some great news, I've just been to the doctor to check...and guess!'

He kisses her and lifts her into the air with joy. 'We have another baby on the way!'

They then sit on the couch cuddling and talking to each other so softly that even I can't hear what they are saying. Their romantic closeness is ridiculous, but at least they are not neutered and have produced new life.

I haven't eaten my dinner yet and would rather not think too deeply about the complications that another baby will bring.

The sun is awake and spreading its golden heat. Oliver is purring in his sleep. I creep out of my basket delighting in the still house. Outside, birds and all creeping creatures are seeking food. I check my territory and mark it. With my first and most important cat task accomplished, I visit the dresser where Bastet sits. I sense the glow of her power and seek her protection for the day. I am hungry and jump on the big bed to wake Karen. Like a cat, she takes her time rolling and stretching before she moves from her bed.

'Come, Bella, breakfast!' she says at last.

The heat is rising. The Humans are spending the afternoon at the pool again. Staring at the blue water bores me, but they seem to enjoy it. Today, George's cousins, Glen, aged six and Angie who is eight, are visiting with their parents. They are active young humans. They dive into the water, then race screaming and splashing. I find a cool spot under the awning near Karen, away from the children. The mother shares her attention between her phone and watching the children.

Tony is restless, eager to show off Oliver's swimming ability to Karen's family. He allows Oliver in the clean pool. Usually Oliver is only allowed to swim after the Humans have been in the pool.

He shrugs. 'How dirty can Oliver be? He swims every day.'

I watch Oliver enter the pool from the steps. He begins to swim his cat paddle with his head held proudly out of the water. Like most Humans, the visitors have not seen a cat swim before. They are amazed and laugh loudly.

A swimming cat is not entertainment or a laughing matter. Oliver is a brave, Swimming Warrior Cat and should be respected. I admire him. Oliver ignores them. He swims until he is tired, climbs out of the pool and runs to hide in a warm place. When he is wet he dislikes being touched.

After yelling endlessly, the children eat huge amounts of watermelon, sandwiches and cookies. George is naughty today, copying his cousins by shouting and kicking.

I am almost asleep under the awning when Glen notices me.

'Look, there's another cat hiding, a ginger one,' he says to his sister, as he walks towards me. Before I can escape, he grabs me. Though he is only ten, his arms are strong. I wriggle, kick and begin to *meow*, but he ignores my distress.

'Can you swim like Oliver?' He says, carrying me towards the edge of the pool. Terror grabs me. The blue is all I see. I struggle desperately to free myself, but I cannot. I hiss and try to bite him.

'What a nasty cat,' he shouts and throws me into the water.

As the water overwhelms me, it is no longer shiny and blue, but dark, dense and deep. As I fall, it sucks me down, down to the bottom of its endless wetness. My paws flail in panic as the Water Monster grasps me. I battle to find a way to escape. I struggle to breathe and lose my cat consciousness.

My eyes open. Firm hands grip me and lift me from the terror zone. Fingertips stroke my soaked head. I recognise Tony's voice talking to me quietly and gently as he places me on the grass.

'There, there, Bella. You're safe now. I'm holding you.'

Karen rushes to me. 'Bella, Bella, my sweetheart!' She strokes my wet, trembling body. 'Everything's fine now, Precious. A bad experience that had to happen eventually. Now you'll learn to swim.'

Oliver is next to me as I look up at Karen, and at the awful boy. Oliver licks my ears and face, and we sit the sun together.

'Oh, I'm so sorry, is the cat okay? We only have big dogs and they like to swim in the river. I saw the other cat swim and I thought all cats can swim,' Glen mumbles looking worried.

When Oliver is certain that I am out of danger, his muscles ripple. Ready to pounce, he rushes towards Glen. Oliver is powerful and when his lean, long body is extended as it is now, he is a mini tiger. As he reaches the boy, he controls his instinctive desire to attack and does not bite. He has sent his warning message.

Glen runs to his father looking scared, 'The other cat wants to bite me.'

'Oliver won't bite you. He's protecting his friend and warning you not to do that again,' Tony says, his voice stern. 'Harming animals is not acceptable.'

Perhaps Glen made a genuine mistake, but I doubt it. He

should've let me go when he saw me struggle. I saw the nasty look in his eyes. I give Glen my longest, most intense cat stare, and turn my back on him. To make my point I shake my soaked coat as close to him as possible.

'Yuck! The horrible cat covered me in mucky water! She did it on purpose.'

'Animals need to be treated with care, Glen!'

I can tell Karen is watching her words because Glen is George's cousin.

Pops places a saucer of fresh water next to me. 'Drink to get rid of the taste of the pool, Bella.'

I drink it all, then he searches in the bag that contains his glasses, hat, book, and his favourite nibbles. He opens a packet of dried meat and gives us both a few pieces.

That mean child threw me into the water on purpose. That was his fault. The rest was all mine. I have avoided water for too long, given into my fear and tried to pretend I could escape it when I should've tackled it head on. I hated the pool and wouldn't go too close to it in case droplets of water fell on me. Of course, I should've tried to swim with Oliver. I will learn to swim now, for my survival, for *Catness*. In another life my ancestors swam across rivers and caught fish in the sea. I need to follow their example, and I will.

My knowledge that Oliver, Karen, Tony and Pops care for me has been reinforced. They will always protect me. Back in the house I stand before the small wooden sculpture of Bastet and thank her for sending my Humans to save me. I am alive and well and didn't even need to use another cat life to survive.

George looks for me. 'Bell-Bell you are a strong cat and you'll be okay,' he says, as he hugs me. I try to escape his grasp. I understand that this is his way of showing his affection and wait until he frees me. He's a young Human, already demonstrating his mother's concern and care.

Oliver is swimming again today and Tony claps his hands with excitement. He measures the distance of Oliver's swim - three and a half metres across the pool and back. His speed and strength in the water is improving. Oliver has incredible *Catness*, both inside the water and out. I admire his courage and perseverance.

My terrifying experience of near drowning is still with me, and I haven't fully recovered. I am aware that I lick myself repeatedly and bite my claws nervously. On the positive side, I am a resilient cat and I will regain my confidence. When Oliver is near, I try to act unconcerned, but I can't fool him. He watches me and knows that I am nervous. Since my nasty experience he has become more supportive. Almost losing me may be the trigger. We cats don't show our affection like Humans, though we care about each other.

As I see it, the word "love" has a mysterious meaning. Humans use it all the time, sometimes without thinking. Perhaps my deep feelings for Oliver and special Humans is love, but I am unsure. I care most about Karen. After all, she feeds me, and I will be enduringly grateful to her for saving my life as a kitten. My loyalty goes to Tony and Pops, who treat me well. George is young enough to live by his instincts and deep feelings. We have an almost cat-like closeness now, but is likely to change when he is older. Are my feelings for Oliver and my Humans love? How will I ever know?

I wonder if Oliver has true feelings for others. He has shown his concern for my welfare. There is no way of knowing if he cares about our Humans like I do. Giving of himself to others doesn't come that easily for him. He is a loner, keeps his distance from strangers and is afraid of them. He is constantly vigilant and rarely relaxes. Having been left in a box in our garden as a tiny kitten by a Human is stamped into his memory. I haven't forgotten that I was thrown near a rubbish dump by a cruel Human, but I have moved on and it no longer bothers me. I have Karen as my protector now and I trust her completely.

When Oliver was younger, I struggled to prevent myself from mothering him and trying to control him as if he were my kitten. It was an instinctive response as I was hankering for a litter of my own.

I have finely tuned cat intuition and common sense. My understanding of others come from experience and listening to Karen help sad Humans. She has taught me a great deal. I have applied the knowledge I have gained from her to my own situations. Oliver's Siamese intellect is undoubtedly higher than mine. He is logical and has a factual approach to cat life that Tony calls "pragmatic". Despite Oliver's intelligence, he is immature and impulsive. He loathes the rules set by our Humans and finds them stifling. We are different in many ways and our life together is never boring.

The sun is resting behind dark clouds and the fresh smell of rain is in the air. After a running energetically through the house I notice that heavy rain begins to fall.

Well Bella, I tell myself firmly, you're going into the rain today whether you like it or not. You must become accustomed to water of all kinds. I force myself to walk through the cat door into the wet garden. My eyes shut tightly as rain wets my coat, dragging me down and making me uncomfortable. Shivering, I shake myself and rush back inside. Just as well Oliver is with Pops and won't be able to comment. This is my first step. I will have to prod myself to go into the rain again and again. Perhaps, once I am used to the wetness, I will be able to sit near the pool with less fear. I run around the house until I am almost dry. As much as it terrifies me, I know I will have to learn to swim.

Oliver

Be friendly but exert feline power if challenged.

How pleasant our garden is in the early morning sunshine. I look forward to a swim later. I am aware that my ability to swim is unusual for a cat. I enjoy being special and it makes my coat glow with pride.

George was sniffling and crying earlier. What a racket! At last I have found peace here under the half-tree. The usual stray, cat visitors sit at the fence and rub themselves against it. How stupid they are! They ought to realise by now that the fence is our territory. Their presence annoyed me at first, but now I ignore them. I am not moving from my comfortable position to chase them away. I know that Bella thinks I am domineering and arrogant. She is mistaken. I am confident, know my own strengths and like myself as I am. No cat should judge another.

A large, brown cat is high up in the branches of a tree glaring down at me from the other side of the fence. Her hissing and bristling frightens off the other cats. I turn my back on her to let her know that I am not the slightest bit concerned that she wants to be noticed, or to become the top cat in the area. She claws the branch and hisses again. To show her how little she bothers me, I close my eyes and pretend to be asleep. It has no effect on her. She growls and puffs up her body to double her size like a monster cat. What a bullying nuisance! Enough! She needs to be taught a lesson from a Siamese cat. *Rrrrrawwwwwwwrrrrrrrr:* I arch my back showing off my powerful muscles. My hackles are raised, my ears drawn back and my pupils are dilated. She can see my teeth as I growl. She is terrified of me and more stupid than I thought. She doesn't realise that she's quite safe on the other side of the fence. As a final act, I make a strong, dismissive kick with my back leg, and with a swish of my tail I leave the garden through the cat door. Strength, intelligence and logic are key elements of our survival. I doubt that this silly cat will live a long life.

The pads under my paws itch. If only I could escape. A taste of the open spaces a year ago and the freedom to roam has made me long for further adventures. Then, a wild cat I dreamed about encouraged me to run away.

After digging a hole under the fence, I raced to the empty field near the house without a thought of the worry or hurt I was causing Bella and my owners. All I cared about was being free to run amongst the tall grass with the wind against my coat. Bella believes that my independence was satisfied when I ran away. Well, she couldn't be more wrong. Every day I relive my experiences of freedom. The delight of smelling the earth, discovering new delectable creatures and rolling in sand, is still in my thoughts. I manage to push away memories of the unpleasantness of lashing wind, rain and numbing cold, living without shelter and fights with the bigger ruling cats. If I failed to catch mice, bugs or rats, I went hungry. No cat shared a catch. I fought with many cats for my place in the field, and as a powerful cat, I was respected. It is distressing that sick and old cats unable to hunt, survived by scrummaging in waste bins for food. Orphaned kittens were the saddest of all. While I was away from home, I realised that a cat without a Human owner who provides food and shelter would have a miserable life and was unlikely to survive for long.

Dogs from the nearby houses were the biggest threat. They were well-fed and came to the field to enjoy hunting for cats and to torment us. They are slower predators than cats and heavier on their feet, but are lethal. Their strong paws and large jaws can easily kill a cat. Cats are solitary hunters while dogs hunt in packs with leaders. Just as well that without their smart leaders, dogs are not as effective hunters. Fortunately, there were tall trees in the field and we cats were able to climb to safety. The dogs barked at the base of the trees but eventually they gave up and ran home. The harsh conditions finally made me give up. Living in the wild was an adventure, but I missed the luxury of a soft warm basket, delicious food provided for me and all the cuddles my Humans gave me.

Though I am a housecat and live in comfort, I keep my claws sharp and my body lean and flexible. Practice has taught me to scramble over rocks and climb trees at a fast rate. I must be fast and strong. Today, I was tempted to climb the tall wire fence. I could climb it easily if I wanted to, but I controlled myself. Instead I raced through the garden and then the house until I was exhausted. I am older now and I will try to resist my constant urge to escape.

Two visitors, a male and a female wearing sun hats and hardly any clothes arrive for a swim. Bella is asleep inside and I watch them from a distance. Perhaps after this summer of intense observation I will understand more about Humans. The visitors do not sit on the grass as we do. They prefer to sit on towels for comfort. Then they stretch and groan with pleasure as they relax in the sun. Once they have covered their pale, hairless bodies with a creamy substance to protect them from the sun, they both search for their small phones and place them on their towels. They pick up their phones when there is a lull in conversation. She is absorbed by what she is watching and often uses her fingers on the small device. The male's phone rings and he moves away from the others to talk. After the call he checks his phone constantly. Humans, even little ones, seem to like phones and other gadgets they carry around. George's grandmother, Liz, gave him a small square tablet for his last birthday. He enjoys playing with it, but Karen encourages him to play with his other his toys or to go outdoors to play in the garden.

The sun's heat is diminishing and the sky is turning pink. It is almost time for my swim. I wait as Tony pours coloured liquid into tiny glasses and offers them to the guests. They sip at first and then drink quickly. He refills their glasses. How weird Humans are - small phones, larger tablets, a lot of chocolate and coloured liquid appears to make them happy.

Tony looks at the darkening sky and searches for me. He smiles as I stand at the pool. The visitors have amazed expressions. I am determined to enjoy another delightful swim, whether I amuse the visitors or not.

Bella

Continue to ignore house rules and refuse to
accept any restrictions of freedom.

Karen is enjoying the last days of her holiday by relaxing on the patio and swimming. She does not mention work. I am on her lap delighting in a sensual tummy rub with the tips of her fingers probing in all the right spots, when the doorbell rings. The postman has a parcel for us and Karen opens it quickly.

'It's for you Bella,' she says excitedly. 'It's your new harness to wear when we visit hospitals. It says, "Therapy Animal."'

I dislike harnesses intensely and hope it doesn't hurt me like the last one. As she opens the box I sniff it. It smells synthetic and I dislike it immediately.

She adjusts it to my size and tries to put the harness around me.

Yeeeeow! Yeeeeeow! I cry loudly.

'Okay, okay, Treasure, I'll make it looser.'

She tries to place the harness on me again. The new harness is heavier and even more uncomfortable than the old one. The awful contraption is too high and rubs my neck. *Meeeow! Meeeow!* I bite the horrid thing and wriggle until she removes it.

'It definitely doesn't fit,' she says, examining the harness. 'I think they mistakenly sent you a small dog's harness.'

Dogs again! Dogs are the culprits that cause me pain and trouble. How could they be so stupid and confuse a dog with a cat. All we have in common is fur, a tail and four legs.

Her face turns pink, a sign of her annoyance, 'I'll measure you and return it,' she says crossly.

Another parcel arrives today. She opens the box hesitantly. A smaller harness emerges. She places it around me and I cannot believe that it fits perfectly, and doesn't hurt. The material is light and has air holes. What a relief!

Thanks to the ancient Cat Gods, the lead attaches easily and I can walk comfortably. The new harness and carry box will make visiting hospitals and homes more pleasant. All my new equipment is an improvement on the old, but unfortunately it is all plastic with a synthetic smell. That's cat life. Nothing is perfect. However, it will enable me to perform my important job.

I rub my cheek against Karen's leg to say thank you.

'I'm pleased you are happier. We're all set to start work now, Bella!'

Work. I wonder if my work as a therapy cat will follow a similar pattern to last year. Will I lie close to sad and sick Humans and purr to help them to relax as before? Or, will I be able to do more this year?

Luckily, the heat has kept Honey from barking at the fence. For such a tiny creature she makes an incredible amount of noise. I see her lying in the shade panting. I don't understand why dogs pant. Perhaps it keeps them cool. Cats don't understand or speak "dog" and naturally I find her puzzling. Her bark is sharp and she growls and whines a lot. Her whining is most unpleasant. Perhaps it means she wants something. Why do I have to bother with understanding a dog? I have enough to do trying to grasp what Humans want, and they're more important. She has a large mouth and strong, biting jaw, a reason not to feel too comfortable around her, or any dog.

Karen is preparing to start work, while Tony is determined to enjoy the last few days of his holiday by sunbathing and swimming at the pool.

'Bella, where are you? Time for swimming lessons,' he calls.

The thought of entering the water terrifies me. I hide.

'Come on, Bella, you know you have to learn to swim.'

Fear stops me from following him immediately. He becomes impatient when he notices my body close to the ground and my tail down. While he places his towel on a chair and applies sunscreen over most of his body, I stare terrified at the deep blue waiting for me. He ignores my fear, lifts me into his arms and carries me to the pool. He doesn't seem to care that I dislike being carried.

'You'll be fine, Bella. I'll look after you.' Reassuringly he pats my head. As he saved me from drowning, I will have to trust him. He lifts me again and places me on the first step. I think of Bastet, the Cat Goddess, and ask for her help. After further calming head pats, he sprinkles water over me. I shudder at the wetness, but I don't try to run away. Tony is correct I must learn to swim.

'Into the water, Bella...slowly,' he says.

Petrified, I stare at the blue.

Remember Catness, I tell myself. I must at least learn to cat paddle. The Water Monster is part of my outdoor territory and I must persevere and conquer it. I survived near death as a kitten, adapted to wearing that awful harness and almost drowned. I will do this too. I am not a natural swimmer like Oliver, but at least I must be able to protect myself from drowning. Oliver is watching from the patio. He doesn't want to disturb my lessons.

Hesitantly, I move forward.

'Right, into the water you go, Bella, you're on the first step,' Tony says, as he holds my body firmly.

I struggle, unable to help resisting.

Holding me, he enters the pool.

On the second step I freeze. The pool is waiting to devour me and stop me breathing. Surprisingly, nothing awful happens. All I feel is wet and uncomfortable. Gently he takes my paws and with him holding me, we move forward slowly.

'That's right! Good girl!'

Gradually he eases his hold on me and I use my paws to keep afloat. I find that my body feels light.

His voice is encouraging, 'That's the way...keep going... I'm here.'

I am no longer aware of the unpleasant wetness. All that concerns me is moving forward. My body seems to know how to keep afloat as I move forward.

His voice guides me, 'Enough for today, Bella.'

Once more, I feel the step under my paws and scramble out. My ordeal is over for now. With a few shakes, most of the water leaves my coat and I lie near him to dry. As I begin to relax, I sense Oliver next to me. He is licking my face and purring to tell me he's pleased with me.

Dark clouds race across the sky covering the sun's happy face. The trees dance in the wind and even the flowers and grasses sway. I enjoy the cooler air and breathe in its freshness. Suddenly banging noises crack followed by bright flashes. The rain comes slowly like a dripping tap.

Then heavy drops fall and the sky spits out white balls. They cover the grass and sound like huge rats jumping.

Our world is turning white.

Oliver and I observe Nature's performance from under a table. Karen and Tony stand at the glass door watching the spectacle and George jumps up and down excitedly. Tony's Grandfather, Pops, is here too, watching from his comfortable chair.

'Thank goodness the cars are in the garage or the hail would've made huge dents in them,' Tony says.

The sky is calm once more apart from fine rain. Oliver moves from his safe position and sniffs the air. He goes to the cat door, locked during the rain, and asks to go out.

'Oliver, the crazy cat wants to go out.' Karen says, shaking her head.

'He's a boy cat and adventurous. He has not seen hail before and wants to experience it, though it is beginning to melt. Bella is far too sensible to be interested.'

Karen mutters as Oliver rushes through the cat door onto the white surface. With a loud *'meow'* he begins to play, kicking the hail and jumping over it.

I stand at the door undecided about following him. One paw and then another touches the whiteness. I feel the icy wet and I'm back inside.

'I want to go out and play with the white balls too like Oliver,' George says.

'No! Definitely not!' Karen says without explanation.

'Maybe when you're older. It's too slippery,' Tony adds.

It doesn't take long for the white garden to melt. Water is everywhere. Tony checks the house and garden for damage and returns smiling.

After the rain, the hot sun is back. Soon the grass is dry and we cats spend most of our day outdoors sunbaking and playing. After the rain, mice, lizards and all sorts of bugs are active in the garden. Chasing them keeps us occupied. Birds are on the grass eating seeds and chirping in the trees. They happily ignore us as if they own the garden. Our little tinkling bells tell them about all our movements. They know they are safe. What a disgrace! Cats that can't even catch birds!

Oliver

Never allow Humans to know how smart you are.

I am proud of Bella. She fought to overcome her fear of drowning and I am certain she will learn to swim well. It has been a boost to her confidence. When I hear her loud contented purr I can tell she is pleased with herself. Her near drowning made me realise how important she is to me. She is undoubtedly the kinder cat. I have deep feelings for her, affection, admiration, respect and I trust her completely. She is generous with her affection, giving it to me unreservedly, as well as to our Human owners. I am not nearly as affectionate.

When I arrived as an orphaned kitten a few weeks old, Karen became my substitute mother and then Bella took over tending to me. I cannot remember my own Mama, Papa or the rest of my family. There are still times when Bella tries to protect and control me as if I were her kitten. Even if she'd had kittens of her own she'd still mother me and worry about my safety. I try not to become irritated with her or hurt her feelings, but she can be possessive and over concerned. She is practical, brave and clever and she has an amazing ability to persevere. Forcing herself to face her fear of swimming is just one example. I doubt I would have her strength. According to her, I am still immature and behave like a teenager in my risk taking and impulsiveness.

Perhaps she is correct, as she often is. She follows the house rules, but I find them irksome and incredibly boring.

I watch her green eyes sparkle in the sunlight. Her luxurious, glossy coat is magnificent. As she moves it forms rich shades of a colour that Humans call copper. Her name suits her perfectly. Bella means beautiful and she is that. She is a tabby, and perhaps it is the mixture she has inherited that makes her so lovely. I have not seen another female cat more beautiful, and I see many at our fence and our front window.

All the Humans say I am pedigreed, special and handsome, and even if I am, all the pampering and worrying about my looks instead of my strength and my character annoys me. Pops thought I was such a "pretty boy" that he entered me in a cat show and I came second. My red rosette sits near the family portraits in the living room. Surely there must be more to me than that!

I struggle to admit my jealousy of Bella to myself. She is a therapy cat, performing an important role and I am only a show cat who swims well.

Bella

Slap Humans on the leg with a paw if they ignore you.

Karen walks towards me carrying my harness and lead. 'Come, Bella, we're visiting Noah again today.'

I roll on my back and then onto my side to escape the harness. I am wasting my time. Karen grabs me. Soon the harness is around me and she pushes me into my carry box. On a warm day like today, I'm not in the mood to compromise. I strongly resent this assault on my freedom of movement. I yowl *meowieeewaaa, meowieeewaa* throughout our journey.

'What is with you today, Bella? Maybe we've been on holiday for too long and you've forgotten that you have an important job to do.'

I like Karen talking to me as if I am a Human who understands, but her sarcasm and disapproval is unpleasant. I am a cat after all with my own needs and ideas. We don't bend to Humans wishes easily.

Once we are in Noah's house, Karen frees me from my carry box.

Noah rushes to me. 'Hello, beautiful cat! I'm so happy to see you.'

He is nervous and teary. I do my job and nestle close to him. He strokes me,and I purr. Soon he is calmer.

Noah's mother talks to Karen about him in a distressed voice. 'I'm so worried about Noah. He wet the bed this week and he screams in his sleep.' She wipes away tears with a crumpled tissue.

Karen nods sympathetically. 'Try to be patient, Noah had a terrifying experience. He saw his father bleeding and unconscious. Though his father recovered well, it will take Noah time to get over it.'

As Karen talks to Noah's mother she looks concerned.

'Does Noah see his father often? Talking and doing things together will help him to overcome his fears,' she asks.

'Since our divorce, Noah spent every second weekend with his dad. And he pops in to see Noah after work during the week as well. They used to go for a burger, and now that Noah refuses to travel in a car, the burger is out. We both want to help him, but it hasn't worked. We argue when we're together and it upsets Noah.'

'Well, for Noah to recover he needs to see his father more often, and without stress,' Karen replies, 'We'll have to find a way around it. Perhaps you and your ex-husband could come to see me together. We need to sort something out to help Noah.'

One thing I've learned about human children that differs from cats is that they need to see both their parents and as often as possible. I'm not even sure which tom cat is my father. There were a few who liked mama a lot.

The mother looks unhappy and nods slowly. 'Yes, I'll talk to him about it.'

While they continue talking, I snuggle close to Noah and purr loudly. Tiredness overwhelms me and I fall sleep. When I hear Karen mentioning my name, I wake.

'Noah, did you know that Bella doesn't like travelling in a car either? Today she was unhappy and crying when we began the journey. She is a brave cat and stopped crying because she knew we coming to see you.'

Karen is an incredible Human even though sometimes she tells huge lies to help people.

'Lovely Bella, thank you for coming to see me.'

'Well, if Bella can be brave maybe you can too.'

Noah looks up at Karen, then at me. He kisses the top of my head.

I'm not in the mood for sloppy kisses in the heat, but I do my best to purr loudly and I don't move away. He needs my encouragement.

Once we are home, Karen sighs and looks out of the window. She does that when she is thinking about a problem. She bends down to stroke me. 'Bella, my treasure, little Noah need lots of help.'

How can I do more to help Noah? I am a cat after all. Karen is the therapist.

The sun is hiding behind heavy, rain clouds. Oliver's tail flicks with dissatisfaction as he sits at the window watching the wall of water. He is bored and wants to go out. At last, there are only a few dribbles and the sun breaks through. He races through the cat door into our garden.

Another poo of a day! The sky is dark and light rain is falling again. I tell myself firmly that I am going out into the rain whether I like it or not. I close my eyes and force myself through the cat door into our garden. My paws are heavy, and the rain wets my beautiful coat, reviving my memory of the overwhelming wetness that almost drowned me. I survived, I tell myself. I am still here. Come on, I encourage myself to overcome my fear. I think of Catness – my desire to survive in all circumstances and I take a few more steps into the mud. I endure the mud and rain on my body for a few minutes longer and then rush back through the cat door wet and shivering. I am inside and safe. I run through the house until I am dry.

At last, the friendly sun spreads its warmth this afternoon. But, the glorious afternoon is spoilt. Tony insists on giving me swimming lessons. After initial resentment, I submit. Since my first lesson, I am less afraid. I know that I must master the art of swimming or paddling. I follow Tony to the pool and wait for him on the first step.

He smiles. 'That's the way. Let's go!'

He is barely holding me as I slide into the water. I swim freely and surprise myself by managing a short distance on my own. I think of Oliver holding his head up proudly, his paws moving and tail helping him to balance. I try to copy him. I am swimming slightly further now and alone. During my swim, Oliver has been hiding behind a bush to watch me. Once I start to paddle, he jumps into the pool and swims slowly beside me following my pace and style. When he notices that I'm tiring he heads for the side of the pool where Tony is waiting to help me out.

Oliver is delighted. I am certain he would like me to practice my swimming so that I will eventually join him in the pool. I need to learn to swim, but I do not enjoy it. I will complete my lessons until I can swim well enough to overcome my fear. After that I'll be in the water as little as possible.

George is here and he jumps into the pool with a huge splash. The exploding water frightens me for only a second. The Water Monster has disappeared. The water on my coat is more of an irritation now than something to fear. Karen strokes me lavishly and places sliced chicken in my bowl.

'Well done, Bella! Tony told me that you swam this morning. You're a champ, Precious!'

Tony stretches and yawns. 'A bit more practice and Bella will be another swimming cat.'

'That's great!' Karen says.

Tony sighs. 'I'm loving being at the pool with Pops and George. I wish I didn't have to go back to work in a week.'

She laughs. 'Don't complain. I'll be working at the hospitals with Bella very soon. Enjoy every minute of the sunshine.'

I am having a snooze in the afternoon cool when the singing doorbell disturbs me. Two Humans enter the house. I recognise his mother's footsteps and her voice. The other Human accompanying her is unknown. At a guess, he is Noah's father. I am not invited into the room this time. From my post at the therapy room door only mumbles escape, until the parents shout. When the mumbles return, I fall asleep, only to wake when the door opens. Noah's parents are smiling and talking to each other. I like that. I hope they will work together to help Noah to recover.

The early sky is rosy as we enter our fenced-off garden to check our territory. Since the heat and rain, the garden is wild with luscious grasses and flowers that pop up between dark leaves. The many new shoots moist with dew are a morning delicacy. We are pleased that the once slim trunk of the half-tree is fat with branches that spread higher. Its top branches are our look outs and its trunk is a useful scratching post.

Tony worked hard to provide us with special features in our garden. He placed rocks in our garden for climbing and hiding spots. A covered area he built catches the sunlight in winter and the shade in summer. He secured a fence around our area, so that wild dogs can't attack us, or feral cats slip in. There is a gate into the fence too for Humans to use. Since the fence was erected it has been reinforced due

Oliver's ability to dig his way out. We are fortunate that Karen added pots of catnip that grow abundantly. We both sniff the leaves or jump into the pot for a roll. We feel lively after our catnip. She ensures we have a bowl of fresh water every day and our food is in the kitchen. I almost forgot about the fruit trees that drop their fruit on our side of the fence. The fruit is like a soft ball and fun to play with.

After an unexciting lunch with my usual food pellets and no treats, Karen calls, 'Bella...Bella, we are visiting Noah again.'

When we arrive, he is sitting on the carpet waiting for me.

'Hello, lovely Bella.' He lays his head on mine and starts to cry. His tears wet my fur but I don't move. He is distressed and needs me. I'm a therapy cat and I know what to do. I snuggle closer, purr loudly and touch his small hand with my paw. Soon he takes huge gulps and stops crying.

The mother looks worried. 'Noah still bursts into tears easily. He's having fewer nightmares now that his father is visiting him more often...but he's still scared of being in the car.'

Karen takes Noah's hand. 'All of us, including Bella want you to be happy, visit your friends, and have fun.'

He stares at his feet trying not to cry.

'Bella won't mind me telling you that when she was little, she was scared of travelling in the car. It shook, made scary sounds and had a strange smell. If she sensed that I was about to take her with me in the car she'd hide under the bed. She still dislikes travelling in the car, but she is a brave cat and travels with me to help people.'

Smart Karen! She's telling Noah about me being brave

to encourage him to be brave too. I will give her one of my long stares to let her know that I am aware of what she's up to.

While Karen and Noah's mother talk softly, Noah tells me about the accident. I snuggle closer and drift off to sleep to avoid the distress of listening to this information.

I wake when Noah and his mother stand to leave.

'Noah, it's time for you to try to be brave like Bella. How about sitting in the car with Bells for a few minutes before I drive her home. It will make her feel better,' Karen says as she takes Noah's hand.

Noah refuses at first and then looks at me. 'Okay, I'll be brave and sit with Bella for a few minutes.'

Karen leads me to the car. It is the first time that I sit on the front car seat. I am usually in my carry box. Noah stands beside the car hesitating.

'Come into the car,' Karen says. She moves me, and reluctantly he sits. I'm on his lap and he strokes me.

He sighs. 'I wish Bella could always be with me in the car.'

'You can imagine she's with you.'

He nods. 'I'll try.'

Poor Noah, I wish I could be with him and give him more help.

Over breakfast, Tony taps a glass with his fork and makes an announcement, 'George, we are very proud of you. You're not a baby any longer.'

He must be referring to George not pooing and messing any longer. He is using a red plastic pot to do his poos in now. Soon he will copy his parents and use the big, white toilet in the bathroom. Maybe it's a good idea for Humans to praise their young ones for basic, physical things that are part of their natural development like learning to make poos. Cats learn early that our Mama's can't look after us for very long. At three weeks old we don't need to be stimulated to make poos. We grow up quickly.

George looks pleased and smiles a happy smile. He is not making smelly messes in his pants any longer, but he is as naughty as a kitten. Today he pulled the cover off the big bed and threw it on the floor. He jumped on it and yelled as he rolled about in the soft material. I remember when Oliver was a kitten, he pulled the cover off the bed and dragged it into the house to show off his strength.

George is a special child. Karen sees many children in her home and at the hospital and I am with her, so I can tell that George is unusual for his age. He began to talk early and understands that we cats have different temperaments – that I dislike being carried and that Oliver is moody often choosing to be distant from his Human owners. George treats Oliver with respect and doesn't pet him unless he receives a tap from his paw. I am closer to George and have an easier cat – child relationship. I jump up to him and sit on him. We play and have an emotional connection as well. The emotional connection is hard to explain. It is inside and I can't touch it with my paw. When he strokes me, I know it is there.

Another swimming lesson today. I am at the pool with Tony. He jumps into the water and swims the length of the pool. Then he calls me. Uncertainly, I stand on the first step. I look at the large area of wet blue, shudder and force myself forward. I must try to swim further today. Tony was gentle and supportive the last time I tried to swim, and I trust him. I dip my paw into the water. He is there, holding me. When he removes his hands, knowing he is there gives me confidence. Now I swim without fear. Gradually my paws paddle and move through the water. I break free and strike the water.

Tony's voice is in the background, 'Great Bella! Keep going, you're doing well!'

I turn about and swim back to the step. My effort has taken most of my energy. Once I'm out of the water I lie in the sun to dry.

Catness demands that I navigate both land and water. I have achieved more than I thought possible and I am pleased with myself. I am no longer afraid of water and I paddled further than I expected – an excellent outcome. I will swim again and again until my paws are able to work faster.

Karen is talking on her phone, 'My holiday is over and I've had an urgent call from an old client who doesn't sound well at all. I'm seeing him this afternoon.'

'You remember Max from last year,' she says. Names are meaningless to me, but I don't forget smells. I follow her to the front room and sit in my work basket that is not as comfortable as my house basket. Just as well, or I'd be asleep all the time. The doorbell sings and Max enters the room. I recognise him. His clothes have the same unusual, vegetable smell. His mouth that smiled before is thin and tight.

His voice is flat and sad, 'Hi kitty cat, a tough world isn't it?' He sighs and sits cross-legged on the carpet with his head bent.

I place my paw on his knee and he responds by patting

his thigh. I sit on him purring loudly. He needs a cuddle and I move closer.

He tells Karen that he has had trouble sleeping and is hardly eating. 'I haven't felt like doing much, just sitting around...and I'm smoking too much grass. I cut down, even stopped, but it didn't last.'

He pats my head and his words tumble out. 'Cats understand, but my parents don't...and we are arguing. They want me to study law and economics, to have a more stable career. I'm a musician, a pianist, and a good one too. I don't want to waste my time at university just to please them. It's dad more than mum. She wants me to be happy in what I do. He's a lawyer and expects me to follow in his footsteps and become a partner in his firm. I don't think he cares about anything else.'

Karen nods. 'It's hard to make a living as a musician and they want the best for you, a profession in case you need it.'

'I know, but I can't change who I am. If I can't earn enough from gigs, I'd rather work in a shop or wait at tables for extra cash than wear a suit in the corporate world like my dad. We had a huge row about my music and me using grass and I left home.' He sighs. 'I'm staying with mates for a few days and my grandma suggested I move in with her.'

He tickles me behind my ears with a gentle touch as he talks. 'She's an artist, so she gets my love of music.'

'If you didn't care about your parents, you wouldn't feel uptight, or have trouble eating and sleeping. You need to sort this out with them. Maybe you need time to find out what you want to do.'

'Yep, I'd like to work and play my music for a year or two before studying.'

Karen suggests he tells his parents where he is staying as they will be worried about him.

He shrugs and drops his head. 'I guess you're right. I

should let them know where I am and give them a contact number. Mum left messages for me, but I didn't phone back.' He stares at the window and sighs again.

I'm warm and comfortable and fall asleep as they continue talking.

He eases me off his lap. 'Sorry, Kitty Cat, I have to go now. No promises, Karen. I'll think about your suggestion of trying to talk to my parents again, and thanks. Sharing helps.'

Karen places a large paper bag on the desk in her therapy room, I eye the bag with interest. Boxes are fun to play in and large packets and bags come next. They have the advantage of being softer than boxes and I can roll in them. My attention shifts to a small, flat object under layers of plastic. When she opens it, I realise that it is a type of computer, smaller than the one on her desk. How will she use it?

This morning she left to do more shopping. Why does one Human need so many things? When she returns she carries parcels to her bedroom. She opens the parcels and out come dresses, pants, jackets and shoes. Why does she need all these clothes when her wardrobe is already full? The ways of Humans are indeed mysterious.

While I lick my paw to clean my face after my meal, I consider my observations. She must be preparing for some new activity. I am certain of it. Thank all the cats in Catland, the suitcases are still on the top of her cupboard, which means she is not about to go on holiday. I will have to be patient until I find answers to the questions buzzing in my head.

Oliver is not interested and hasn't the patience to

consider Karen's possible movements unless I present facts. He deals with practical things as they happen. Unimpressed, he turns his back on me and goes to sleep.

After dinner we are all in the television room when the conversation turns to Karen's plans. As she talks, the pieces of the puzzle begin to make sense.

'I've decided to make changes. I've had an offer to work three half days at the hospital with Bella. They like my work and they are all extremely impressed with my therapy cat.' She smiles and strokes me tenderly. 'It will be a positive change and there'll still be time to see a few clients at home.'

'Great! I know you enjoy working at the hospital and I think Bella likes it too,' Tony adds.

Ahah! She needs the small computer and all her new clothes for visits to the hospital. The change will be stimulating, and I enjoy helping sick Humans. I will meet lots of different types of Humans at the hospital who will adore me. On the negative side, I will have to endure being in my carry box during the dreadful car journey more often. And I'll have to wear my harness and lead all the time which is uncomfortable. Oh well, that's a cat life. There is usually at least one tasteless pebble in a food bowl.

Oliver is quiet and acting oddly. His paw steps are soft when he passes me, so that I barely hear him. He disappears for short periods and when he returns he won't look at me. What is he up to?

This morning Tony yells, 'Karen, have you seen my black striped socks? I'm sure I saw them in my drawer yesterday. And some of my underwear is missing too.'

'It's probably at the back of your drawer.'

Tony searches his drawer and the washing basket. He

can't find his socks anywhere and leaves for work wearing red socks.

That evening Karen is dressing to attend a meeting and is running late.

'Have you seen my gold necklace, Tony? The one that belonged to my grandmother. I can't find it.'

'No, sorry darling. Anyway, you look great without it.'

'I haven't the time to look for it now. I'll search later.'

When she returns, she is like cat hunting for a mouse. She turns all her drawers over, looks under cushions, carpets and under her quilt. Then she goes to the bathroom and kitchen and searches there. No necklace. Other items are missing as well – two fancy teaspoons, one of Karen's earrings and George's hairbrush.

'I last wore my necklace a week ago when we went out for dinner. I was tired when we came home and left it next to my bed intending to put it in its box. It's a precious item. I should've treated it more carefully.'

'Bella or Oliver could've seen it, played with it and then hid it. When I was a child we had a cat that stole food and hid it under the sofa,' Tony says.

'I guess it could be the cats.'

Karen looks at me accusingly. I am suspect number one. When I was a kitten, I hid her watch under the bed to keep it safe. That was a long time ago. I give her one of my disgusted stares, kick my back leg in her direction and turn away from her. I'm an adult cat now and not a thief. I would never consider stealing her possessions. I wonder about Oliver. He's mature in years, but he does silly things despite his smartness. My cat intuition tells me that he has something to do with the missing items. I search his favourite spots, behind the soft chairs and under carpets. There is no sign of the missing items. Karen looks under the beds and shakes the soft cushions with no result either.

'They will turn up,' Tony says hopefully.

Now that I am working with Karen again, Oliver has become secretive and jealous. When I first accompanied her to hospitals I sensed that he would've like to be a therapy cat too, but he knows he doesn't have the necessary temperament. Poor Oliver! I feel sorry for him. He is a proud cat who wants to be included in everything. Not being able to excel as a therapy cat upsets him. It should be enough that he is smarter than me, powerfully athletic and an extremely handsome show cat. If only his jealousy wouldn't make him unfriendly.

He growled at me today when I passed his food bowl. He hasn't done that before. Last week he took a ball from my basket and hissed at me. He is acting like a bully. Another strange thing I've noticed is that lately he is leaving his poo uncovered in his litter box. Usually we both cover our poo with litter or sand if we are outside. Most cats cover their poo to keep their presence unknown from possible predators. When cats don't cover it, they could be displaying their dominance by allowing other cats to smell it. We haven't had dominance issues until now. I guess he is sending me a message, telling me that he is the dominant cat in the house.

When my frustration with Oliver subsides, I think about him. Perhaps there is more to his bullying. What is bothering him? He is a highly sensitive cat, and Karen says the Siamese breed are particularly sensitive. Though I am not at all happy about his behaviour towards me, I will put up with it for a while. He is bound to settle down soon.

We are visiting Noah and his skinny mother again today.

Noah smiles as he runs to greet me. 'Hello, beautiful cat. Guess what?'

I wait.

'I went in the car with mum to the café for ice-cream two blocks from home. I was scared to go in the car. I remembered that you were scared too, and I was brave like you.'

'That's great Noah!' Karen says with a grin. 'Bella will be pleased, I'm sure.'

He nods and smiles shyly.

'Where do you want go next time?'

'Dad is coming to see me tonight. He promised to take me for a burger and chips. It's close by so I think it will be okay.'

'I'm proud of you Noah, you're doing well.' His mother gives him a hug.

Karen smiles broadly. 'Soon you'll visit me and Bella at my house and meet Oliver, our other cat.'

Noah's mother phones Karen to tell her that Noah is longing to see Bella but he's afraid of the long journey in the car. We will have to drive to his house again!

Noah is waiting for us at the gate. As we walk into the house, he talks to me in my carry box. Once I am sitting on the carpet, he hugs me excitedly. His hug is tight and uncomfortable and I dislike him breathing into my face. I am a therapy cat and must endure it.

'Love you lots, Bella, missed you!' he says.

I purr for him and touch him with my paw.

Noah's mother is smiling. This is the first time I have seen his mother relax with a smile that brightens her tight face. There is joy in her voice as she tells Karen that Noah's sleeping has improved and he is eating well now. The best news she leaves for last. They went to visit Noah's cousin who lives in the next block by car. The two boys played all afternoon and Noah enjoyed himself.

While Noah strokes me, Karen tells his mother that this is the last time Bella and I will visit their house. The following week they will have to come to us. Well, that will be an improvement!

This morning Tony is moving something heavy and panting like a dog. He has a long drink of water before talking. 'I have something special for you and Oliver.'

Oliver's ears prick up and we move closer to each other as we watch Tony and wait.

'Come and have a look, cats! I've made a toy for your garden. We don't want the two of you bored and sleeping all day.'

We run through our door into the garden. A long tunnel made with strong wire inside and fine wire outside sits on the grass outside. Oliver touches it with his foot and it rolls.

'Go on, run through it,' Tony says enthusiastically.

Neither of us move. It is a new object that smells strange, invading our garden. I will have to get used to it.

Tony mutters and walks away, 'I go to all the trouble of making a new toy and you both ignore it.'

I sniff the long object. Oliver sniffs it too. I'm not sure why Tony made it.

Karen is watching us from the kitchen window. She has a ball in her hand and enters our garden.

'Let's play, cats!'

The ball glints temptingly in the sunlight. She bends and throws it though the new tunnel.

'Go on, fetch it!'

Oliver runs after the ball and returns it to her. She keeps throwing it and I retrieve it. It's fun!

She leaves and calls out, 'Now play together!'

We run through the tunnel a few times to please her. Tony has wasted his time. Since he has gone to such trouble for us, I will wait until he returns and run through the tunnel a few more times. We might like the contraption eventually. It takes me a long time to become used to any new equipment or to like unusual food.

Soft rain falls again. We are both tired of being muddy and lie on the patio tiles. Oliver is bored and runs through the house. I follow him as he disappears into the big bedroom. I hide to watch him. He is in Tony's cupboard. Out he comes with a rolled-up pair of socks in his mouth. He runs off and I wait. He doesn't spot me and rummages in the cupboard again. Cautiously, his head pops out and then the rest of him. In his mouth is a long tie Tony wears around his shirt collar. I continue to follow him, making certain he doesn't see me. He heads for the kitchen to a rusty, seldom used cupboard under the sink. He opens the cupboard door with his paw and deposits the socks and tie inside it. As he runs off, he purrs his excited purr. Tired after his thieving, he jumps onto the couch, curls up and sleeps.

I retrace my steps to the kitchen and open the sink cupboard. I have discovered Oliver's lair packed with a hoard of his loot – Tony's black socks, his underwear, the tie, Karen's necklace, George's hairbrush and one of Karen's earrings. I meow loudly. Oliver hears me and joins me in seconds. His eyes are wide with fear and his tail is guiltily between his legs. I flick my tail at him in disgust.

When Karen goes to the kitchen she finds the cupboard door open. She peers inside.

'What's all this?'

Out come all the missing items.

She examines the black socks and notices fine white hairs stuck to the wool.

'Oliver's work!'

She calls Oliver. He has disappeared and she searches for him throughout the house. When she can't find him she gives up.

'Naughty cat!' She says loudly. 'I don't want to see you all day.'

At dinnertime she calls him. He comes to the kitchen with his body low and ears back. He eats with his eyes on her.

Much later, he is in the television room with the family. Karen pats her lap for him to jump up. She whispers to him about how loved he is, and he purrs.

The episode is over, hopefully.

The doorbell sings. Noah and his mother have arrived.

Karen welcomes them. 'Great to see you both. Well done, Noah! At last, you're visiting us!'

Noah clenches his fists and looks away. He is unsettled after the drive and doesn't come to me immediately. After sitting quietly, he gives me a cuddle. I purr to let him know I am happy to see him.

'Noah has some good news,' his mother says with smile.

He forgets his nervousness as his words tumble out, 'Mum bought me a kitten. She's orange like you, Bella . . . pretty and purrs a lot. I'm calling her Amber.'

Proudly the mother tells Karen how well Noah is caring for his kitten and making her comfortable in her new home.

'She's still a baby and I love her lots.'

'I'm happy for you, Noah. Amber is a lovely name.'

Noah interrupts, 'Dad took me for another burger last night. I had a single burger and a small shake, and he had a triple and large shake. It was great!'

Karen's face is bright with smiles. I purr with pleasure, nestle closer to Noah and give his hand a lick. I don't lick Humans very often, but he deserves it. Noah tells me about his kitten while Karen and the mother discuss new plans for Noah and their hopes for him to return to kindergarten.

'I'm so proud of you, Noah. You're a brave boy doing so well. I hope you'll go back to kindergarten soon,' Karen says.

Noah stamps his foot and bursts into tears. 'I don't want to go back! I haven't been there for a long time. I won't have any friends and the teacher won't know my name.'

While he moves about restlessly, I try to comfort him.

'Noah my darling, don't worry, I'll go with you, make sure you find your old friends and that the teachers are kind to you. I promise, if you are unhappy there, we'll come home.'

'You promise, Mum?'

She hugs him reassuringly. 'Of course I do.'

After they leave, Karen sighs happily and strokes my head. 'Thank you for helping Noah my beautiful Bella. He is gradually recovering.'

Being thanked and appreciated by Karen makes me glow from head to paw.

 # Bella

Don't come immediately when called. Store the message.

The moon is fat, full and glowing, the air sultry. I am alert, waiting and watching, ready to shift my position or pounce. Oliver lies next to me staring up at the sky, his Siamese nose quivering as he sniffs the night's fragrances. His ears flicker as he listens to the zing-zing of cicadas and the croak of frogs.

Above us, in the ceiling, shrieks are followed by tiny thuds. Creatures larger than rats are invading our territory! Under the lowest part of the ceiling we hear screeches and clicking noises. We run to the window. In the dark we can just make out furry creatures about the size of cats climbing the tree and jumping onto the roof. They appear to be placid if left undisturbed. I know that their young make a tasty treat.

'Did you hear the possums last night?' Tony asks Karen over breakfast.

'They were having a party in the ceiling and woke me.'

'They're an endangered species. We'll have to call a possum catcher to trap them and take them somewhere else.'

I sigh with relief. Our territory will be safe.

After dinner, Pops tells stories about his past. His favourite story is about his cat Cocoa and his life on the family sheep farm. We have all heard it before. He enjoys telling his story and everyone likes to listen. Pops' mother, father, and sisters lived on the farm together when he and his cat, Cocoa, were young. He chose Cocoa out of the many cats on the farm due to her nature and colouring. He smiles as he describes how his cat behaved like a dog, herding stray lambs. Suddenly his mood changes. He looks sad as he describes the fire that destroyed the farmhouse and took the lives of his son and daughter-in-law, Tony's parents. I don't remember him talking about the fire before. As tears roll down Pops' face, Karen puts her arms around him and kisses him.

'It's a sad story and it upsets you. Perhaps Tony can continue. I don't know much about the fire and neither does George.'

Tony wipes a few tears from his eyes. 'It's time we talked about the fire openly. It shaped our family history.'

Pops nods. 'You tell the story, Tony.'

'Farming can be tough especially during droughts. We had just come through a devasting drought. Neither the land nor the animals had fully recovered and mum and dad were worn out with the battle of running the farm with only my uncle helping occasionally. My uncle wanted to buy the farm from them, but they wouldn't sell it. They had lived there all the years they were married. The farm was part of them. They must've been exhausted from the day's work and had fallen asleep when the fire took hold. It was too late when they realised the farmhouse was on fire. They were overcome with the smoke and flames and couldn't escape.'

Karen gives Tony a hug. 'Fires are monsters. I'm so sorry darling. I know you miss them terribly. Just as well you are close to your grandfather. He has been like a father to you.'

Tony and Pops hug each other.

Humans can suffer so much sadness, but some, like Tony and Pops, bounce back like cats.

Oliver

Why do Humans talk to us in the same soft,
strange voices they use to talk to babies?

The Humans are complaining about the extreme changes in the weather this summer and I'm not surprised.

'We've had days of heat followed by endless rain and storms. I can't remember a summer like this before,' Pops says.

Karen looks up from reading the newspaper. 'I wish the unpleasant weather would settle. Apparently, this strange weather has happened before, years ago, but it concerns me.'

Pops looks through the window and sighs.

I stare at the heavy clouds racing across the sky obscuring the sun. The air is electric. I hear rumbles, a yellow light flashes and howling winds drive through the trees at incredible speed. A horrendous storm is about to strike. At the first clap of thunder Bella hides under the big bed. I follow her and we huddle together. Wind rattles the windows and hammering rain hits the roof. The storm is fierce and terrifying.

Throughout the night heavy rain falls and wild winds lash our house and garden. I hear a loud thump. Tiny bits of gravel fly hitting the windows. A tree must've fallen. George is afraid and cries so much that Karen carries him to their bed. Pops can't sleep and wanders through the house. A most unpleasant night.

In the morning, the winds ease though the rain is endless.

Tony covers himself in a plastic coat to check for damage to the outside of the house. Inside, I notice water dripping from a patch on the ceiling onto the wooden floor. The Humans have not noticed it. I meow loudly, with a long warning *meeeeow*. Even Karen ignores me. Too much is happening around her, but she ought to know better. I don't demand attention without good reason.

Back inside, Tony dries his head, lifts off the plastic and complains, 'What awful weather! A small tree has fallen on the roof, only slight damage to the roof, easily fixed.'

The house is pleasantly quiet now apart from the sound of soft rain like mice on the roof. Bella is asleep, Pops is in his room, Karen is working on her computer and George is playing with a new toy. I begin my morning wash. I am fastidious as usual and follow a cleaning routine. I believe I am cleaner than Bella. Naturally she wouldn't like to hear that. After I have cleansed my entire body, my next task is to check my territory and leave my scent in every corner and on all the furniture. Once again, I follow a strict routine, far stricter than Bella's. Of course, I'm a perfectionist. She complains about that aspect of me often, though I am sure that she secretly admires it.

An unsettled feeling passes through me, as if an unpleasant event is about to occur. George is bored with his toy and throws it down. He whizzes past me looking for his mother. Then I hear it – a slipping sound, a sharp cry and then a bang, as loud as a tree falling. I find George lying in a pool of water on the floor where rain has dripped from the ceiling. I jab him with my paw. He doesn't respond. If George falls, he cries loudly. Now he is quiet and still, much too still. I am scared. Where is Bella? She knows what to do in a crisis. I race to find Karen. The door of her room is open, and I run to her meowing as loudly as I can.

'What's up Oliver? I have left you food. Don't bother me.'

Meeeooooow Meeeooooow!

I scratch her leg.

'Oliver! Stop it! You're hurting me!'

Meeeooooow...meeeeeoooow! I cry desperately.

I run to the door and look back, indicating to her that she should follow me.

At last, she leaves her desk to follow me.

'Oh, no! Georgie!'

She is on the floor feeling him all over. Then she lifts him gently and kisses him. Slowly he opens his eyes and starts to cry.

I breathe slowly again. George is making sounds. All is well.

'Do you hurt anywhere, my darling?'

He continues to cry loudly and points to his leg and then his head.

'Right, I'm taking you to the hospital in case you've broken a bone.'

By now, Bella is next to me and watching worriedly. Quickly Karen phones Tony and then runs to Pops' room. She rolls George in a blanket and carries him to the car. The car disappears, and we wait.

When Karen returns with George, who is limping, she helps him into the house. Pops has been waiting worriedly for their return and gives George a kiss. By the time Tony arrives looking concerned, George is tucked up in bed.

Tony questions Karen endlessly about George's accident.

'George is fine now, Tony. He's a lucky boy. It's nothing serious, just some bruises and a bad headache. He slipped and hit his head. Now all he needs is quiet and rest.' She takes Tony's hand. 'Thanks to our quick-thinking Oliver for alerting me. I didn't take notice of him at first and he went on meowing until I did. I hate to think of what could've happened.'

Tony bends to stroke my head.

'He's okay, that's the main thing.'

Karen strokes me and then calls me to the kitchen.

'Treats for Oliver, my hero, and for Bella,' she says, placing some salmon on a plate for us.

Once George is asleep, Karen cleans the muddy floor and puts buckets under the hole in the ceiling. Tony phones for help with the leaking ceiling.

At least our house will be safe and intact again. I lie in my basket and think about George. My concern about this little Human surprises me. Perhaps I am here to watch over him and the new baby when it comes. I will wait to find out.

A Human with heavy footsteps is on the roof. Once he is back on the ground, he talks to Karen, 'Rats and possums have moved the tiles. Some of the wooden structure is eaten away. I'll have to do repairs and replace tiles. It will take me a day.'

He stomps above us and we put up with lack of sleep. At least once the roof is repaired rats, mice and possums will have to find a new place to live. Security of territory is a key to a positive life for cats.

 # Bella

Let all Humans know that you own the house and them as well.

We play in the blazing sun for short bursts and then rest to cool down. After Oliver wins another game of hide and seek, we both sleep. All is well in Catland.

I dream, not of my past as I often do, but of the future. Karen, my most valued Human is caught in a violent storm with howling winds and thrashing rain. She cringes in fright as green light streaks the sky. Bastet appears stretching her paws out to calm the storm. Bastet calls me, and in a whispering voice tells me to do my cat job to look after Karen.

I wake confused. Karen is carrying new life and I am trying my best to look after her. Does she require extra attention? I can't discuss my dream with Oliver. He is far to practical and he doesn't believe in Bastet's powers. He won't admit that the unusual sensation he experienced before George slipped and fell was a warning, an omen. What can I do about a cat who doesn't believe that strange sensations or omens can foretell future events?

While Oliver is asleep, I stand before the small statue of Bastet to seek clarity about my dream. Sadly, none comes. I will have to find my own answers.

A sense of disquiet descends on me. I watch and listen attentively. The night is humid, and my sleep is interrupted by buzzing insects. I scratch my nose, itchy from a bite, and try my best to understand my dream. I decide that Karen appears to be well, but I will take precautions and watch her more carefully. I will try to purr loudly for her and concentrate on helping her to breathe slowly and relax.

Karen is wearing her serious face today. 'Bella, next week we will start working at the hospital again. You've learned a lot about being a therapy cat and I am certain you'll be even better at it this year. We will have to prepare with a bath and clipping your nails.'

She is talking about baths again. Her instance on perfect cleanliness is illogical when cats are already clean. How dirty can I be after swimming in the pool?

'Come, Bella, time for a bath,' she calls.

I accept my fate and don't run from her as in the past. In the laundry I flick my tail in annoyance as she decides on which shampoo to use. She fills the tub with suds and I shudder. Humans seem to relish the feel of water. If it isn't swimming, it's showers. Some are even crazy enough to like the rain. She lifts me into the water. I try not to struggle too forcefully and accept the wetness. I loathe being washed, especially the bubbling soap slithering all over me and rubbed into my coat. The showering after the soap is another trial.

'You've changed, Bella. You're such a good girl. We will be going to the hospitals a lot this year and that means lots of baths.'

The bath is far from enjoyable. I allow her to rinse the soap from my coat without trying to bite her. Soon I am out. And after a quick dry with a towel I run off to shake my coat. I dry completely in a sunspot.

Just as well I decided to try harder to get over my water "thing". It will be an advantage. I'm surprised at how much I enjoy having a soft, fluffy coat after my bath. I can't believe it. I no longer fear water – the monster has gone. I've been out in the rain and had a bath without it distressing me excessively. It shows me what I can do if my head makes up its mind. At least I will be able to manage paddling in the pool on the weekends. I have no intention of trying to swim for pleasure. Cats know when enough is enough.

The singing doorbell wakes me from deep sleep.

'Jodi's here,' Karen calls. I ignore her, stretch, roll and blink to adapt to the bright sunlight. Jodi, Karen's cousin, will have to wait. She must have free time from her studies and be here to care for George while Karen catches up with her work. In the sunlit room Jodi's brown hair sways on her shoulders. Her large cat-like eyes search for me.

'There you are Sweetie!' She makes meowing noises and bends to stroke me. I roll on my back for her and allow her to tickle my tummy. Life is pleasant, perhaps too pleasant. I try to be optimistic with a tinge of caution. Experience has taught me that change is like fate. It is fickle and can have serious consequences.

Jodi and Karen are drinking tea and chatting in the kitchen. I sit at the door listening to their conversation that takes as long as a cat stalking a mouse.

'Do you remember Brett? Jodi asks. 'He was in senior school with me a class ahead. We started off being friends then drifted into a relationship. We've been together through Uni and I've always loved him.'

Karen gives Jodi a hug, 'That's great. I'm happy for you.'

Jodi nods. 'We're lucky to have found each other but living together isn't always a breeze. He still wants to go out with his mates and have me there waiting when he comes home.' She puts down her cup looks at Karen. 'He talks about a more serious relationship, but I don't think either of us are ready for it.'

Karen smiles and takes Jodi's hand, 'Give yourselves time. You're both very young.'

'You're right. We need to grow up a bit.' She looks up and notices me. 'Look who's listening at the door?'

I rush towards her and jump onto her lap. I anticipate a long, petting session. She has a perfect touch – gently sensual. While they keep talking, I'm in cat rapture and I don't hear a thing. Jodi's strokes become slower and softer as bliss ends.

She knows how distressing suddenly stopping a heavy petting session can be. Humans don't realise how awful it feels to be pushed off someone's lap when the juices of joy rise to a height. They should know. They're animals too, even if they have fine hairs and are without lustrous body fur. It must be their lack of insulating fur that makes them so peculiar. I purr and smile a secret cat smile that Humans can't see. They hear my purr but sadly they are limited. I shouldn't expect too much from Humans after all.

Both of us are wary of George since Karen started working again. He has changed from the young, placid child we knew and now has spells of wild naughtiness. When Karen dresses him in the morning, he squeals, making the start to the day noisy. He has found his voice and wants to be independent, except he isn't.

Another thing, he appears to have lost interest in us cats during his mood change. On his short, little legs, he chases us and pulls our tails. Neither of us bite him. Instead, we run from him to hide. A little later he calls us, 'Sorry Ollie, sorry Bell.'

When will the cat-loving child return?

While Karen was talking on her phone, he went into the bathroom and found a tube of toothpaste that had fallen onto the floor. He stomped on it and smeared creamy, white snakes all over the bathroom floor. That wasn't enough for him. He covered himself in the white cream too. When Karen saw it, she threw up her hands in horror and took a deep breath. I've noticed that when George is naughty, and it happens a lot now, she takes deep breaths. Maybe it is to stop her shouting too loudly or smacking him. Only once I saw her smack him. He yelled afterwards but she was more upset than he was. She hasn't done it again. I don't think she will.

Yesterday, he scribbled on the new sofa cover with his crayons. Karen gathered up the cover and squeezed it into the machine that churns as it washes. George ruined the previous sofa and Tony had to buy a new one. Now the sofa and all the chairs are protected with strange-smelling covers.

'He's trying to get my attention,' Karen tells Tony. 'I give him lots of love when he behaves well and ignore him when he does things like that. I hope it stops him.'

All cats in Heaven! This morning he is painting the long wall with his poos. Karen hasn't seen or smelled the stink yet. She will be cross. It is the type of behaviour that Karen will consider extremely naughty.

She shrieks when she sees the poo covered wall, 'Naughty, naughty boy...no!' She says loudly, picking him up. She rarely uses the word naughty, so she must be cross. She carries him to the shower. She does not squirt him with water in the way she squirted Oliver and me, but washes and rinses him, and not gently. Then she locks him in the small laundry that smells of dirty clothes for what she calls, "time out". His yelling is louder than Oliver's Siamese yowl and reverberates through the house. Karen ignores him for longer than usual. Eventually he stops crying. After a while Karen opens the door to let him out.

I can't help wondering if George is learning. His memory is short, much shorter than a kitten's memory. Now he is pulling vegetables out of the special tray in the kitchen. Karen will be cross again. Will she ignore his behaviour or put him in the laundry again? Oliver is smart and says that George knows that he is being naughty. That he is standing up to his mother and expressing his independence. Oliver says too that it will pass when he learns that he cannot win against his mother. Oliver is usually correct.

Over her lunch break, Karen makes George his favourite sandwich of cheese, tomato and lettuce. He is behaving well and eats without messing. She sits with him and tells him that he is her special boy.

'You're a big boy now. I can't be with you all the time my darling, but that doesn't mean I don't love you. I am here for you if you need me,' she says, kissing him again.

I purr when he says, 'Love you lots, Mum.'

Tony, Karen and Pops are in the television room discussing George.

'If he wants your constant attention now, Karen, what will he do when there's another little one?' Pops says.

'It is a worry, Pops.'

'Maybe you can ask Jodi to care for him when you're busy or at work. He likes her and behaves well when he's with her,' Tony suggests. He touches her hand. 'He is going through a naughty stage. If Jodi looks after him, you won't worry constantly about him.'

'It's worth thinking about,' Karen replies distractedly as she tidies the table in the television room.

I hear Karen's alarm buzz. She is slow in killing the noise today. I wait for her to come to my basket. Perhaps she has rolled over like a cat and gone back to sleep. Tony didn't wake her as he usually does. He made his own breakfast and left for work earlier. Softly I pad into the bedroom. Karen is asleep, and late for her appointment. I jump onto the bed and nudge her gently. Her eyes open with shock as she looks at the clock.

'Oh my goodness, I've overslept.' She tries to sit up and falls back onto the pillows, 'I'm exhausted.' Tears fill her eyes. 'I don't think I'll manage to work today, with all the worries about George and the new baby. It has built up and is tiring me.' Slowly she heaves herself out of the bed. 'I must check on George.'

I hear Pops talking in the background, 'Go back to bed Karen, you need rest. I'll look after George this morning and I'll phone the hospital to give your apologies.'

Karen is back in bed. I lie close to her. Tears of tiredness trickle down her face. I lick her tears and shift closer. We both sleep. I wake to the sound of Pops' heavy footsteps as he carries in a tray with a sandwich for Karen. She nibbles her food and takes a few sips of tea. She tosses and turns in the bed. I sense her exhaustion and wish I could do more to help her. If only I could give her more energy to recover. Maybe that's what my dream of helping Karen was about. Instinctively I know what to do. I concentrate on Karen through half closed eyes. I send her a message about a garden filled with beautiful, perfumed flowers and purr loudly. She likes flowers so it might help her. Instead of falling asleep I watch her breathe slowly and relax. She smiles at me, touches my head.

Karen is fatter now with a big bump in her middle. She tires more easily and is relieved to have Jodi helping her to care for George. This morning, Karen rushes past me.

'I'll be working at home today Bella. I won't need you in the therapy room. Enjoy spending time with George and Jodi.'

Jodi moves gracefully and sings to herself like a purring cat. She likes cats too, a definite plus. I like it when Karen talks to me as if I was Human. Maybe she really does know that I understand human language.

Oliver has come indoors after running about in our garden. He is in his favourite summer spot on the cool stone tiles. He likes Jodi too, and lifts his head to listen to her lilting voice. Once George is asleep, Jodi relaxes on the sofa. She picks up her phone and flicks through her messages. Her eyes shine and then she types furiously. Perhaps she is sending a message to Brett, her boyfriend. When she talks about him, she smiles a special, warm smile. Her eyes are misty. I lie next to her on the couch and sleep. There is only so much young, Human romance a cat can take.

Karen comes out of her room to look for George. Jodi points to George asleep on the sofa. 'There he is! Fast asleep with a cat on either side.'

'Let him sleep.' Karen sighs. 'He was restless last night, didn't sleep much. He kept us up and we didn't sleep much either.' She glances out of the window, up at the sky. 'The forecast for the weekend is warm. Hopefully, we'll be able to swim this weekend. You and Brett are welcome to come for lunch and a swim.'

'Thanks, Karen, I'd like that. I'll check with Brett.'

Sunday is a warm day with low, hanging clouds. Karen ignores the signs of rain as she prepares for her guests. Liz, Karen's mother, Jodi, Brett and Tony's work friends are expected for lunch. Tony and Pops are on the patio heating up the barbeque contraption to cook yummy meat and sausages.

George allows Karen to dress him with no complaints today. He looks neat in his shorts and tee and he is behaving himself. Will it last?

Tiny plump pearls of rain begin fall hissing on the barbeque. Tony looks up at the sky and scowls. 'With luck, I'll manage to cook our lunch. Such a pity, we won't be able to sit outdoors to eat it.'

Karen looks up at the sky. 'Let's hope the sun will be back later.'

Liz arrives and joins Karen in the kitchen. She places a plate of biscuits on the kitchen table and then gives Karen a hug and kiss.

Karen smiles and takes her mother's hand. 'These look yummy! We'll have more than enough food now.'

Whenever Liz is here our lives are disrupted. She dislikes cats, and us in particular. Oliver is unhappy. His tail sways and I growl softly. We hide inside behind the curtain, listen and watch. Tony's friends from work, Dave and Gavin arrive with their girlfriends. They are carrying bottles as gifts. The men talk and shake hands and the women kiss, the strange thing humans do when they meet. When Jodi and Brett arrive with a cake, the Human greeting ritual begins once again. The rain dances on the roof as they all stand in the television room staring longingly at the pool.

'Where are the cats?' Tony asks looking around.

Liz looks at Tony pleadingly.

Karen pretends not to notice her mother's complaints and we stay in the television room with the guests. A divine aroma trails her as she carries platters of cooked meat and sausage into the room. She places the food on the long table and Tony follows with bowls of salad – just grass and leaves. Humans eat an enormous amount of grass. After serving the guests, Karen gives us two separate plates of meat and sausage.

After our scrumptious meal we leave the noisy talk to find a quiet place to relax. I think of how much I dislike Liz and remember the stinky poo I made on the carpet next to her bed when she last came to stay. I won't "freak her out" again today. I'll save it for another time.

All the guests have left apart from Jodi, who is chatting to Karen on the couch. George is asleep with his head on Karen's lap.

'Brett shouldn't have gone off straight after lunch to meet his mates. It's rude!' Jodi says, looking unhappy.

Karen gives Jodi a reassuring hug. 'We don't mind. He's a great young, guy and fun, and he can't keep his eyes off you.'

Karen closes her eyes and rubs her tummy. 'I feel like some ice cream. Lately I've been craving for it. Tony, Jodi are you joining me?'

They both nod enthusiastically. Karen brings a tub from the fridge, with spoons, bowls and small plates for us. She opens the tub and a delicious milkiness melts into the meat aroma still in the room. She scoops out small spoonfuls for us. We have not tasted ice cream before and approach it cautiously. The Humans make slurping sounds as my tongue touches the cold sliminess. I lick some and like it. Oliver smells it and won't touch it. He doesn't eat milky foods – a Siamese thing. I lick up his portion. The day has ended well, after all.

Max is here to see Karen again this morning. He looks fatter and he smiles.

He stretches to pat my head. 'Hi kitty cat, so nice to see you again.'

'You look happier,' Karen says.

'I am, but I still have things to sort out. It's dad more than mum who is setting all the rules.'

Max rubs his hands together and his breathing is fast. I snuggle up to him.

'Hey, Bella, beautiful kitty, you understand about stress, don't you?'

'She does, and she's gone through a bit of stress in her life.'

'It's the same old story. Dad accepts that music is my thing, but he wants me to study law or accounting. He says at least I'll have a profession.'

Karen nods. 'That's true, a profession is an excellent backup in life.'

'He reckons he'll pay for my studies and give me enough cash so that I can join a band part-time.'

'That's reasonable as long as you're happy with his choices of study for you - law or accountancy?'

'No way! I'm not a corporate guy. If I'm going to study it would be journalism.'

'Have you discussed this with him?'

'Not yet. When he makes up his mind, he can be unmoveable.'

'Well, if you don't talk to him, you could end up studying subjects you dislike and leaving Uni. He wouldn't be happy about that, would he?'

'No he wouldn't, you're spot on.'

'Why aren't you telling him what you feel, Max?"

'I guess I'm scared of disappointing him, though I'm an adult now and shouldn't care.'

'He is still your father, Max.'

'And he was a strict father while I was a kid. He didn't beat me, but I had to keep to his rules.'

Karen nods.

'I know, it's time I asserted myself, spoke up for myself. I'll talk to him tonight.'

Now that I know Max will stand up to his father, I am relieved. My eyes feel heavy and my body wants to sleep, but my mind makes certain that I stay awake. I know that I have more work to do, more than purring or Max will take a long time to become confident and happy. Cat instinct leads me. I stare at Max, concentrate and close my eyes. Holding a sense of him, I send him healing, powerful purrs from deep within.

Jodi is caring for George again today. While he is asleep, she is on the phone talking to a friend. I listen to the first part of her conversation. She is discussing Brett in a breathless way and her eyes shine like a hungry cat who smells food.

'He's a darling, he never forgets my birthday. This year he sent me red roses and gave me a lovely gold bracelet with a heart. It's gorgeous and I wear it all the time.'

I look at her and see something on her arm that shines. It must be Brett's gift.

As she talks to her friend about "love", I drift off. I understand attraction but this "in love" thing Humans do is weird. When I was incarcerated in the cattery last year, during Karen and Tony's holiday, an athletic Bengal in the cage next to me caught my attention. Not only was he handsome with his spotted coat and green eyes, but athletic too. That dreaded word "neutered" enters my mind. Well, if the vet hadn't killed that special part of me, I'd have wanted kittens like him. We cats do not have long term relationships with sickening, romantic sentimentality like Humans. We mate if we haven't been "fixed" and move on. I think too of the white cat who waits for me at the fence of our garden. He smells good – a wasted opportunity. I live with Oliver who irritates me as much as he pleases me. We have no interest in each other than friendship. Perhaps we are too different, and then he's neutered. Pity about that!

When I wake, Jodi is still talking on her phone. I think she is talking to someone else now as she is repeating her story about Brett. Why Humans talk so much on the phone is another mystery.

For George each day is one of experimentation and what appears to be Human curiosity. Oliver compares George's behaviour to his own wild streak as a younger cat. I know that Oliver's wildness still lurks like a mouse under a carpet. Beneath his silky coat he is a stalking predator, biding his time. Will he run away as he did last year, or has he grown up enough to control his instincts?

Tony is on duty again tonight, cooking a dinner of lamb chops on the barbeque. The smell is tantalising, and my tummy can barely wait for our treat. Waiting is always a battle.

Tonight George's naughtiness comes to a climax. It had to happen eventually. He smells the meat cooking and when Tony isn't watching, he creeps too close to the roaring flames.

'No George! You'll burn yourself!' Tony shouts.

'But, I'm hungry.'

Of course, he doesn't listen to his father and tries to grab a chop. He drops it immediately and runs from the flames crying. Learning can be tough.

A shiver ripples through my fur as I wake this morning. The sky is dark with a malevolent tinge. Winds race wildly across the sky and thunder booms. The pace of blasting winds is terrifying. This has been a crazy summer of heat, rain and storms. A morning sleep is out of the question. I must remain vigilant and take preventative measures. I secure our house from the impending storm by spreading my scent widely and by making a quick detour visit to Bastet to seek protection. The storm begins by raining like mice and rats. We both hide under the big bed while rain and winds lash our house. Just as well the roof is secure now.

Outside, the grass and bushes are stripped of their leaves and debris floats on the murky water. The smell is disgusting. Our garden is in a sorry state and will take days if not weeks to dry. We are stuck indoors with George. Pops is as thoughtful as ever and makes us clever toys, tiny balls dangling on bits of string and furry bits of cloth on the end of elastic to chase. He takes large boxes from the back room, cuts holes in them and then assembles them for us to play in. Thanks to Pops we are occupied for a while.

The wild winds and soft ground keep George indoors. We follow our routine of sleeping, running through the house and chasing each other. George is restless and though he plays with his toys for short periods, he nags to go out. As he is forced to stay indoors, Karen encourages him to draw. Soon he is bored with that too. This morning he scribbled on the walls with crayons.

Karen is angry and takes deep breaths to keep calm as she grabs him. From the laundry, I hear her explaining to him why he is being punished. Then she closes the door and ignores his loud cries.

Later she opens the door. 'Every time you do naughty things like scribbling on the walls you will be locked in the laundry, George. Now you can help me clean your scribbles.' She collects brushes, soap and water and starts to show him how to clean the marks from the wall and expects him to help her. I don't think he'll do that again. Karen is a good mother who tries hard. She comments on all the positive things George does by saying "good boy" and giving him a hug. He is quietly playing with his toys now. Perhaps he is beginning to learn.

I am not a moody cat, but I am fed up with the howling wind, George's naughtiness, and hearing about Jodi's love life. The routine inside the house is too predictable and unstimulating. In bored desperation, Oliver slips outside and runs back in quickly. His eyes are red and irritated from dust and his coat matted with mud. Brushing and combing follows. I doubt his short visit outdoors is worth the consequences.

After what seems an endless stay indoors, cloudless, warm days dry our garden. The first day outside is a thrill. Many of our plants have disappeared, but our catnip has withstood the flood. Within days, new shoots spring up in the warmth. Karen plants some flowering shrubs that were inside and have grown too big. They will grow quickly and improve our garden. Soon, we will have a flourishing garden once more. Our lives are pleasant. As usual when life is pleasant, I tend to worry about possible change. With such unpredictable weather, it cannot be far away.

I was correct, the fine weather does not last. Trees sway in blustery winds. Karen peers out of the window. 'It's been a strange, short summer. Autumn will probably come early this year.'

I am curled up asleep when I feel a gentle tap. I open one eye and feel another tap. I mutter a cat curse and open both eyes. A rustle and a flutter. I sniff the air. It is Samantha. Why is she bothering me by roaming the house when she should be at rest? I can't help wishing she would leave. The moon is hidden in the dark sky. All I see of her is a furry, moving outline. Is she asking me to follow her? Reluctantly, I climb out of my basket. She is in the big bedroom now, hovering over Karen. Is she trying to tell me something about Karen? The early hours of a moonless night are not the time for cat philosophy. Slightly irritated, I return to my basket.

Karen's face is tight and worried as she tells Tony about George's latest exploits.

'Perhaps early kindergarten will help,' Tony suggests.

'I've been thinking about it. He's fine with the toilet and feeding himself, but he will be unhappy about leaving home and me.'

'It's has to happen eventually and playing with other children is what he needs,' Tony adds

On and on they talk, changing their minds like a cat that has lost its way. Sleep is an escape from it all.

They must have decided to send George to Kindergarten, as early this morning Karen dresses him. Then she fills a plastic box with fruit and a sandwich. Reluctant to go,

George digs his feet into the carpet like a scared kitten, and yells.

'Take your little bear Billy with you,' Karen says. He clings to Billy as Karen urges him towards the car. After more crying, at last, Karen drives off. They are back earlier than I'd hoped with George sobbing and clinging to Karen.

She gives him a hug. 'Mama is here and you know I love you lots. You're my big boy and you're going back to kindergarten tomorrow.'

After a quiet night, the morning begins with George crying again, refusing to leave the house. Finally, he agrees to go. Karen must be using magic to keep him still and take him to the car.

They return later, and George is not crying. Progress!

Two mornings a week, the house is peaceful while George is at kindergarten. When he returns, he is tired and sleeps for a few hours. He says he is enjoying kindergarten and Karen is smiling. So far, all is well with a small Human like George. One day there can be too many mice and the next day not a single mouse to catch.

I am on the back seat of Karen's car in my carry box on the way to a hospital. I don't complain about the early hour or wearing a harness, but the car lurches during the stop start journey and the air is foul. At last, she pulls up and parks. As she lifts me out of the car and I recall the smell of the earth and trees and the smell of the large hospital. Karen says that sadly that two Humans we once visited have passed over the Human, rainbow bridge.

We stop at the glass door and Karen talks to the Human

who watches everyone who enters like a guard dog. She shows him papers, he nods and allows us to enter the hospital. It is an overwhelming place with Humans of all ages walking, talking and rushing. We go down a long corridor and then we stop. Karen pushes a button on the wall and we enter the tiny moving enclosure she calls a lift. It is packed with an unpleasant Human smell. We stop and walk along another corridor – I take a deep breath. The air is fresher.

'We're here, at last. The teenage cancer ward,' Karen says.

I notice beds, teenage Humans, their parents and many nurses. Some of the young ones are in the beds with their parents next to them, others are in a different part of the ward playing or painting. There is a kitchen too, for coffee and tea. It is a busy place.

A nurse stops for a moment to greet us. 'Karen and Bella. Great to see you both today! So many patients adore cats and miss their own cats at home. They will enjoy a visit from this ginger beauty.'

'Bella will enjoy it too. She likes doing her job.'

The nurse lifts her foot uncomfortably, obviously wanting to move on. 'A young man you have both visited before, Benjamin...Benjy, is back in hospital for further treatment. He's been asking for you two.'

She points to his bed and dashes off.

Benjy is sitting up in bed waiting for us. 'Hi there! Great to see you Karen, and hi, Princess. It's ages since you both visited me,' he says excitedly.

I jump onto his bed to greet him with rubs and deep purrs.

He strokes me and looks into my face, then his eyes blink slowly with "cat kisses." I return his eye blinks and snuggle close to him.

'So, how're you doing?' Karen asks.

'Up and down. I had a good break for a few months after treatment, but some of the symptoms have returned. Nothing serious, I just need more chemo to make sure it's gone for good. The doc is optimistic.'

Karen nods. 'What have you been doing since we saw you last?'

'I've been studying massage. The nurses have been great and allowed me to practice on them. They like my massages and I have a queue waiting.' He laughs. 'I have passed all the theory subjects with high grades. Only a little more practical experience and I'll have my certificate.'

'That's great, Benjy. You've used your time here well.'

'As soon as I'm strong enough, I'll carry on studying an advanced course and animal massage therapy too. I want to massage animals.'

Karen smiles broadly.

He turns to me. 'I wonder if you remember your massage, little one?'

I think of the wonderful massage Benjy gave me during our visit last year. Will I be lucky again?

'Since you were here last, I've massaged one of the therapy dogs. He enjoyed it. I've been waiting to try some new tricks I've read about for cats. Another special massage coming up just for you, Bella.'

He begins to talk to me softly as I move closer. He rubs my neck and back slowly and oh so gently with such a caring touch. He smooths tight muscles and sore spots. Divine. Heaven. It must not stop. Unfortunately, it ends, and I tingle with pleasure. Purring loudly, I turn my head to look at him and give him one of my rare licks.

'That must've been good,' he says with a smile.

'Listen to Bella's deep purr for your answer.'

His expression changes and he looks away.

'All going well, I'll have my final treatment in three weeks. After that, they'll check me out from head to toe. Then hopefully, they'll allow me to go home. I can't wait!'

I'm grateful to Benjy for the magnificent massage he gave me with a full heart. Now I want to give him my gift of healing. I slow my breathing, and half-close my eyes. Holding a sense of Benjy, I purr from deep inside and imagine a shower of white, healing light spreading over him. When I open my eyes again, he is relaxed and smiling.

'Wow, Bella, you sent me a deep, warm healing purr... I felt it."

I look away.

'You have an incredible cat there Karen. She's breaking new boundaries with her purrs.'

'Yes, Bella is an amazing cat.'

Karen has no idea of what happened between Benjy and me. One day she'll find out.

We leave Benjy with a promise to visit him again if he is still in hospital. Karen has a list of teens she wants to visit and keeps me tightly on the lead while I follow. We find the teens in another ward. Their eyes are on are on me as soon as we greet them.

'What a pretty cat,' one says.

'So friendly and I love her ginger coat,' another comments. They gather closely around me. I feel trapped, but I don't pull at the lead to escape. Karen reads me well and lifts me into her arms.

'One at a time, or poor Bella will be swamped.'

I hear their names as they chat to Karen and stroke me. There are too many young Humans for me to tell them apart. Most have no or little hair and look the same, but each one smells different.

'This is our first visit this year. We'll be back to see some of you individually,' she says.

We are about to leave when a tall Human who has kind vibrations approaches us. He introduces himself as the doctor in charge of the ward. He looks ordinary and doesn't even wear his white coat. As he talks busy nurses and patients gather around him.

'Bella is one of the special therapy cats who visits the hospital. Few people know that cats provide us with more than just emotional support. They contribute to our well-being with their soothing purrs.'

He goes into more details about our purrs and two of the teenagers seem bored and leave the group.

'Too much for me,' the one says.

He continues, 'Research is in its infancy about the therapeutic value of cats. From what we know so far, when a cat purrs within a frequency range of 20-140 Hertz, we Humans can benefit from the vibrations. It's all a bit technical,' he says with a laugh. 'We think the frequency of purrs corresponds to the frequency that scientists use in vibrational therapies to promote tissue regeneration.' He smiles. 'It's easiest to remember that purring can lower stress and improve our wellbeing. Whatever researchers say, cats and other animals improve our mood and ease our worries. They are our precious friends.'

As we move away from the group a nurse takes us to Heather. She looks around thirteen, and is in bed holding a book in her hand, though she is not reading it. She has sparse golden hair, her skin is milky cream and her eyes are blue like Oliver's. I cannot help staring at her.

Heather puts her hand out to me shakily. 'Hello there! What a gorgeous cat. What's your name?'

''Bella,' Karen replies.

'How weird that is. My middle name is Bella.'

'Then, you two have a lot in common.'

Heather pats the side of her bed. 'Come sit, Bella.'

I jump up and she strokes my head.

'Beautiful, loving Bella, you are so calm, and you look happy. I wish I felt like that,' she sighs. 'The chemo has shaken me. I feel so sick each time I have a treatment. I've asked, but they won't stop it. Will I ever go home?'

Karen draws her chair closer as I nestle into Heather's lap. She talks to Karen in low tones about how sad and hopeless she feels. I can tell Karen is concerned about Heather by the deep furrows on her forehead. Lines appear on her face when she is worried or upset. They talk until tea and cake arrive. There is no food for me. I am hungry and disappointed.

Heather pushes her tea and cake aside and tells Karen she's not hungry. After their chat, Karen asks to speak to Heather's nurse. While Karen waits for the nurse, I want to use my new skill of sending healing. I follow the same process I used with Benjy. When the doctor arrives, Heather is relaxed.

'Something happened that made me feel warm deep inside. I am certain it came from Bella. Thank you darling, Bella.'

Karen and the doctor discuss Heather in soft tones.

When we are about to leave, Heather clutches me. 'I wish you could stay with me, Bella. You are a lovely cat and you make me feel calmer.'

Karen, scratches her head. 'What about taking a few photos of Bella? Then you can look at her and remember how calm she made you feel until we visit again.'

After Heather has taken photos of me, we leave promising to see her again soon. At the door, the tall doctor in charge of the ward approaches us.

'I hope you'll be back often, and with Bella. The patients adore her and you both help them so much. They seem calmer and more positive after you've gone.'

'That is excellent feedback and it makes our work worthwhile. We'll be back soon.'

Once we are out of the hospital, I breathe fresh air and relax.

I enjoy the stimulation of visiting Humans in hospital and using my healing gifts to help them, but by the end of the day I am exhausted. I know that I'm never satisfied. Even a cat asking for more may not want to eat a whole bowl at once. If I'm tired Karen must be tired too. She has a sense of duty and forces herself to carry on even when she needs rest.

Today, we are in a small hospital for elderly Humans. I am being passed from one lap to another for petting sessions. The old people enjoy stroking and cuddling me and I'm pleased that they are happy. Karen's phone rings but she ignores it.

When it keeps ringing she answers. 'Yes... Oh, Oh dear! He's upset and crying? I'm at work, but I'll leave immediately.' She apologises and hurriedly places me in my carry box. Half running to the car, she jostles me about mercilessly and almost throws my box onto the back seat. She drives faster than usual.

'Sorry, Bella, Sweetie,' she says at a traffic light stop. 'George is very upset. I have to fetch him from kindergarten.'

When we arrive at the kindergarten, she rushes inside and I am left on the back seat with the windows open. I recognise George's cries from a distance. They are like the yowls of an upset cat. Before Karen straps George into his safety seat, she kisses and hugs him. He sobs all the way home. Nothing Karen says comforts him. Once we are inside the house, Karen frees me from my box. I run to my litterbox, eat and drink. Then I search for George and Karen and find them in the television room.

George is on Karen's lap while she talks softly to him, 'Now, Georgie, tell mama what has been happening.'

He blurts out his words in such a jumble that not even Karen understands him.

'Slowly, my love.'

'That big girl, Sophie, says horrible things to me and Liam does too.'

'What did they say my sweetie?'

'That my lunch stinks more than my poos and they tell lies about me that I wet my bed every night.'

'You know that none of it is true, my love. They're just nasty.'

'And today she punched and pushed me ... and took my Billy...'

'Did she hurt you?'

'Na...but she's got my baby bear.'

'What happened?'

He busts into tears again and talks between sobs, 'She pushed me hard, I dropped Billy, and then she took him.'

'My darling, I don't want you to worry about Billy. I will try to find him. Meanwhile, I'll help you to undress. Then lie in your bed and try to sleep a little.'

Once George is in bed, I jump up next to him. He needs lots of purrs and a special head butt. He is still little and has been treated awfully – like a kitten who has been bitten and his best ball stolen. Karen will fix it. She always does. When George is asleep, I look for Karen. She is talking on the phone and sounds angry.

'Mrs Atherton, I have to tell you that your Sophie and her brother Liam are bullies. At kindergarten today she and Liam pushed and punched my son, George, and took his bear.'

There was silence.

'Well, The teacher saw it happen,' Karen says.

As Karen listens, she taps the table impatiently. 'Well, George is extremely upset and wants his bear, so please find it and my husband will collect it.'

When Tony arrives, Karen tells him what happened to George. He is both angry and upset. 'I can't believe that children under four can already be bullies.'

'I'm going to complain to the supervisor about bullying at the kindergarten. It's not good enough. The teachers should've intervened and sorted it out,' Karen says angrily.

The phone rings and Tony answers. 'It's Mrs Atherton,' he whispers to Karen, 'She's looked everywhere for the bear. Sophie didn't bring it home. It must still be at the kindergarten.'

'I'll try to find it when I go to the school tomorrow to talk to the supervisor. Bullying behaviour is not acceptable, especially at this young age!'

She clenches her fist. I haven't seen Karen as angry before, like an enraged mama cat whose kitten has been threatened or hurt.

George is awake now and eating dinner. He asks Karen if she has found Billy.

'Not yet, my darling. We'll try to find him.'

He pushes his food away and starts to whimper. 'I want my Billy.'

Only Karen's hugs and kisses calm him. In bed that night Karen and Tony discuss George again.

'Perhaps he shouldn't go back to kindergarten,' Karen says. 'It's my fault, I didn't realise that he's not ready emotionally. He will have to learn how to get along with other children his age first, become tougher and more confident. Before sending him to kindergarten I should have taken him to special children's play activities or to the park where he can learn to play with other children. I won't leave it to Jodi, I'll go with him myself now.'

'Yep, he's not quite ready. There'll always be bullies and I guess he'll have to learn to ignore them. If that doesn't help, to go to his teacher or come to us for help.'

Karen sighs. 'Those young bullies and their families are a worry and could do with some counselling. I don't want to think what they'll turn into later.'

Pearly light streams through the windows. Karen is already in the kitchen. Why is she up so early? She usually sleeps late on the weekend. Oliver is awake too and we creep towards the kitchen to investigate.

Karen spots us and laughs. 'The wonderful smell of a chicken roasting in the oven has woken you two. Of course, you'll have chicken treats.'

The word "treats" is one of my favourites as it results in something delicious. I sniff. Spicy fish is cooling on the bench top before she moves it into the fridge. Spice burned my mouth once and taught me a lesson. Never again. She is cutting and chopping heaps of green stuff that doesn't look or smell at all enticing. Two full bowls go into the fridge. Now she is filling a platter with tiny bits of bread and covering it with plastic.

She wipes her forehead and sighs loudly. 'Done at last.'

Tony has arrived in the kitchen. 'You're up early,' he scratches his head. 'Liz is coming for lunch today, isn't she?'

Karen nods.

'I'll make myself scarce after lunch. While you and your mum chat, I'll work on my computer.'

A day of Liz. How awful! Oliver gives me one of his knowing looks. Liz is a special category of Human to be totally avoided. She is not worth our wasting a moment of cat time.

She arrives early. Karen runs to her bedroom quickly to wash and change her clothes before greeting her mother. Liz is quick to make sharp comments about her daughter's appearance. Whenever Liz visits, she brings George a present. Today she has a small package for him. He pulls at the bow and paper. Once it's opens, he looks at it quizzically. It is a minute toy animal – one I haven't seen before.

Karen smiles. 'You're a lucky boy, George. A tiny monkey that will play with you, a new toy popular with children in the USA. It's an expensive toy Mum. You're spoiling him.'

George stares at the monkey and doesn't touch it.

'Look how cute it is, George. It moves, blinks its eyes and blows kisses, Liz says.'

The artificial animal winds itself around Liz's finger. Then George holds it and plays with it unenthusiastically. He gives Liz a quick kiss, places the tiny toy on a cushion and looks at Karen. 'I want my Billy!'

It is beyond reason why Liz has brought her grandson this tiny monkey creature – a dead thing that pretends to move, when he has two real cats as friends and lots of soft bears. Oliver flicks his whiskers in disdain, a habit of his. We both walk away.

While Liz and Karen talk, George looks for us.

'Bell, Bell...Ollie,' he calls.

Oliver doesn't respond, but I go to him.

He strokes my head with his tiny hand.

'Let's play!' He says.

I don't feel like playing his version of hide and seek. I try to please him by allowing him to hide and then pretend to find him. When he is bored with this game, he calls me to run around the house with him. His little feet make small steps and the game is slow. I tire of playing and run through the cat door into our garden to sleep in the sun.

Oliver

Maintain independence except when hungry or affection is required.

The mystery of Billy's disappearance continues. George is distressed and still not sleeping well without Billy. There are two words Karen uses often to describe the precious qualities that George must develop – confidence and resilience, both hard to achieve for a young Human. Then, I am a cat equipped with those attributes. Like all cats, I had to learn to be tough and independent from a young age.

Today, George brings a friend home he met at his art classes during the holidays. They eat together, play their strange games and laugh at their jokes. I am pleased he is enjoying himself. Best of all I watch them play. When they bore me, I sleep.

Logic has deserted our house. Not only is the weather unpredictable, but Samantha's spirit has returned and Bella's religiosity has increased. Her daily visits to Bastet's statue concerns me. Since chaos appears to have hit the house, Bella seems to find comfort in the certainty of her belief that Bastet will shield her from all her troubles. As for me, I am sure more challenging events are on the way.

As I have no control over them, I will fortify myself with food and sleep.

The moon is a slither in the navy sky when I hear Bella leave her basket. She is unaware that I am following her as she visits Bastet in the sitting room. Then she checks on our Humans as they sleep. Stepping delicately on my fine, Siamese paws, I follow her at a distance. Samantha's spirit is here again to visit Karen. Though Bella thinks I am not aware of the ghost cat, I sense her presence but chose not to bother with her. It perplexes me that I am unable to find a logical answer for her appearance. After all, why would a cat's spirit return to roam in this house rather than rest forever? Something significant must be drawing her here. Her pale outline is in the bedroom hovering over Karen. Tiny, diaphanous buds on her shoulders quiver. She is a cat with wings, an angel cat. I hide and watch, attempting to find answers for her visits. The only plausible answer is that she is worried about Karen now that she is carrying a new baby, as well as caring for George and working hard. She is here to protect Karen. But I don't understand why she needs to visit Karen when we are both protecting her? I find it insulting that she doesn't trust us to guard and care for Karen.

Today is a happy day for George. Karen found his bear, Billy. He hugs and kisses the filthy toy.

He smiles at Karen. 'Thanks for finding Billy, Mama!'

'He was hiding behind a couch at the kindergarten. I'm glad you're happy to have him back. We'll wash him when you have your bath.'

Swimming is fun and I am mastering it as well as a cat

can. I doubt I could swim any faster or adopt a different style. Tackling a new project would challenge me more, but at this moment there is nothing worthy of my attention or perseverance. Bella is a true companion, but she is predictable. She follows the rules of the house and hasn't a creative idea in her ginger head. She is smart in her own way and knows me as well as the inside of her basket. She pulls me into line if I disobey the house rules. My wild side niggles restlessly. I look out of the window at the distant hills and long to run free. I dream often of the red paper flying in the sky on a string that Tony made for George. I long to be like it, kissing the low clouds, seeing the trees, the tops of houses, gardens, and further towards the blue mountains in the distance. When I think of alluring females calling me, choosing the one who appeals to me and fulfilling my purpose of fathering our species, I am resentful.

I wake from a sleep and an exciting dream.

I am a wild cat, born in the forest living with my Mama, sisters and brother among a group of cats on the mountain side. Though we are lone hunters, we sleep together for safety at night to protect ourselves from our predators – owls, hawks, wild dogs, racoons and foxes. Each night, one cat keeps watch, hidden in the branches of a tall tree. The rest of us sleep deeply to recover from an active day and restore our energy.

While hunting for food, I sense movement – a brown fox with a long, bushy tail is behind a rock waiting. As the juices of fear rush through me, I am alert and ready. I am no match for its big jaw and sharp teeth. It nears, stalking me, and then chases me through the high grass. To escape,

I jump across a rocky ravine and scale a tree. Bushy tail is unable to jump across the ravine. I am safe, for now.

After taking a long route home, I cuddle up to my friend, a stripped cat and sleep. I wake in the pink light. The guard cat jumps down from the tree to rest.

While Bella is visiting sick humans with Karen, I am with Pops and George in the television room. George is building with coloured blocks. When he tires of them he kicks them away. Pops helps him to open a box of new toys – tiny creatures. There are cats, dogs, larger four-legged animals I have not seen before, creeping things and birds. Humming to himself, George places them on the carpet as he creates his own animal world.

I like George and protect him as I have in the past. It is my duty, though I am not as attached to him as Bella is, and doubt my feelings will change. I am sorry about his experience of bullying at kindergarten. Since he has been back home, he's been a nuisance. He is demanding of Jodi and robs me of extra time spent with Tony. Hopefully soon he will be less dependent on others, grow stronger and have adult muscles like Tony. Then his childhood bullies will be forgotten. How peculiar it is that his parents make a fuss of his every new word or achievement. Soon Karen will bring another little human creature into the house to obsess about. I wonder over and over how George, who is the centre of attention in the house now, will cope with the competition of another little one.

Pops puts his newspaper down for a moment, looks at Bella's empty basket and resumes his reading. I can tell he misses her. He looks about and then calls me. Since the recent cat show, I have been less affectionate towards him and pretend I don't hear him calling me. The show was an appalling experience, the grooming beforehand, then the parading and judging was almost more than a sensitive cat can tolerate. I fulfilled his expectations by winning a rosette for him. He knew I loathed all the shampooing and fussing, being stared at and prodded by judges, but he didn't consider my feelings. I feel used. Merely a creature to satisfy his needs rather than mine. Of course, I am aware that as a cat my place in the world is lowly in comparison to Humans, but he ought to care more. I can't help my feelings of resentment. And cats can store resentment for a long time. I certainly do.

After dinner, George is in his bed and Bella is asleep next to Karen, who is too fat and uncomfortable to allow Bella to sit on her lap.

Karen stretches and sighs. 'I'm so tired lately.'

Tony sighs too. 'Work is demanding and some days it's hard to keep up.' He sits up and turns to her. 'What about going away for the long weekend?'

'A great idea. George will be with us, but what about the cats? Remember how they hated the last cattery we took them to and caused a virtual revolution.'

'Well, we can't leave them with Pops. He is too forgetful lately He told me that he won't look after them again. They're a responsibility.'

'I've heard of a great cattery where the cats are treated royally and don't even want to come home.'

I hear the word "cattery" and my ears snap in fright. No matter how well they treat us at this cattery, we'll be shoved into our carry boxes and endure a car journey, which I loathe. Then Karen and Tony will leave us at a strange place that stinks of cat excrement and is covered in the scents of other cats previously incarcerated. How dreadful! I won't tell Bella yet. Why upset her unnecessarily. They may change their minds, as often happens, and decide not to go.

 # Bella

A Human's lap is my lap, and it is comfortable too.

A crowd gathers around us in the cancer ward and teenagers clamber to touch and hold me.

'Hi pretty kitty, let me pat you.'

'Wow! You have such lovely, soft fur.'

'Come to me, gorgeous.'

'I want to hold the cat.'

I feel overwhelmed and try to move away from them.

'Please wait and give Bella some space. You'll each have a turn with her,' Karen says with an edge to her voice.

I am on a bed with the teens around me when a doctor rushes up to us.

'Karen, I need you and your cat to help us urgently.'

'Sorry folks, we must leave you all for a while, we'll be back later,' she says to the group of teenagers.

Karen hold's my lead and I follow her and the doctor to a bed further down the ward. All I see is black curls poking from the sheets. A frightened face emerges.

'Hi Tanya,' the doctor says. 'You asked to see Bella, the ginger cat. Karen is here to visit you with Bella. She'll help you to feel better.'

'Hello, Bella.' She places her small hand on my head. 'You're such a lovely cat and have beautiful eyes. I have a cat at home called Simba and I miss him,' she says in a sad voice.

She sits up as I jump onto her bed, and I purr loudly.

'Tanya is upset, she needs an injection, but she's terrified of needles,' the doctor says.

'No...no! I don't want an injection,' she cries and twists her body away from him.

I am sorry for this little one. Karen sits next to the crying child and wipes away her tears with a tissue. I move closer to Tanya and keep purring.

Karen speaks softly, just above a whisper, 'Our vet gave Bella an injection last week and her friend Oliver had one too.' She picks up her phone and searches through her pictures to show one to Tanya. 'This is our handsome Oliver.'

'He's a beauty and with such gorgeous blue eyes. You have two lovely cats.' She strokes me and looks up. 'Why did your cats have injections? They don't look sick.'

Karen explains that every year we both have injections to prevent us from developing infections from other cats and to keep us well.

'Were Bella and Oliver upset about having injections?' She asks.

Karen smiles. 'All they felt is a tiny prick that didn't hurt and they were fine.'

'They are brave cats,' Tanya says with her first smile.

'If Bella stays with you do you think you can be brave too?' Karen asks.

'Can I hold Bella and shut my eyes?'

'Of course you can.'

A nurse arrives, and Tanya holds me a little too tightly for comfort, but she has her injection and loosens her grip.

'I'll bet you hardly felt it,' Karen says.

'It didn't hurt at all. With Bella here I am brave,' she says and gives me another pat.

'Close your eyes and think of Bella whenever you need to have another injection,' Karen says, giving her a hug.

We return to the group of teenagers so that they can each have a turn at stroking me. I enjoy the way each one touches me differently. I am lucky to be wanted and needed. I purr for them all.

Karen glances at her watch. 'Sorry, we have to leave now. We're visiting others in the hospital. We'll be back soon. Feel better all of you!'

In the long corridor, a man with dark hair looks at Karen as he passes us. He stops and smiles warmly at her as if he knows her. But she does not return the smile.

'Let me see…what a cute cat you have in the box.'

'Thank you,' Karen replies coolly as she walks away.

I think he fancies Karen and was looking for an excuse to chat to her. Human males aren't that different to feline ones.

We are visiting Benjy next and find him easily. He is sitting in an armchair and grins when he sees us.

'Hi Karen and gorgeous Princess! What a great surprise!'

Karen smiles. 'It's good to see you sitting up, but I'm surprised you're still here. Any news about going home?'

His smile is gone, and his eyes are teary. 'Unfortunately, it's been put back a bit. More treatment first. I'll be here for a while. The doctors have found a few more problems.'

'Oh, I'm so sorry.'

'Well, it's better sorting things out than going home and having to come back again.'

Karen nods.

He taps his lap. 'Come and sit with me, Gorgeous.'

While he talks to Karen, I have the benefit of his expert touch. He certainly knows how to give a cat pleasure.

One of the nurses join us. 'Benjy is a wonder. He's been giving us nurses foot massages. Absolutely wonderful after a day's work.'

Karen asks if he needs any books or information to help with his studies.

He points to a pile of books and papers next to his bed and shakes his head. 'Thanks, that's kind of you, I have all I can manage for now.'

I am sad that Benjy is struggling, and will try to send him healing. I close my eyes and breathe deeply until I feel warmth in my chest. Then I purr and send my healing to Benjy. I am pleased to see light around him in a circle of white.

'I feel your warm, healing purrs, Bella, and I feel great. Thank you.'

Karen takes Benjy's hand. 'I'm sorry, we must go. I hope the treatments help and you feel better soon.'

I nudge him with my head, place my paw on his arm and move away.

We look for Heather. She has been moved into another ward and is difficult to find. A nurse helps us to locate her bed. But she's asleep.

'She hasn't slept for nights, so I don't think we should wake her,' the nurse says. 'Leave a note, and I'll see she gets it.'

Karen writes her a note and gives it the nurse.

'We'll try to visit again soon.'

Something is about to happen. Karen is dragging suitcases from the top cupboards in the back room. When I see a suitcase of any size, I know what it means – a holiday for them and misery for us. In panic, I hide among the rocks in our garden. Oliver finds me and tries to calm me. He knew about the holiday two weeks ago. But he didn't want to upset me and kept the news to himself. I creep back inside the house. More than anything, I need to know when they are leaving and if they are taking us to the same disgusting jail of a cattery they took us to previously. Leaving our house wherever they take us will be distressing. The house and garden are our world.

From under the bed, I watch Karen remove clothes from the cupboard and place them in a suitcase. She changes her mind several times, replacing one item with another. Why does she need to take so many clothes with her? Perhaps it's a human characteristic. We have only one coat, fuller in winter and lighter in summer – enough for us.

Later, Tony repeats the process of packing. He is faster than Karen and fills his suitcase with fewer clothes. Humans are indeed strange!

Karen sees me hiding under the bed and calls me, but I refuse to go to her.

'Bella is under the bed and Oliver is hiding behind the curtain. They know we are leaving. Poor cats had a dreadful time at the last cattery. I hope that they will be happier at the new one.'

So, it's a new cattery they are taking us to, another place of torture and incarceration. I know we will hate it. Oliver joins me under the bed. He snuggles close and licks my head. At least we will be together during this horrible period. We sleep fitfully under the big bed, knowing that at any time they will snatch us from safety and place us in our carry boxes.

In the dark of the new morning, Tony crawls on his hands and knees and tries to grab me, I manage to escape and run to hide under George's bed. Oliver hides too.

Tony sighs. 'Now I'll have to search for you both.'

Karen helps him search. 'Our poor cats hate leaving their

home. I wish we didn't have to put them in a cattery. It's a pity Pops can't care for them and Jodi is too busy.'

Karen knows our hiding spots and doesn't take long to find us.

We are in our carry boxes on the back seat of the car next to umbrellas, coats and hats as the car twists and bumps. At least I smell flowers and trees during the journey.

When we arrive, a Human with a sweet voice greets us. 'Welcome Oliver and Bella, you'll enjoy being here with us.'

Karen and Tony discuss the food we eat with the Human, then we are carried to a small room with an intense cat smell. They watch as we jump out of our boxes to inspect the room.

We are in a cat room with two low couches, a box of toys and large windows with views of plants, a spurting fountain and relaxing music is playing. Now for the food – a choice of dry pebbles, water and a bowl of fishy bits for each of us.

'Have fun my treasures. I'll be back to take you home soon,' Karen says, as she bends to stroke us each in turn.

We are too distracted by our luxury accommodation to hear her. We investigate thoroughly, sniff the furniture and scratch poles. We discover that we have our own cat door that leads to a private fenced courtyard that catches the morning sun. There is a small grassy garden as well. It has bushes and a tree trunk with wide branches that resembles the half-tree at home. What a pleasant place for a cat's holiday, where we can play, sleep inside or on our sunlit patio and enjoy the tasty food. After a complete cleansing of past inmates and our own scent rubbed throughout the room and its furniture, we are satisfied with our accommodation.

The couches are low and wide, built for cats to stretch, cuddle or lie together. Balls, dangling, coloured mice and squeaky toys in a box are not exciting. We prefer to relax to the music and watch water spurting from the fountain. Outdoors, flowers and plants grow in abundance. We nibble petals and enjoy the scratchy feel of spiky succulents. A generous amount of catnip is planted in deep tubs and we eat and roll in it. Birds congregate near the fountain. As usual, our jingling bells warn them of our presence. We have a friendly, white cat on one side. We talk and rub each other through the fence wire. Our other neighbour, a green-eyed, brown cat, is shy and spends most of her time inside. The gentle carer visits often and when she strokes me I sense she respects cats. The weekend passes in the flick of a cat's tail. When we hear Karen's voice we wait at the door to greet her. The stay was a delightful holiday. This time we don't turn our back on her as we did previously when she left us.

Karen is awake early. She calls me to the kitchen to eat while she has her breakfast.

'My work at the hospital has piled up since I've been away, so we'll have to leave early,' she mumbles between mouthfuls of cereal. She is eating well now and is even fatter. The short holiday must've helped her to relax. The tone of her voice tells me she is happy again.

The heavy traffic slows us down jolting the car as it stops and starts. Parking is difficult to find and Karen curses loudly. My ears flicker. Karen doesn't curse! This is new.

My box swings uncomfortably as she hurries towards the hospital entrance. We squash into a lift filled with smelly Humans and she carries me through endless newly washed corridors that stink of disinfectant. Usually we visit hospitals later in the day when the strong smell of the disinfectant has worn off. An officious security guard stops us to demand that Karen removes me from the hospital corridor. It is a lengthy business, and nothing new, but Karen remains calm as she shows the guard papers that confirm my right to be there. Shamefaced, he apologises.

First, we visit Heather who was asleep last time. She looks up from messaging on her phone and waves.

'I was upset that I missed you both when you visited me last time. I'm so happy to see you today.'

She pats her bed. 'Come and sit up here with me, Bella.'

I jump up and she strokes me from my head to the tip of my tail. How delightful! I notice she has changed. Not only is she skinnier, but all her hair has gone. Despite the changes, she is optimistic and happier.

'Since I saw you two last, I've had chemo treatments. Not easy with the nausea, and aches and pains in my hands and feet. I am coping and feel that I'm getting better. Only two more treatments to go and then x-rays to see if there's a positive change. All going well, I'll be allowed to go home. Then I'll be seeing my doctor as an out-patient.'

Karen squeezed her hand. 'That's great, Heather. I'm so pleased you are more positive.'

Karen and Heather chat. The sound of their talk reminds me of the rumbling noise of my food pellets being shaken in their bag. When they stop talking, I give Heather my special gift of deep healing purrs. She smiles with pleasure and relaxes back against her pillows. Perhaps my healing is helping her.

'I hope all turns out well for you,' Karen says as we leave.

From the smell of male Humans and sound of their voices, I realise we are in the adult male ward. Karen opens my box and clips on my lead. Heads of brown, blond and black hair, and no hair at all, stare at me.

'A cat!...a cat!...cat is here!,' reverberates through the ward.

'How wonderful to see you, Karen and?' The nurse's voice rises in a question.

'This is Bella, we're here to see Grant.'

She looked puzzled. 'Oh, yes, Dr de Lambert mentioned you would be bringing a cat to see Grant. He's recovering from a car accident but he's still in pain. Follow me.'

We find him sitting in a padded chair so large that it consumes most of him. His gloomy eyes look up at us.

'Hi Grant, I'm Karen and this is Bella.'

'Thanks for coming and for bringing Bella.' He looks at me and his eyes brighten, 'I'm crazy about cats.'

There is a sadness in his voice, 'I have a cat called Biscuit at home...and I miss her a lot.'

In seconds I am on his lap. He strokes me and remains silent as he stares ahead. Karen talks to him, but his answers are short and flat. When they discuss his recent accident, he covers his face with his hands.

'I try not to think about it, but the pain reminds me all the time and I'm having awful dreams about it.'

Karen nods and he continues, 'The future looks pretty grim. I was slightly over the alcohol limit and the accident was my fault. My employers aren't at all sympathetic and I've lost my job. At forty-five I can't imagine retraining.'

While Grant strokes me, Karen tries to reassure him.

He looks away. 'No point in talking about it. I can't do a thing while I'm stuck in hospital. The doctors say I'll probably need an operation and will be here for at least another month or longer.'

Karen asks him if he has talked to his wife about the way he is feeling, and his worries.

He shakes his head. 'We don't talk much and a lot of it

is my fault. I don't want to burden her, she has enough to cope with.'

Karen nods. 'Does she visit?'

'She pops in every day and tells me about the children.'

'Perhaps you can try to have a talk. It will help to be open with each other.'

He stares at a painting on the wall. 'I'll try.'

I purr for him and he smiles.

'You're such a loving cat, Bella. You make me feel much calmer.'

Karen wishes him well and we leave.

In the hospital carpark, the man with masses of dark hair who smiled at Karen before, gives her a long look and grins at her. 'Ah, the lovely lady with her beautiful cat is back.'

Why is he trying to chat to Karen? He smells strange and I don't like him. He is not interested in me. He's like a tomcat on the prowl. My job is to protect her and keep her safe. I growl at him and then hiss loudly.

'Okay, cat! Cool it! I'm not talking to you. I'm talking to your owner.'

I hiss again. Louder this time.

'Get lost!' Karen mutters as she pushes past him and hurries to the car.

'Thank you, Bella, my sweetie! He's an awful man and you're looking after me. I don't think he'll worry us again.'

Karen is as feisty as a cat, and I am proud of her.

Oliver

Show important Humans affection with gifts of small dead creatures.

'Oliver, Oliver my beauty, come,' Pops calls. I look up, lift my paw and move slowly in his direction. I hope for some slices of dried meat as a treat, and petting too, of course.

Pops looks at me and smiles. 'You are such a handsome cat, Oliver.'

Oh no! The word handsome is not necessarily a positive one. I hope Pops is not considering entering me in another cat show. All that shampooing, combing and gel on my fur. All those Humans staring at me and touching me. Bella has a great expression for things she despises, *Meeyuk*! I'll add to that, *Catavolting*!

He stands at the shelf where my red rosette stands. He dusts the shelf, shakes my rosette and returns it to its position. 'One last show for us both and a blue rosette for the best neutered cat. Win this one and it will be our shared trophy.'

I loathe the idea of another cat show. I thought I was free of it, that it was over. Now all Pops wants is for me to win, and I don't think he cares how I feel about it. I'm not at all interested in winning a prize at another show. I glare and turn my back on him, but he doesn't even notice. Perhaps Pops is clinging onto the past. He has become frail, his body has shrunk and his beard is white. He is slower and more forgetful and has been losing his glasses.

After dinner, he talks excitedly to Karen and Tony about showing me again.

Karen tries to dissuade him. 'Oliver has had enough of cat shows and he won a rosette. Enough it's enough, Pops.'

'I think it's an excellent idea. One last go, and I'm sure he'll win!'

I recognise the determined look on Pops' face. It is there when he sets his mind on a course of action. He looks at me, as he begins to gather up bottles and brushes. I hear water running. Now he is filling the laundry trough with warm water.

No! I hide under the big bed in the front room at the other end of the house. He won't find me here. George spots me clawing the carpet.

'Oliver's here, Pops, catch him quickly!'

Karen leaves her computer to find out what the noise is about. She crawls under the bed, and gently carries me out to the laundry. Being carried is so demeaning for a cat when we can walk perfectly well, when we want to.

'Sorry, Oliver, I know you hate this, but Pops has set his mind on another show. It will be over soon.'

I endure the thin comb raking my coat. After the combing, the brush caressing my coat is pleasurable. At least, all my dead hairs are collected. It saves me the trouble of rolling on the grass to remove them. The less said the better, about cleaning my ears and trimming my claws. Both are humiliating for a proud cat. Swimming is fun, but being dunked into warm water, and having shampoo rubbed into my coat is horrible. When I see Pops pick up the loud hairdryer, I refuse to put up with it. I run from Pops to lie in the sun to dry naturally. The worst part is yet to come, the final insult is the shiny gel applied to my coat. Humans like combing their hair and primping, but I can only take so much fussing. Frustrated with me, Pops mutters as he throws up his hands.

Tony and Pops are up early. As stealthily as cats, they grab me from my basket to carry me to the laundry. With no escape, I am brushed and more sticky gel smeared on my coat follows. With two of them holding me, I can't even wriggle. When Pops is satisfied with my glossy appearance, he claps his hands.

'You look magnificent, Oliver. You'll be a winner.'

My coat feels stiff and I look forward to rolling in grass to feel like a cat instead of an ornament. They collect my cage, papers stating my vaccinations, as well as food, a liter box and a water bowl. This is going to be a day I will not want to remember. I wait apprehensively.

Tony drives as Pops holds my box at the back of the car. Travel is always unpleasant. Bella is more tolerant of discomfort. Once we arrive, I am surprisingly nervous. Winning has not been a concern until now. Though I won a second prize at the last show, I hope Pops won't be disappointed if I don't win today. The noise is overwhelming with cats yowling and Humans shouting. Tony can tell I'm upset and he whispers to me reassuringly.

Once the boring fuss about registering me is over, we progress a bit further. I am given a number and category. I am number thirty-five, an Adult Neutered Seal Point Siamese.

I remain in my box while Pops decorates my "showing cage" with shiny curtains that Pops says match my eyes, and a cushion for my comfort. At last, I'm in the cage with food, water and a small litterbox. The caterwauling around me is horrendous, but thanks to the privacy of the curtains, I can't see the cats next to me. More unpleasantness, as

Humans peer into my cage trying to decide whether I will win my category or not. Some even take bets that I will win for them. Humans can be sickening.

One says, 'His head is shaped well, the full thirty points and his blue, expressive eyes are perfect. He's a winner.'

'A beauty with a silky coat,' another comments.

I wait until Tony carries my cage to the judging area. I remember that this is the worst part of the show. A fat Human pulls me out of my cage. She is an expert at handling cats and though I would like to scratch her, I don't. My behaviour is admirable. After all, I'm a Royal Siamese cat. I wait, and eventually another older Human smelling of pungent foods examines me carefully, feels me and measures parts of my body with his fingers. It is embarrassing, to say the least.

'An excellent Siamese specimen,' he says, as he moves on to the next cat.

All the while I hear Tony's and Pops' calming voices.

'Oliver has an excellent chance of winning,' Pops whispers, 'The judge looks impressed.'

Tony places his hand on Pop's shoulder. 'Don't get your hopes up too soon, Dad.'

The judge returns. 'It's between these two cats for first place,' he says, pointing to me and another cat. He looks down and rubs his head for a minute or two before speaking again. 'I've decided. First is number thirty-five and second is twenty-six.'

'Oliver's won!' Tony and Pops shout with joy. Tony kisses my head, Pops strokes me from head to tail. They are thrilled, but I wish they would take me home. They hold up my big, blue rosette, smile and nudge each other.

I am number thirty-five, an "excellent, Siamese specimen," the winner with a huge blue rosette and a prize of a year's cat food.

At home, Karen, Georgie and Bella stand at the door waiting for the result.

'Our champ, he won! He won,' Tony shouts as he opens the door to the house. Proudly he holds up my blue rosette and grins. Pops is beaming and his eyes shine.

George bends to hug me and I struggle to free myself. 'You're the best, most beautiful kitty!' He whispers, 'I love you Ollie!'

Karen waits to congratulate me too, 'Wonderful Oliver! Some shrimps for you and Bella to celebrate.'

While Karen prepares the shrimps, Bella gives me a loving lick. The shrimps are spectacularly delicious. As always, they disappear too soon. The Humans open a bottle of something fizzy and click glasses of the pale liquid. 'To Oliver and Pops, and happy days.'

My ordeal is over and I hide behind the curtain. I don't want anyone near me, not even Bella. Number thirty-five has brought them all joy, but I don't feel it. Well, I have met their expectations and brought Pops pleasure. Now that the show is over, there is an emptiness inside me. Am I just livestock – a winning cat with no other value or purpose other than to win rosettes and free cat food? Apart from Tony's lap cat and Bella's friend, I am nothing. Am I without purpose? At least Bella does something useful by helping Humans. Everyone says what an excellent therapy cat she is. I am pleased for her, admire her ability and warm nature, but within me, the seeds of jealousy grow.

When I hear Honey barking at the fence my mood lifts and I sneak outside. Her owner opens the fence gate to allow her into our garden. She bounds in with a yelp, her tail wagging furiously.

Her dog odour is not as overwhelming today. She turns about to show off her clean coat, as golden and fluffy as the new rug Karen bought for the television room. She wants to play. We run through the garden chasing each other. When she's about to reach me, I climb the half tree. She sits under the tree and barks with frustration until her owner calls her.

After playing with Honey I am more philosophical about my win. The discomfort of the show is over. I won, after all, didn't I? I should be proud. I am an exceptionally handsome and athletic Seal Point, Siamese cat. Even if my original owner thought I was unfit to be cared for, I turned out well thanks to Karen, Tony and Pops. The nasty human didn't know that my breed is elite. We Royal, Sacred Siamese are highly regarded. Nevertheless, I wish I hadn't been given a number at the show like a chicken. I will try to forget that I am number thirty-five.

Pops calls me but I do not respond. He looks about and spots me. 'There you are enjoying the sun under the curtain.' He sigh. 'I get it, you're angry with me, Oliver, for subjecting you to the cat shows. I'm sorry you're upset, but you are a magnificent cat and you should be recognised.'

He puts his newspaper on the floor and holds onto the side of the chair as he stands. As he walks slowly towards the kitchen, I notice he is limping. He was always slow, but his limp is new. I hear the cupboard door open and a clatter from the kitchen.

'Lunch, Oliver,' he calls.

Food motivates me, but my pride won't allow me to answer his call immediately. I wash myself thoroughly first and then join him.

'A treat for you. Some chicken as well as your dry food.'

I'm bought for now. I eat the chicken quickly and leave the dry food for later. I rub past Pop to say thanks and leave. From the kitchen, I hear him sigh. He knows that I am still resentful that he insisted on showing me again. He continues to try to win my affection. Gradually I forgive him. I sit at his feet while he reads his paper. When he puts it down, I jump onto his lap. He whispers to me and I allow him to stroke my head, but I turn my face away from him. He hasn't fully recovered my trust.

His health has deteriorated this week and I notice that he is struggling to stand and walk. Bella is concerned about him and watches him carefully. When he almost slips one morning, Karen suggests he visits the doctor. Pops dislikes doctors as much as I dislike vets. After a long battle with Karen, he allows Tony to drive him to the doctor.

When they return, both Pops and Tony look unhappy. Immediately, Pops goes to his room and closes the door. Once George is in bed, he joins Karen and Tony in the television room. We pretend to be asleep and listen to everything they discuss.

Pops sighs deeply. 'The day after tomorrow I have to go to the hospital for tests and x-rays. I wish I didn't have to, but I'm in pain and the doctor insists.'

'I'll take some leave from work so that I can drive you to the hospital and I'll stay with you during the tests,' Tony says.

'Are you sure?'

'Every employee is entitled to special leave. I'll be there with you.'

'Go to bed Pops and relax. I'll bring you some hot cocoa,' Karen says.

Later, Tony tells Karen that the doctor is concerned about Pops.

'Let's wait for the results before we worry,' Karen says wisely.

Tony takes her hand and kisses her.

Tony and Pops rise early and leave for the hospital. When they return Pops is exhausted. He is anxious about his test results and stays in his room.

The following day, I overhear the Humans talking. Pops' tests and x-rays show that he will need an operation soon. Poor Pops!

This morning the sun peeks from behind the clouds in greeting. Pops is awake and calls us both.

We sit on his bed while he talks to us, 'I am having a big operation and I may not come back. Maybe, I'll be gone like the sun leaves each day. I care about you both.' He strokes us and plants a kiss on each of our foreheads.

I have been aware for a while that Bella is doing something new and rather strange. It's a form of spiritual cat healing she has developed. I watch her doing it now as she closes her eyes, breaths slowly, purrs loudly and then allows herself to drift. Whatever she is doing, I hope it helps Pops.

He closes his eyes, smiles, looks at her and nods. 'Thank you, Bella, I feel much calmer now.'

Tony arrives to help Pops pack a small suitcase. Then he drives him to the hospital. Tony and Karen are anxious about the operation and sit near the phone. We are worried too and sit at their feet.

After a call from the hospital Tony's tense face relaxes. 'The operation has been successful and we can visit him.'

Karen sighs with relief.

Before dinner, Karen and Tony take George with them to visit Pops. When they return they seem pleased with Pops' progress.

As soon as he can walk, he asks to see us both. Bella is busy with Karen, so Tony takes me to the hospital in my carry box. As I am not a therapy cat, and I haven't been checked by a vet, I am not allowed in the hospital wards. I sit with him on the garden balcony.

He pats my head. 'I've been looking forward to seeing you all day, Oliver.'

I sit close to him and purr. He strokes me and says my purrs are healing. 'Oliver, you're my therapy cat now,' he says with a smile.

After several days in hospital he is allowed home. Initially, I lie on his bed to comfort him and then Bella joins me. Soon I become restless and bored. I leave his bed to run outside. Pops may think I am a therapy cat, but I don't have Bella's patience.

# Bella

Always find a safe place to hide while sleeping.

We are basking in mellow sunlight when I look up. My friend the duck, absent since last summer, is hovering, unsure whether to fly down to greet me or not. Perhaps the sight of Oliver is confusing him. When he visited last year, Oliver wasn't here.

I call, *meow, meow* inviting him to join us, but he has spotted the swimming pool and ignores my call. I hear him splashing in the water. After a swim, the wet duck sits on the fence and greets me. Unimpressed by his slow acknowledgement, I walk away. He follows me and tweaks my tail. Then he flies up to Oliver who hasn't seen a duck before. Oliver eyes the flying creature with webbed feet. They stare at each other until the duck playfully nips Oliver's ear. Soon we are both chasing it. Another duck hovering above joins the fun. We climb the half tree and the ducks fly up to chase us. They are bold and then tackle us playfully on the ground. We frustrate both ducks by climbing down and hiding quickly behind the rocks. They lack a cat's sense of smell, but their amazing vision ensures that they will find us.

After watching us play, George places his yellow, bath ducks on the grass. Karen laughs and calls Tony. They hold each other and laugh loudly. The real ducks would not appreciate the joke. Humans find strange things amusing.

At first, Pops appears to make a good recovery, but the healing of his wound is slow due to his age. He is irritable and frustrated and sighs a lot. Karen is concerned that he is not eating much and sleeping poorly.

'I think poor Pops may be depressed as a result of his lengthy recovery. He says he doubts he will ever be free of pain again,' she tells Tony.

After Tony visits the hospital with Pops, the doctor suggests new medication and some gentle exercise. The result is positive, Pops smiles and dresses each day for his walks. As a result, his pain lessens and a little of his former strength returns.

Tonight, he joins the family for dinner for the first time since his operation. Karen prepares his favourite roast dinner and Tony places a large bottle of red stuff on the table. They touch glasses and drink to Pops' improved health.

As soon as the Humans are in bed, we sit together on the edge of the couch to look through the window. The sky is black without a moon or shimmering stars. We sniff the air and listen. Nothing alerts us other than the rustle of the wind, tiny animals scuttling along and a cat in heat calling.

Oliver yawns and we head for the big bedroom and our owners' bed to sleep. Every few days we change our sleep spots. This is an instinctive aspect of Catness, an echo of our early days in the wild – protecting ourselves while we are asleep. If we become too predictable in our habits we become vulnerable to predators.

Tonight, I lie on Karen's side of the bed and breathe her aroma.

We have the run of the house now. When George was tiny our Humans locked us out of their bedroom at night and away from George. It is upsetting to think that they were afraid we would harm him. Due to Oliver's frustration at being locked out, he persevered and practiced until he could open the high door knob that separated us from the rest of the house. One night he was racing through the house when he heard George breathing in a strange way. He called me to listen to George's breathing. I could tell he was struggling to breathe. We both rushed to his sleeping parents, roused them and led them to George. They called the ambulance and George was taken to hospital. They were extremely grateful and since then have trusted us to protect George.

Life in Catland is perfect, or as close to perfect as possible. I must be a cat pessimist. I can't help wondering what will spoil our bliss this time?

The early morning peace is broken by Honey's barking. As tiny as she is, her bark is irritating.

'I wish Honey would shut up,' Tony says.

'She will eventually if she's ignored,' Karen says and goes back to sleep.

Honey wakes George who runs to his parent's room holding his ears. 'Honey is making a big noise.' He walks to the window to look at Honey. 'But, she's a pretty doggie,' He stamps his sturdy, small feet. 'I want a puppy like Honey.'

'Georgie, she's just had a bath that makes her look like a cute, fluff ball. We have two beautiful cats and that's enough. No dogs for us.'

At last, Honey stops barking.

Did I hear correctly? He wants a dog. A puppy. Why? Honey stinks when she isn't clean. Cats are always clean. Aren't we enough for George? Puppies pee and poo all over the place until they are trained, like young Humans in a way. I hope he changes his mind, but if he's like Karen, he won't give up. I guess she is like a cat in that sense. Once she's set on something, she doesn't change her mind.

Karen gives George a hug. 'You don't need a dog, Georgie, and we are not having one. A dog would cause the cats too much stress and they don't deserve it. I don't know if you can understand this. The cats have been in the house with us for a long time. It is their place and they won't want to share it with a puppy. It's different if puppies and kittens grow up together when they are little and can learn to live together peacefully.'

Well, I hope that's the end of talk about dogs in our territory.

Our Humans are going out for dinner. Karen has changed into a swirling dress and smells of flowers. Tony is wearing a shirt and pants and George is dressed in a new outfit. Even Pops is in his best clothes. They are celebrating the new baby and talking to each other loudly. There is a sense of anticipation and excitement in the air.

Once they leave, the empty house is ours. Once we have checked our territory, we play by having a mock fight.

Oliver is on top of me, then I'm the top cat. We butt heads, chase, bite and slap each other in fun. Then we sleep.

When they return, they smell of strange food and liquid. The only thing they want to do is to go to bed.

Tony and Karen are sitting close to each other on the couch in the television room.

'I am certain of it, George is a gifted child,' Karen says.

Tony laughs. 'All mothers think that their children are gifted.'

'I'm not like that. I can tell he's advanced for his age and smart with a big vocabulary for a three-year-old. He is already learning to read, count and asks questions about the cats and the world around us. This morning he asked me who makes the clouds. Yesterday he asked why cats are small.'

Tony smiles. 'Let's wait and see what happens when he starts school.'

Karen's fat tummy is taking up most of the space on her side of the bed. There isn't much room for me next to her. As the glowing sun breaks through the sky I move to the comfort of the couch.

George is up and his small footsteps pad through the house waking me. 'Where are you Bell-Bell?' He calls.

I ignore him and close my eyes for more sleep. Unsatisfied by lack of attention, he grabs me hugging me so tightly that it hurts. I wriggle and meow loudly until he lets me go. He was gentle when he was younger. Now he is like male kitten experimenting with his strength. Cats don't like Humans controlling their bodies and their space. I don't think he realises that cats feel pain like he does. If he wants me to cuddle him he must learn to treat me with respect. I am not one of his toys.

His life is changing. With Karen busy he sees less of her than before and misses her. Like a cat, he listens for her car as it turns into the driveway. He runs to her for hugs and cuddles as soon as she is in the house. When the new baby comes, Karen will have even less time for him. I hope he'll adapt. What a pity that Humans have more trouble adapting to changes in a family than we do.

Karen is studying on the computer, "doing research", she calls it. I wait expectantly to find out if any of the information gleaned will affect me or Oliver. Karen does not waste her time studying unless she uses the material. I sit near her attentively.

White papers fly from the noisy printing machine like magic. I try to catch the papers, but they are too fast for me. She clips the papers together with one of those shiny little things I enjoy playing with, and then all is quiet. I peep through the partially open door. She is sitting at her desk enjoying a quiet time. With her hectic life I'm sure she needs moments of solitude when she can merely sit and relax. I can understand that, as cats enjoy being alone for periods too. She is alert now and leaves the study to head for the kitchen. I follow. She searches through the cold fridge and the food cupboard and then writes a long list.

The list is in her handbag when she dresses and leaves. She must be taking it to the food shop again. Lately, she is buying the usual meat as well as well as many horrid vegetables. Then she cooks it all until it stinks. I am hoping that with all her cooking there will be treats for us.

'Well, now we have all we need to start our Paleo diet. It is high in protein and fat and has fewer carbs. I bought Paleo food for the cats too. They'll eat like their ancestors once ate and it should keep them healthy,' she says to Tony.

'Wonderful,' he replies, not sounding truly enthusiastic. He eats his dinner slowly without giving Karen his usual complements about her cooking.

Cat's above, what is Paleo? I am used to the food she provides and like it. Why is she changing it? Whatever she is concocting I hope it tastes good.

Oliver sniffs the cooking smells in the kitchen and runs away. After dinner, Tony complains that he is still hungry and goes to the kitchen for a cheese sandwich with his coffee. He tries to eat it quickly so that Karen won't notice, but she catches him eating a crust of bread.

'You should try harder, darling. We'll both need to lose a bit of weight and feel good. It is worthwhile doing.'

'Good luck with the cats. They won't like change,' he says with a scowl.

She opens a bag of food that looks nothing like the food we usually eat. Oliver turns his head away as she spoons some into his bowl. Then she fills mine.

'Venison my treasures. Special organic cat food,' she says.

I approach the bowl slowly. *Meeyuk!* It smells like a dead rat. We both turn our back on the food and leave the kitchen. In the background we hear her muttering. A little later she refills our bowls with our tinned food. What a relief!

Today she has another organic food bag in her hand. As she opens it an unusual smell wafts into the kitchen. I approach the food hesitantly. Oliver eats his food immediately and licks his lips. I follow his lead. The food is delicious.

'Rabbit, my sweethearts,' she says, as she refills our bowls.

Oliver knows about rabbits. At the beginning of summer, two appeared on the other side of our garden fence. Now there are many more tiny ones. Oliver watches them. If he could, I'm sure he would stalk and catch them.

The new food trial continues with meat that we both dislike and refuse to eat. Her final attempt at changing our diet comes with a mouth-watering concoction of mackerel and lamb. The blend of flavours is a cat's delight.

'Two out of four. Not too bad,' Karen says with a happy sigh.

After Karen has tidied the kitchen, we all sit in the television room. They are watching something with many Humans talking.

George spots a tiny dog on the screen. 'Look...such a cute doggie.'

'Yes, it's cute,' Karen replies.

'I love the cats lots, but please, please, can I have a small doggie?'

'We've discussed this. Cats don't get along well with dogs, George.'

'Our cats are clever, and they would if they tried. Please!'

'Let us watch the movie, George, we'll talk about a dog another time.'

This will not be the end of George whining for a dog.

My friend, the sun, is back to dry the garden after a night's rain. I go out to greet it. The ground is soggy and I jump from one rock to another to avoid the mud. When I brush against a flowering bush, I receive a thorough drenching. With the combination of rain and sunshine flowers and plants grow abundantly, but hold the wet like suckling kittens. I find a dry rock to sit on and observe the garden. The birds are singing and hopping on the branches overhead.

There is a swoosh above me. I look up at a familiar blob in the sky. The duck is here. It flies lower, and lower still, almost touching me. To tease me with a greeting, it hovers indecisively. Then it ignores me and heads for a mud puddle where it drills small holes with its beak. It is so busy digging for worms and bugs that it forgets me. It shakes itself with a tail quiver. Muddy water sprays and droplets fall on me. I watch it while I lick myself clean. Then it remembers me, and our fun begins. It flies around the garden on its strange short legs, flapping its wings. I jump onto a rock. It flies close, pecks my nose and then my tail. The rain has made it mischievous. I am enjoying chasing it until it flies up onto the fence wire. We rest, stare at each other, and then start the game again. Suddenly, like the tap of a cat's paw, it is above me flying away.

Karen looks at my matted, muddy body and laughs. 'You've been playing in the mud with your friend the duck. Sorry my Sweetie, I'll have to wash you.'

Wash me! Surely not! I can't be that dirty. I start to run from her, but she's smarter than me. The laundry doors close. The tub fills. I am trapped.

'Come Bella, you'll be nice and clean after a wash.'

I'm plunged into the tub and covered in shampoo. The drenching water follows.

'Out you come, Bella,' she says, as tries to dry me with a towel. I escape to the sunny window to dry. Was playing with the duck worth all of this? Yes. I need fun in my life and I'll remember it. The disgusting wash I intend to forget.

Karen drinks tea looking tired. Her tummy is huge and the weather is too hot for her. George took a long time to grow inside her and she was much fatter before he came out. I doubt the new baby will be here for a while.

George is behaving like an upset cat. One day he is almost

a kitten scared its Mama won't feed him. The next, he turns his back on Karen. He is a clever child and must realise that Karen is thinking about the baby growing inside her. He is jealous already and the new baby isn't here yet.

Pops goes to bed early. Since his operation, he tires more easily than months earlier.

Karen is worried about him.

'It's nothing serious, Pops is just getting old,' Tony says, trying to reassure her.

I observe Oliver, but I do this carefully as he doesn't like being watched. Since the cat show he has been unhappy. He no longer walks proudly with his sinuous tail held high. He has not been interested in playing or attending to grooming his cream coat with his usual care. I am sad to say that he is grubby and doesn't smell fresh. At night, he sleeps fitfully. Most alarming are his low-pitched, mournful yowls.

I would try harder to be kind to him if he wasn't exerting his dominance through his strength. Yesterday, he pounced on me while I was sleeping. This morning he tried to block my way to the garden. Why is he doing this? I try to seek answers before acting wildly and striking out to assert myself as my ancestors would've done. I pace about our garden thinking while he sleeps. He's had spells of aggression before and they passed. This time, I cannot find a reason for his unhappiness that has turned him into a bully.

I consider several possible reasons for his behaviour. He is jealous of me in many ways. Perhaps it is George's affection for me that is bothering him. The small Human pets us both. George is growing and changing, one day favouring me and the next Oliver. Perhaps he wants all of

George's affection. Then there's Pops. I am certain that Pops is closest to me. He confides in me and spends more time with me than with Oliver. Of course, Oliver wants to be the most loved cat.

My answers don't satisfy me. Oliver's sadness and bursts of aggression must be more complicated than merely wanting affection. Perhaps he lacks purpose since the shows are over and he is jealous of my work as a therapy cat. Now that Pops is too frail to be involved in a cat show, Oliver is no longer a show cat and it is unlikely he will be again. Now he is just a lap cat and I doubt it is enough for him. I am fortunate to have a useful job. He is smart and needs to be useful too.

Though I would like to help him, he will have to sort it out himself. He is too aggressive towards me. No cat, not even Oliver, is going to interfere with my life or confront me in this way. He is too cat centred and can do with a shakeup. I let him know my feelings by turning my back on him and ignoring him. I am vigilant about my territory and flick my tail rapidly if he dares to try to move into my areas. Shocked, he glares at me, stretches, shows his muscular body and grooms his claws. He is trying to exert his dominance again. I will not allow him to intimidate me.

Unfortunately, today we had our first fight in ages, a real cat fight with hissing, brushed tails and biting. Karen was so upset with us that she sprayed us with water. I am still wet.

The air is heavy and the hot days have returned. The heat has stirred our irritation with each other. The coolest places in the house are in the bathroom and a spot on the carpet directly under the big fan in the television room. I head for the bathroom and he follows. We find the door to the bathroom is closed. The ceiling fan is our next destination. My heavy coat makes me much hotter than Oliver with his fine, silky one. With my vital need for cool, I consider that I ought to have first choice, the prime position in the cool. Most days he prefers to be away from direct breezes against his more delicate coat, but he is like a silly attention seeking kitten today, trying to draw me into another fight. As I find a place directly under the fan, he tries to push me aside. He has succeeded in annoying me. He's behaving selfishly. I growl at him, with ears tense, back arched, claws out and ready and my tail like a brush. Driven by the intense heat, I lose my usual calm and become my wild self ready to defend my right to cool down.

When Oliver is angry and on the attack, he looks ferocious. Acting on instinct, I bite his tail. Soon he is biting and scratching me. Karen hears us fighting and runs towards us holding a spray bottle.

'Fighting again! I'll cool you two down,' she yells, as she sprays us, 'Out...both of you!' This time neither of us mind the cold water.

I move away to lie alone on the patio. The breeze cools my body and my temper. I am not pleased with myself. After all, I am a therapy cat and I should know better than to be drawn into the worst kind of feline behaviour. Oliver has been unhappy most of the summer and the heat hasn't helped, but it isn't the real reason. He is acting like depressed Humans, like Pops who had a down mood after his surgery. Humans don't realise that cats can be sad and feel depressed, and especially sensitive ones like Oliver.

I must put my annoyance with him aside, he needs my help.

I wake in the dark, and just as well. I need some time alone to work out a plan to help Oliver without him realising what I have in mind. Karen's sessions with unhappy Humans are worth thinking about. Perhaps I can use some of her techniques to help Oliver. By morning light, I have a few ideas.

After breakfast, I call Oliver to play outside. I ignore his snappiness and insist on playing. We play our old game of hide and seek and I allow him to win. Then I ask him to help me to clear the rats from the garden. He is reluctant to help, but tries to satisfy me. We hunt together. When he has killed many more rats than I do, he is pleased with himself. The activity does him good and we sleep. Over the weekend, Tony is home and as much as I dislike swimming, I suggest we swim together. I force myself into the water and agree to a race. Naturally he wins. The spark in his blue eyes is returning and he eats a huge meal after all the exercise. I hope he will be able to motivate himself now.

Karen is resting on the sofa after lunch with George on her lap. She whispers loving words to him and strokes his head in the same way she strokes ours. She pats the spaces on either side of her. 'Where are you Bella, Oliver? Come!'

We approach slowly, making sure that there is space for us to sit comfortably. Oliver jumps onto the couch first. I follow and cuddle up to Karen. He moves close to her too.

'I have you all with me now. My favourite boy George, and my much-loved cats,' She kisses all our heads. 'It's time for jealousy and fighting to stop.'

Oliver and I purr loudly, relishing the sense of shared affection.

When Karen leaves, Oliver butts my head and licks my face in thanks for helping him. We will be closer than ever now.

Karen is planning a big celebration for George's third birthday. She will show the children a film about cats and dogs, a topic that is always popular. George's cousins, a few friends and all their mothers are invited.

George is thrilled and asks his mother, 'Please can Oliver swim? He is so funny and clever.'

'He'll be able to show off and he'll like that. I'll make him a party swimming costume. He'll look adorable,' Karen says, giving George a hug.

Pops orders a birthday cake and Jodi helps Karen to prepare sandwiches, tasty snacks and cookies.

On the morning of George's party, George is delighted with his gifts and plays with them quietly. Karen and Tony prepare the house for guests. We eat an early breakfast of pebbles with a large spoonful each of cooked egg as a treat. *Yummow!*

We hide behind the curtain so that the Humans forget about us while they prepare for the party. We are in an excellent position and can watch all that is happening. In the television room. There is a great deal of activity. The entire room is changed as Karen and Tony move the couches against the back wall, roll up the rugs and carry the patio table into the room. When a noisy truck arrives, Tony helps a large Human carry chairs inside – small yellow ones for the small Humans and big brown ones for the adults. They place a tall white hanging thing, a "screen", against the wall.

Such a lot of trouble for one little Human, only three years old. Today is a good day for Pops. He was up early and is involved in the birthday celebrations. He leans against the doorway and makes suggestions. 'The screen could be a bit higher, Tony. Put the children's chairs closer together or you won't fit them all in and leave a bigger space in the front.'

'Okay Pops,' Tony says good-naturedly, even though I can tell he is a little irritated.'

The house is almost ready for the party. Tony looks

around and shakes his head worriedly. 'All this will cost a fortune, but it is the last time George will be an only child. I want him to enjoy his birthday.'

Why do Human always talk about cost and money, I thought that money is used is to buy a place to live comfortably and food to eat. As long as I have my basket and pebbles. I am happy.

The birthday cake is covered in blue, has three candles on it as well as sweet flowers and small men. What a waste of time if they are going to eat it. This is another one of those strange Human things. For the children, she puts tiny toys and sugary things on the table. Tony blows into skinny, coloured, plastic shapes called balloons until each one is round and full. Then he stands on a chair to attach the round wavering things to places in the room. He even hangs a few from the lights.

Once Karen is satisfied with the table decorations, she dresses George in new clothes. He is so excited that he jumps up and down with excitement. *Wooooeee, woooeee,* he calls.

When Tony carries us both to the back room neither of us complain. This birthday party will bring too many Humans into our house for us to handle.

We hear everything from our safe position. Tiny and larger feet arrive and an assortment of voices – shrill, small ones and loud ones. The noise grows louder with singing and shrieking. The sound of the film follows.

Then Tony enters the room. 'Time for your star performance, Oliver. Karen has made a cute costume for you in blue to match your eyes.'

Oliver sees the blue costume and attempts to hide under a chair.

Tony bends and grabs him. 'Gotcha. Now, no nonsense, Oliver.'

151

Oliver obeys, for once, as Tony pulls the costume onto Oliver.

'You look amazing!'

Oliver cries loudly in protest. The material around him is constricting and uncomfortable, but Tony lifts Oliver into his arms ignoring his objections.

'Come on, join us, Bella! Let's go to the pool.'

I follow Tony through the patio door and down across the grass to the pool. The children and their parents are waiting for us. I run to Karen and hide under her chair.

'Come, my handsome boy,' Tony says, as he places Oliver on the first step of the pool, 'Swim for George, it's his birthday.'

'He looks incredible!', 'What a cute kitty,' and 'I don't believe he can swim,' are some of the comments I can make out in the noise.

'Shushhhhh!' Karen says putting her finger to her lips, 'As quiet as mice. Oliver doesn't like noise when he swims.'

Oliver glares and turns his back on Tony. It looks as if he is will refuse to swim. Tony strokes Oliver's head and whispers to him. Oliver looks up at Tony. I know he thinking I am doing this for you. He steps into the pool and starts to swim. Down the middle of the pool the blue of his costume glistens as his paws strike the water and he completes each paddle stroke. The children are flabbergasted and don't utter a sound. Oliver manages to swim a record distance, the furthest he's swum yet.

Tony jumps into the pool and holds him up high. 'Isn't he absolutely incredible?'

The intensity of the applause almost sends me running back to the house.

'Come, George,' Tony says motioning to George.

'Luv you, my Ollie,' George says, as he strokes Oliver's head.

As the Humans leave, they are still talking about Oliver. His eyes are glowing, his tail is high and he struts with pride. He has enjoyed being the centre of attraction, even outshining the birthday boy.

Jodi and her friend help with the cleaning up and we hear the furniture moving back into place. When Karen opens the door to let us out we rush to the kitchen where a plate of food is waiting for us. We eat hungrily and then look for George. We find him asleep on his bed.

George rushes inside carrying a bird to show Karen, 'Why is the bird lying so still?'

My ears prick up when I hear the word 'bird'.

'It won't fly or sing again.'

George looks at her perplexed. 'Why?'

Karen cuddles him and tries to explain that it is time for the bird to rest. It has crossed the Rainbow Bridge and is in Bird Heaven where there are green meadows, trees and hills. 'This is where all our special friends who have passed can play,' she says.

He puts the bird down and sobs.

'We'll bury your bird in the front garden,' she says, putting her arm around him. 'First give it a name.'

He stops to think. 'Sunshine... because birds sing in the sun.'

Karen smiles and takes his hand. We watch through the window as she digs a hole in the earth under a flowering bush in the main garden. She wraps the bird in tissue paper, lowers it into the hole and places sand over it.

'Come, George, put a flower over Sunshine's grave and let him rest.'

What is Heaven and where is it? It must be a wonderful place because Humans often talk about it. Rainbows with so many beautiful colours and green meadows too. I have seen them both. Crossing the Rainbow Bridge to this place called Heaven must be an ideal place to be. It's all too hard to understand. Even Oliver looks perplexed.

Karen is an incredible Human. She cares so deeply, but caring with such intensity can be dangerous, even for a Human. They are big creatures and can hurt a lot.

The hot air is as thick as soapy water, cicadas buzz and birds twitter. To cool down after work Tony, Karen and George rush to the pool. All I want to do is lie in the shade and enjoy watching the sun die. I lie under the shelter and Oliver rests under the half tree. Though Tony has cut away the top half of the tree to stop us from climbing it to a dangerous height, the tree's branches have grown outwards providing us with excellent shade. I spread my body in the hope of feeling cooler. A breeze allows me to sleep peacefully.

A loud yowl wakes me. It is Oliver writhing as if possessed. His body is coated in stickiness, I don't know what to do to help him. Our Humans are at the pool drinking red liquid in small glasses and nibbling something that resembles our food pellets.

I rush to the pool for help. *Meeeeeow, Meeeeeow* I call, trying to gain Karen attention.

'Goodness! What's the matter, my precious?'

After I call again and stare fixedly at her, she follows me. At least she is learning to respond to my cries for help.

'I won't be long, there's some problem with the cats, just checking,' she calls to the others. She frowns when she sees Oliver covered in goo. His trembling body is almost stuck to the ground. He is unable to move and he is yowling in high pitched, frightened tones.

'I'll call Tony to help us.'

Tony arrives with George. 'My poor boy! What on earth have you been up to?'

While Tony talks to Oliver reassuringly, Karen searches for the source of Oliver's misery.

'The sticky stuff is tree sap,' she says, pointing to the weeping bark of a tree.

Tony nods. 'Wow… it is certainly yucky stuff! How are we going to clean him?'

Karen scratches her head as she does when she's thinking, 'Maybe something oily but gentle. I'll try cooking oil and then wash him in his special shampoo. I remember my dad cleaning our dog with oil once before washing him, when he rolled in a mess.'

Tony hands Karen the bottle of cooking oil. While he holds Oliver firmly, she pours oil over him. I haven't seen a cat look more miserable. Seeing Oliver covered in oil sends shivers through me. He lies on the ground defeated without even a whimper. The shampooing in the deep laundry trough is too much for him. His yowls are loud and desperate. Then I yowl to accompany him.

'Bella, I'm not killing Oliver,' Karen says. 'Just a bit of patience. He'll be fine in a few minutes.'

A bedraggled, wet Oliver emerges from the trough. Tony carries him to the open patio door. 'The heat will do the trick Oliver, you'll be dry soon.'

Oliver's fur regains its glossy shine. As soon as he is almost dry, he scuttles away to hide under the big bed.

While Karen strokes my head, she talks to me in her sweet voice, 'Bella, my treasure, I've been busy and haven't spent enough time with you. I have a treat for you.'

I follow her to her computer and wait. Unfortunately, the treat won't be food. It is something especially for me and not Oliver. She clicks on the computer and spends time searching.

'I know that you don't see the images like we do. I think you see a blur, a flicker of light and movement, but you can hear the sounds, and you'll like this.'

Then I hear it, two cats are purring and having a relaxed conversation. They are saying caring things to each other as they rub heads affectionately. How delightful to listen to them. I wish I could see them clearly. I talk to Oliver like that and sometimes he responds in the same way. I purr loudly at the cats on the computer and look up at Karen asking her to play the pictures again for me. What a pity Oliver hasn't the patience to watch moving sound pictures of cats. He is missing out.

'Now for something tasty to eat for you and Oliver,' she says.

Oliver

*Humans will discover that an angry cat is like a
vacuum cleaner with teeth and claws.*

George's party was enjoyed by all and my swim
entertained the children. Hearing clapping and the
positive comments about my swimming made me feel
good. If I have any purpose at all it must be to entertain
and amuse Humans. I suppose I can't expect much more
though. I would like to be of value.

Thanks to Bella, who is more help than she could ever
know, I am out of my down mood. Well, I was out of it until
the despicable episode of the tree sap. Being trapped by
revolting tree sap was an uncomfortable and degrading
experience that no Siamese cat should be expected to
endure. I don't recall feeling as afraid or vulnerable since
I was a kitten trapped in a cupboard. Siamese cats are
proud creatures. We dislike being totally dependent on our
owners. Undoubtedly, I need Humans for my sustenance,
care and a comfortable, safe place to live, even though I
pretend that I am independent. As humiliating as it is, being
covered in sticky slime demonstrates how much I depend
on them. They came to my rescue by washing the goo off
my body. I couldn't have done that alone.

I sleep and dream, an important, recurring dream of my
past life that I cannot stop thinking about.

Many cat lives ago, in ancient times, I was in a distant land inside a grand building. The walls were adorned with exotic silks, paintings, ornaments and a yellow metal called gold. Huge lights glimmered from high ceilings. Outside were patios, fountains and endless gardens. Cats like me ran contentedly through the building and in the magnificent gardens. We belonged to a nobleman who fed us and treated us well. We were all plump with shiny coats. I'm not at all surprised as we ate as much as we pleased – irresistible delicacies from seafood to slithers of chicken in sauces cooked to tempt the fussiest cat.

Many Humans served the nobleman. I knew by their downcast eyes and bowed posture when we passed them that they were in awe of us. A temple was attached to the grand building and our vital job was to guard it. We were involved too with certain spiritual matters connected with the Human soul. When an eminent human died, one of us received their soul. I have no real appreciation of how this came about, but during a ritual with pungent, floral aromas and incantations by the priests, one cat was selected to receive the soul. It was an impressive occasion.

I was the chosen cat to be imbued with a Human's soul, taken from the household to live a ceremonial life of luxury and respect among the priests in the temple. I had the unique power of interceding with the Gods for the souls of the departed. The Gods were incredible creatures, half-human and half-cat, with rippling muscles. I was treated royally. The relatives of the deceased person provided me and other chosen cats with delicacies on gold plates and satin embroidered cushions so that we would be comfortable, and their loved ones receive some good fortune. My life was bliss.

I was disappointed to find myself in my basket when I woke. I can't help wondering why I had this magnificent dream. Was I truly dreaming of a past life? I am from royalty, a Sacred Royal Siamese, after all. But I had no idea that a cat's life could be so privileged.

It is midday, and I am alone in the house. Bella is with Karen at the hospital and Pops is asleep. I am bored and lonely with no one to play with, so I curl up on the couch to sleep. A key opening the front door alerts me. I recognise Tony's footsteps. Why is he home early?

He goes to the fridge, removes several dark, small bottles, sighs and sits near me.

'Ten years of service and this is what I get, made redundant with the flick of a pen,' he mutters.

He opens one bottle, drinks its contents, then the next as he wipes away a few tears. 'I'm not looking forward to telling Karen. She was right, I should've left when she said I was working for a company who couldn't care less about their workers. She's always right!'

Yes, Karen does appear to be correct in most cases. She is formidable. I am sorry for Tony. I edge closer to him. What can I do to comfort him? Bella would know, but she's not here. I will try my best. I place my paw on his thigh and purr loudly. My Siamese purrs are even louder than Bella's. He touches my head and closes his eyes.

'You're a loving cat Oliver and your purrs relax me.'

I'm delighted that I can help him. Perhaps I have this wonderful "thing" Karen says Bella is born with – empathy. I will have something important to share with Bella when she returns.

The atmosphere in the house is dismal. Tony is slumped on the couch all day wearing his pyjamas and gown. He hardly eats or talks. He drinks more from his bottles than usual, as he sinks into a dark mood. I stay near him to comfort him. This is a new role for me and I am enjoying it. Karen tries to talk to him, find ways to help him, but he pushes her away.

This morning, he snapped at her when she offered him breakfast. 'Leave me alone, I'm not one of your patients. I'll sort things out myself.'

He is not sorting things out at all. He is barely sleeping and paces through the house at night. I sense his sadness mixed with intense resentment. He even threw a plate on the floor and kicked the door. Just as well Karen was out at the time or she'd have been upset. His moodiness persists all day.

Karen is incredibly patient and attempts to encourage him. 'Tony, darling, come and look at this,' she calls from her desk at the computer.

He moves slowly, like a cat that has woken from a long sleep.

'Okay, okay, I'm coming.'

I follow him and watch them both hunched over the screen.

'This could be quite good, and with a higher salary,' she says tentatively.

'Ummmm, possibly.'

'With all your experience it's a good fit. What do you think?'

'I'll think about it overnight.'

He dislikes her telling him anything. Bella is correct, Humans are decidedly weird, but I haven't given up, I still hope to understand them.

Karen watches Tony like a Mama cat. I can tell by the furrows on her forehead that she is worried that he isn't eating enough. Instead of nagging him to eat, she prepares pancakes with sticky syrup for his breakfast. Tony drinks his coffee and eats. She smiles with relief.

Today, he is dressed in a white shirt and a suit and tie. He leaves the house early.

'Good luck with the interview, my darling,' she says, giving him a kiss. 'I'm sure you'll go well.' She is home working on her computer and stops regularly to check her phone for messages.

We cats are in the kitchen with Karen eating lunch when Tony bursts through the door. He grins. 'It went well. We chatted for ages. I think they are impressed with me. I like them too. They promised to let me know by the end of the week.'

She hugs and kisses him. 'It will be fine my darling. Try not to worry.'

He hugs and kisses her too.

This morning the phone rings. Tony answers and calls out, 'I've got the job and the terms couldn't be better!'

Life will be happy in the house again.

Karen smells of fragrant flowers. She wears a shiny dress and shoes with points and high heels. The shoes are dangerous weapons to be avoided if she mistakenly kicks or stomps on us. Tony smells fresh and woody and wears his favourite shirt.

'I've made a booking at a restaurant to celebrate my new job.'

'Yes, we have a lot to celebrate, my love,' she says with a smile that makes her eyes shine.

We sleep while they are gone and wake to hear the door opening and their laughter.

He kisses her, lifts her and twirls her around. They head for the bedroom.

Joan Zawatzky

 Bella

Unlike Humans, we do not suffer from insomnia.

This morning the air is cool, and a dull mist covers Catland. I look through the window at the magnificent red, amber and gold leaves floating down from the trees and collecting in our garden. There is movement in the garden. Some birds have already left for warmer places. Mice, rats and all tiny creatures that creep, hide in the dry grass and leaves.

Honey barks at the fence, scratches the ground and wags her tail furiously. She wants to play. I have learned that when dogs wag their tails they are happy or excited. Dog language is strange - almost as strange as Human language. I am certain that Honey doesn't grasp our wonderfully expressive, cat language and the way we show our emotions in our tails and ears. It's too complicated for Honey, but Karen and Tony understand that a wildly flicking cat's tail can mean we are angry, frustrated, or even bored. A frightened tail is often tucked under our bodies. When a tail is held high, all is well. They know about our ears – that if our ears are back and flat against our heads it could signify that we are afraid or defensive. Naturally, The meaning of each cat's tail and ear positions depends on the situation as well as the cat. There is so much of our other behaviour to learn about and Honey wouldn't have a clue about that.

As Karen opens the fence gate, Honey bounds into our garden. With a yelp, she runs towards me with her tail wagging. I stand my ground while she runs closer wanting to play.

Wuff, wuff, wuff, wuff!, she barks in exasperation, as I pretend to be slower than her. Just when she thinks she has caught up with me I climb the half tree. Oliver takes over. They chase each other, roll and pretend to fight. I watch. Unable to catch Oliver, she barks shrilly in annoyance. Then we both enjoy teasing her until she runs home through the gate. Now Oliver and I play together – chasing, pouncing, stalking each other until we drop onto the grass, exhausted. Then we rub each other affectionately.

Later, I think about dogs. I have made a mistake about Honey, one of my worst mistakes ever. She appears to have no intention of harming us, but that doesn't mean that I like her. Then I think of therapy dogs who visit sick people like I do. My personal experience as a kitten has biased my thinking against dogs. There is a lot I must learn about them, it seems. I made the error of thinking all dogs were the same dangerous cat haters. I need to be more flexible in my thinking in future.

Two sour smelling Humans are here today. After talking to Tony, one climbs up onto the roof and makes a great deal of noise with his heavy boots as he steps on the tiles. The other measures the wall and windows.

'Yeah, I think we might be able to extend the existing house into the garden, and add another bedroom with an enclosed patio. It will be cool in summer and nice and warm in winter.'

Karen looks at Tony. 'It will be lovely for the baby.'

'But we don't need a patio for the baby.' She looks down and then nods.

We had builders making alterations to the house before George was born and I remember the noise and mess well. Oliver is groaning with dissatisfaction. Tony sits in the television room pouring over drawings for the proposed room. He makes notes on a pad. When Karen looks at the drawings she shakes her head. I can tell she is not satisfied. She has the last say on everything.

They already have a huge house, why do they need more space? Humans don't know when to stop. There are only three adults, a child and two cats in the house. They want bigger and better territory all the time. I don't understand why a tiny baby needs a separate room. There is a messy room at the back of our house that Karen calls the "box room" filled with old furniture and rubbish. If they cleaned it the new baby could sleep there when it is ready to come into the world. I guess that like cats, their territory is important to them. I don't know why I'm complaining. A bigger house means we will have more cat territory and sunspots.

A van arrives. A man and a woman ring the doorbell. Then Karen and Tony talk to them. The woman is wearing an unpleasantly, powerful, perfume and the man smells of perfume too. They are all discussing the extension again. The woman talks and makes pictures on her small computer, while the man is outside looking at the walls and then climbs onto the roof. Tony looks happy about what the woman tells him and Karen smiles.

'We like your ideas. We'll discuss it and get back to you,' Tony says.

The woman gives Tony a small card and they leave. We hear our Humans talk about the extension for days.

Today, the woman is back without the man. I can smell her perfume before she rings the bell. They talk a lot and she fiddles on her small computer to show them a picture.

'We're happy with your quote and ideas. We can go ahead,' Tony says.

They do that strange thing Humans do of holding each other's hands and shaking them. A groaning *meow* comes from Oliver.

This morning two workmen dressed in dark clothing spattered with dirty spots and splashes of colour arrive. They begin by creating a deep hole outside with noisy machines. When one machine stops they use another deafening machine. They appear to be satisfied with their mess and leave. Karen has not locked us up yet. I expect it will happen soon.

What a relief, the workers have not returned for two days. Oh no! Others have arrived. They are carrying huge pieces of wood and banging them together. Karen is eyeing us. Bad news! She carries me to the back room. Oliver is too fast for her and hides. She calls and calls, but he won't come to her. When she finds him there is anger in her voice. We are both incarcerated for the day. At least she has left us our baskets, food, water and most importantly, a shared litter tray. Having one each as usual is too much to expect. I have learned not to expect too much from Humans or I'll be disappointed. I don't expect too much from Oliver either. He is nothing like me, apart from being a cat.

Our day is exhausting due to the banging machines that prevent us from sleeping and the workers talking. We know that the noise will continue for a few days as it did when George's room was built. Cats do have excellent memories that protect us in case we need to draw on our experience to manage a situation. We try to amuse ourselves by jumping on the furniture and running in and out of boxes. Soon we tire of it. When the men leave, Karen allows us out of our prison for dinner. Quickly, we run to investigate whether the room outside is ready yet.

Oh, No! It will take far longer than we had hoped to complete the basic structure, and day after day we remain locked inside the back room.

Karen wakes me to tell me to eat quickly as we are visiting the hospital. She hardly eats now, just sips a cup of coffee before she carries me to the car. The short drive tells me we are going to the small hospital. A nurse leads us into a room where an old Human sits in a chair.

'Good morning, Mrs Lorimer, I'm Karen and I've brought my cat Bella to visit you. I believe you like cats,' Karen says.

At the word 'cat' the grey head lifts. The woman sighs with pleasure.

'What a lovely surprise, and please call me Leticia.'

Within minutes I'm out of my carry box and on her lap.

While they talk, I'm stroked by an expert cat lover's hand. She finds the exact pleasure spot under my chin and gently caresses the tips of my ears. I stop listening as I take a trip to cat paradise and then fall asleep. I wake when Karen is almost ready to leave.

'Thank you, Karen, for the chat, I feel less upset about my son not visiting me now. He is young and has a busy life. And thank you for bringing Bella, she is such a comfort.'

Karen nods and smiles.

'I know I shouldn't ask because you're busy, but do you think you could both visit again?'

'Of course we will, Leticia.'

'What a delightful person Leticia is,' Karen says, as she carries me to the car.

Karen talks to me in the car as she often does. 'You were so gentle and comforting with her, Precious. She is ninety-four in human years.' She counts on her free hand. 'That makes her about nineteen in cat years. Many of her friends and relatives are dead and all she has are her two children who are busy and don't visit her often,' she says in a sad voice.

At home, the workers have left. From past renovations I can tell that they have not finished the job and will return soon. Now we can run freely in the quiet house and in our garden. Karen sweeps up the rubble they have left and mops the floor. Tiredly she clutches her tummy and breathes heavily.

'You're overdoing it Karen. Are you okay?' Pops asks looking worried.

'I am tired. I'll have to sit down.'

'Some tea?'

She nods. 'Thanks, I can do with it.'

I watch her and worry. She is doing too much and needs rest badly. I stay close to her but her tummy is too large for me to sit on her lap.

When Oliver goes to the kitchen to look for food, I run off and stand before Bastet. 'Please look after Karen and the baby she is carrying,' I implore.

When I return, Oliver is licking his lips and Karen's eyes are closed. Pops is in the kitchen making a meal while he waits for Tony to come home.

I lie on the new, velvet couch, the couch that Karen says is out of bounds to us. The coloured cushions she bought to match the couch are uncomfortable. I kick them away, trying to avoid the large platters on the table. I broke a platter last week with a swish of my tail. The luxurious couch is like cat heaven. As I burrow into softness for a long sleep, the builder's van draws up with two workers. Oliver joins me on the couch, and we listen as the bigger worker shouts at the smaller one. The smaller worker's voice is sharp, and he sounds like a frightened cat. The two workers don't chat and laugh like the previous workers. Oliver says the big one is a bully like a top cat who bullies the other cats.

At last, the workers leave and the house is pleasantly still. I sleep and then dream. When I wake, I think about my brief dream and worry.

Bastet appeared in a swirl of light. She carried a message, or perhaps a warning that change was in the air. The change would not be in the weather, but in something far more significant. 'Be prepared', she said and then disappeared.

There is no point in worrying about my dream or Bastet's prediction I will handle whatever is in store for me.

Karen is working in her room, even though she promised Tony and Pops she would reduce her home clients with the baby coming soon. If she is not at a hospital she is busy on her computer. This afternoon, she goes out and takes George with her. They return with parcels.

She gives George a kiss, 'Thank you for helping me to choose new curtains and a carpet for the baby. Your brother or sister will have a lovely room.'

Pops makes Karen a cup of tea. 'You should rest and look after yourself,' he says looking concerned. 'I hope you'll give up work soon.'

She smiles. 'Not yet Pops. Thanks for worrying about me.'

'Do you think you will have a brother or a sister, George?' Pops asks.

George shrugs. 'I don't care.'

Karen has started to make dinner. She sips her tea and slices vegetables while cooking on the stove. She is doing too much at once. She is rushing like a tired cat listening for her owner to return while battling to catch a mouse. The more she tries to do at once, the slower and more tired she becomes and the mouse escapes.

Crisp red and brown leaves fall from the trees and spread their colours over the drying grass. Dust is everywhere and the sun shines only briefly. I lick my coat that has grown thicker to warm me in the cooler weather. A good wash like mama taught me is necessary every day. I wet my paw with my rough tongue and begin with my heaviest fur. The tiny barbs on my tongue do a great cleaning job, I stretch and roll on the carpet to remove any dead hairs.

'Come to the therapy room, my treasure. Work!' Karen calls.

A child and her mother are sitting in the room.

'This is my cat, Bella,' Karen says. I as look at the young child clutching her mother's hand. I wonder if I am imagining seeing this child. Before me is a Human kitten. Fronds of her long, red hair flick her skin and her green eyes filled with tears, stare at me. Like two cats we make an instant connection. I look away, not wanting to overwhelm her.

The mother places a hand on the little one's shoulder. 'Amelia is eight,' the mother says. She wipes away a few of her own tears before she continues. 'She's being bullied at school. I hope you can help her.'

'Hello there, Amelia! I hope you like cats,' Karen says.

'I love cats.' She moves towards me and extends her small hand, allowing me to smell it.

'She's a beauty. She has such lovely fur and green eyes too. My Auntie is also called Bella.'

Amelia leaves her mother to sit next to me on the carpet. We snuggle together while Karen asks the child's mother questions about her daughter. My tail disappears into Amelia's long hair and we mingle, cat and child. I fight my desire to sleep and instead I listen. This young Human is unusual and I want to know more about her.

'She is a clever child and enjoyed school until the bullying started. A group of children are upsetting her so much that now she hates school.' The mother explains that Amelia is an only child with few friends as they live on a large farm. The only neighbours with children her age are a distance away.

Fat tears stream down Amelia's face. 'They're horrid! They call me names like "carrot top" and "strawberry". They push me and stick out their tongues at me. One of them even drew a picture of rooster with my name and posted it on the Internet.'

The mother bends to stroke her daughters head. 'Karen will help us my darling. We'll sort it out.'

I move even closer to Amelia, ignore the tears falling on me and her wet hands holding me too tightly. I want to comfort her and I send out my loudest purrs.

The mother wipes away her own tears again. 'I talked to Amelia's teacher and she tried to help, but so far it hasn't stopped the bullies. I don't think moving her to another school is the answer. The same thing could happen. I don't know what to do to help Amelia. She begs me to dye her lovely ginger hair to brown so that she can be like everyone else in the class.'

Eventually I succumb to sleep in the child's arms. When I wake they are almost ready to leave.

Karen takes Amelia's hand and promises to speak to her class teacher.

'Bye, Bella,' Amelia says. 'I think you understand because you're a ginger too.' She gives me a last glance and is gone.

Karen strokes my head. 'My precious, my beautiful, ginger cat, you are a wonderful therapist.'

The blasts of wind and heaps of dry leaves don't stop us from running outside. Exercising in the garden is preferable to running through the house. An old tabby cat from one of the houses in the street is at the fence again today. He visits most days, meowing and looking lost as he wonders from one side of the fence to the other. His fat tummy tells me he is being well-fed, but his matted coat shows that he is not caring for himself. Cats are fastidious creatures and his lack of grooming is not a positive sign. I greet him by trying to rub noses though the fence wire. He is old and forgetful like Pops. I am not looking forward to growing old.

Visiting hospitals with Karen is becoming even more enjoyable. I am accustomed to the harness and the travel now. Once my harness is on, I jump into my carry box. Oliver eyes me jealously. He would like to escape from the house too. Despite the pleasure of the visits, I am uneasy about Karen. Her face is pale and sweaty and she sighs with tiredness. I remember that when she was carrying George inside her she was healthier. She wasn't as fat then, or nearly as tired. I wait for her to relax and I concentrate on sending her my healing purrs so that the baby will be strong, and that she will stay well. My dream warning from Bastet is not forgotten, I must look after Karen.

Once Karen has parked in the hospital grounds, she rushes as she carries me though the big door into the hum of the hospital. She walks on until we find the ward. A nurse introduces her to Lucas.

Karen smiles. 'Hi Lucas, this is Bella.'

'Hello, lovely lady, with a lovely cat.' A bald-headed, young Human of about fourteen stretches out his arms to me. 'Bella, beautiful cat, come and say, hello.'

Karen opens my carry box. I jump into his arms and burrow into his warm chest. I sense I can trust him and allow him to tickle my tummy.

'Just what the doctor ordered. I adore cats, especially cuddly ones like you, Bella.'

He looks at Karen. 'How did you know I'd like a visit?' He asks.

Karen smiles. 'The nurses thought you might appreciate a chat with me and a visit from Bella.'

'So, you're a shrink... a therapist,' he corrects himself, 'and she's a therapy cat.'

'Yes.' She smiles.

He frowns. 'I haven't had any visitors apart from my parents since I've been here for treatment. None of my classmates visit me. They bullied me at school and feel guilty . . . think they've upset me. Well, I'm not at all worried about them. A scrawny kid like me looks like a victim. Well, I'm not, and I'm not pretending either,' he says with a smile.

'Tell me more.'

'I'm smaller than the others, but I had good grades without doing much work. They were jealous of me and the bigger ones pushed me around, hit me, even drew blood. I was too small and weak to defend myself and I didn't know how, not then, anyway. My parents were at work all day, tired at night and I didn't want to hassle them with my sad stories of bullying.'

He takes a sip of water. 'One day a huge boy hit me so hard that my nose bled. My answer came naturally, "You poor guy, all that blood on your hands. What will the teacher say?" The others laughed and he scuttled off to wash his hands. The next day, when another bully pushed me, I turned around and said loudly, "Hey, couldn't you find anyone smaller, like a mouse?" The class laughed and from then on none of them attacked me again.'

'So, you sorted them out with your smart comments,' Karen says with a smile, 'Good on you!'

'Yep, and I had no further problems with them after that.'

Lucas and Bella talk for a while longer. When Karen stands to leave he thanks her for visiting and kisses the top of my head. 'Please come to see me again with Bella if you're in the hospital.'

'A lonely, clever, young man,' Karen says to me.

Karen is breathing fast and heavily as she hurries through the hospital passages. She is tired and my carry box must be heavy. Suddenly she stops and makes a sound, partly a sigh and partly a call. Struggling to hold on to the passage wall, she totters and then falls to the floor with a thud. My box follows her. A doctor and nurses gather around her. When I hear her voice again, even though it is slow and uncertain, I am reassured. She is alive. Nurses help her onto a narrow bed with wheels while I lie in my box forgotten.

'We'd better bring her cat with her,' one of them says at last.

They take us to a tiny area surrounded by curtains. Karen is moved to a bed and I am placed on a chair. *Meow, meow, meow,* I cry softly. Nothing must happen to Karen.

A doctor speaking in a hushed voice feels Karen all over while nurses stand by for instructions.

'The baby seems to be fine,' the doctor says, 'She is exhausted, and I doubt she is eating enough.'

Tony arrives panting. He has been running. 'Is Karen okay? And the baby?'

The doctor talks to Tony too softly for me to hear her. Then she gives instructions to the nurses, 'She's to stay overnight for observation. Check her every hour and if everything is fine discharge her in the morning, after I've had a chat with her.'

Tony sits with Karen and talks to her. She is too tired to answer.

He stokes and kisses her hand. 'I'll take Bella home and I'll be back later darling.'

It is dark outside when Tony carries me to his car. He sits in the car, before starting to drive and cries. Then he wipes away his tears and drives home.

Oliver is at the door waiting for us. When he notices that Karen is absent he meows nervously. After I tell him about Karen's collapse he paces restlessly. Tony feeds us and George. He and Pops eat a quick meal before they go back to the hospital together.

The house is empty and I miss Karen. I cannot eat or sleep, even though the doctor wasn't concerned about Karen or the baby, I ache inside when I think how tired she is. I can't imagine my life without her. My feelings for her are not about Catness, about my food or comfort. I scoffed about Humans who love, and Jodi in particular. Now I understand those feelings, the searing fear that something awful could happen to her, and the overwhelming emotion that has no name in my chest. It must be love. I love Karen. Now, I am certain of it.

Tony helps Karen from the car. Once she is in the house, George cries and clings to her.

'You're off to bed with a nice cup of tea and a sandwich, Doctor's orders,' Tony says.

Karen tries to argue but it is useless. She needs nutritious food and rest. Tony has taken time off from work to make sure she has it. After a day of lying in bed Karen is up and about. She agrees to rush less and rest more between seeing a few of her clients.

Amelia claps her hands in delight when she sees me. 'I've brought you a present, Bella,' she says opening her hand.

It is a toy mouse, much too small to be of interest. I purr and throw it up in the air to please her. She is happy that I am playing with it and pats my head.

'Amelia is still complaining of bullying,' her mother says looking worried.

'I hate school, they're all so horrible.' She looks at Karen pleadingly. 'I don't want to go back to school. Bella understands.'

'Well, I talked to your class teacher and she promised me that there will be changes at school that will help you.'

Amelia shrugs and looks away. 'My teacher makes promises she doesn't keep.'

Karen and the mother talk quietly while I lie next Amelia's ginger head, breathing her sweet scent.

'Love you, Bella,' she says.

'Your mum says that you like to draw and paint, Amelia. Please bring some of your art next time you visit us.'

Amelia nods and smiles. 'Okay,'

I am tired today and don't have the energy for healing Amelia. While they talk, I sleep.

'Bye, bye, Bella,' I hear her saying as she pats my head.

Oliver

Humans do not realise that we understand what C.A.T. means.

Pops sits on the couch with Karen. He wipes his forehead and takes a deep breath. 'I have amazing news. A television station rang me. This morning they saw some pictures of Oliver winning the first prize at the last cat show, and they want to feature him on one of their programmes, called "Winning Animals".

'What do they want Oliver to do?'

'It seems that they want him to sit on a cushion and wear his rosette. They say he is incredibly handsome and they would like him on their show.'

Karen doesn't answer immediately. 'Pops, you know how he hates all the shampooing and preparation.'

Oh No! They want to shampoo me and then put me inside the television. That talking box with pictures. How horrendous!

'Oliver... Oliver,' Pops calls.

I run to hide behind the curtain for safety and I'm not coming out.

'Oliver my boy, don't be scared. You have been paid an enormous compliment. The people from the television company want to take pictures of you and show them to everyone on television.'

I step forward slowly, meowing loudly to express my displeasure.

In the background, Pops explains in detail, but panic blocks my ears. I cannot hear a word. The box in the front of the room looks bigger than usual as my fear erupts into terror. Deep yowls escape from my throat and I run to hide under the bed. If I lie under the middle of the bed and my claws grab the carpet, they won't be able to shift me. I lie trembling. All I can think of is imprisonment in the box.

Later, Pops sits on the bed 'It's okay Oliver, calm down. I'll say "no" to the offer. It isn't worth upsetting you for a television show. We all know what a magnificent cat you are and that's all that really matters.'

I crawl from under the bed and place my head on his soft slippers. He has saved me from the worst imaginable situation. Since the phone call, I have been too afraid of the television box to join the others in the large room. I will recover eventually.

After dinner, Tony reminds Karen, 'The men are coming back tomorrow to finish working on the baby's room.'

Karen stretches and stands. 'We'd better do some tidying before they arrive or the entire house will be covered in dust.'

'I'll do it, you relax.'

Tony whips round the house like a storm, putting glass objects in a safe place and covering the couch and chairs with sheets. He rolls up carpets, lifts small tables and chairs and places them in other rooms. We hide together under the big bed among forgotten slippers and old socks, away from the wild rush of activity. It is a place of refuge.

With a screech and a shuddering stop, the men arrive. Their loud voices, banging and knocking disturbs our routine sleep. Worse, is the dust laden air that makes breathing hard. By the late afternoon, the house is quiet. We inspect the parts still covered with plastic and a wooden barrier, and avoid them. I wonder if the room will be finished before the baby arrives.

 # Bella

*Why do Humans need so many clothes? All we have
is one coat and two pairs of paws with claws.*

I wake to hear Karen calling, 'Bella, come! Amelia and her mother are here.'

After a stretch and roll on the carpet, I follow her to the room. Amelia has brought a large folder filled with her paintings to show Karen. She drops the folder and runs towards me. 'Hi, beautiful Bella!'

I purr and roll on the ground exposing my tummy and neck to show her my trust and affection.

Karen spots the folder. When she opens it her face glows with delight.

'Wow! What a gorgeous painting of Bella! You've captured her easy-going nature and her colouring.' Karen looks at another painting of me and throws her hands up in amazement. 'You're a wonderful artist, Amelia, incredible for your age.'

There are more paintings in the folder and Karen places them on the carpet. Amelia has painted children from her class, her teacher and the bullies.

Karen smiles wryly, 'I see a few bullies in your paintings. I can pick them out easily.'

'They're in my class and belong in my pictures.'

'You have captured everyone's expression and features.

Your paintings are far too good to hide in a folder. What about showing them to your teacher?'

'Maybe,' Amelia replies shyly.

'Think about it. You're too good an artist to hide your talent.'

Now that the builders have finally completed their work, the door to the new room is open. We cannot contain our curiosity and pad across the soft carpet into the room. Awful smells greet us. The new carpet has a vile odour and the colour on the walls smells disgusting. It is a large room, larger than George's room. No doubt, the size of rooms will be a topic to argue about one day. The white bed, table and armchair Karen placed in George's room when he was a baby are in the room as well as new posters on the walls and soft curtains. When the present smells disappear from the room they will probably be replaced by baby powder and poos. What a lot of trouble for a second room much like George's. What a waste! Couldn't they share a room or use the box room? Strange indeed, but I've forgotten male and female humans don't share when they are young.

After dinner, George wanders into the new room.

'Stinky,' is all he says, holding the tip of his nose as he walks out of the room.

The spatter of rain is over and the last of the sun's rays attempt to dry the soaked grass. Birds are chirping, croaking frogs sit in the wet and the sky buzzes with tiny flying insects. I step out cautiously, attempting to avoid puddles.

I stop to listen. 'Quark, quark.'

The duck is here, enjoying itself, gliding on the surface of a mud pool and then drilling into it. It pulls out a long worm and swallows it with a gulp. What a strange creature. It is not interested in me today. Reluctantly I turn my back on it.

As I search for a dry spot, I detect ripples of movement in the wet undergrowth. Rats. Streams of them are heading for the house, where it is warm and dry. With so many to chase, I will have to risk getting wet. I rub my scent around the outer walls of the house and pee, so that they smell my cat smell to warn them to keep away. A cat knows what it must do. My duty has made me filthy. My paws and coat are caked with mud and dirt. I had better hide from Karen and clean myself before she sees me, or a bath will follow. I find a dry spot and begin my rolling on the wet grass and licking job.

'We'd better hurry,' Karen says. 'Amelia's teacher has invited us to visit her school.'

There will a lot of children looking at me and wanting to touch me. I needn't worry though, Karen will look after me. One thing, I hope I don't spot the bullies in the class. After all I've heard about them I'd like to bite them, but I will behave well, as Karen expects of me.

At the school we are greeted with overwhelming noise.

'Karen has brought her cat, Bella, to visit. Quiet now, and give them some space,' the teacher shouts.

Karen lifts me out of my cage. I recognise the sound and smell of one familiar, small human, Amelia.

'Hi, darling, Bella, thank you for coming today,' she says, giving me a gentle pat.

'Will she bite?' A little one asks tentatively.

'Bella doesn't bite, she likes children,' Karen says in her sweet voice.

'She's beautiful,' another says.

'Wow, her fur is the same colour as Amelia's hair.'

'And her eyes are like Amelia's too!'

'Lucky Amelia to be like Bella!'

'Go to your seats children, you'll each have a turn with Bella,' the teacher says loudly above the noise.

Here I go, doing my rounds. Squeezes, prodding with small, sticky fingers and some gentle hands too. As a caring professional, I close my eyes and tolerate it all.

After each child has had their turn touching or holding me, Karen taps on the front table. 'Enough! Bella has been patient and allowed everyone a chance to pat and cuddle her. She is tired now. I must take her home, feed her and allow her to rest.'

'Let's thank Karen and Bella for coming today,' the teacher says.

We leave amid cheers from the children. At last it over and I am back in my carry box, safe from tiny hands. I am relieved to be in the car with Karen even though the traffic is slow and travel is bumpy. I will wash my coat well when we are home. If all I endured helps Amelia to be treated well instead of being bullied my discomfort will be worthwhile.

Winter

 # Bella

I wish they wouldn't interrupt my cleaning rituals.

Winter announces itself with icy blasts lashing our garden. The trees are bare, the grass is stiff and brown and the flowers have perished. A few brave birds sit on the naked branches and mice scuttle between their underground burrows. I shiver and lie inside next to the heating vent. Oliver is restless, and when the skies are clear he runs about in the cold garden. I had forgotten how cold winter could be after the long period of warmth.

We are all in the television room tonight. Karen's tummy has grown even bigger, and when I sit next to her I can hear and feel the baby moving around inside her. Oliver is excited about the tiny whooshing sounds and slight activity. I remind him that it won't come for a while. Human babies take ages to develop inside, unlike kittens.

Karen lies on the couch, rubs her tummy and sighs a tired sigh. 'Thank goodness the baby's room is finished.'

Tony gives her hand a squeeze. 'It looks beautiful.'

Karen rubs her tummy again and closes her eyes.

'You need a break. It's been too tough for you with work, George and the baby coming,' Tony says.

She nods. 'I haven't seen my dad or my sisters for ages. They're spending a few weeks at their beach cottage, maybe we could join them.'

'A great idea and a forced rest for you.'

'But, what if the baby comes early?'

'The doctor told you it won't come for at least six weeks, and on the off chance it does, there is a local hospital about ten kilometres away from the cottage.' He gives her a reassuring hug. 'I'd like to go away too. I'm not enjoying my job. It is not what I expected at all. I could happily resign and look for something else.'

'I know you're not happy at work, but with the baby coming we need the money,' Karen says, looking concerned.

'Try not to worry, I've had other offers. I didn't want to bother you with it right now.'

I give Oliver a long look. His ears shift back and fear is in his eyes. Any talk of our Humans leaving home is disturbing. What will be our fate? We decide to sleep on the big bed at night, hoping to overhear more from our owners about their holiday plans.

We learn nothing further about the holiday until tonight.

Karen yawns. 'A break is a great idea. There will be a lot to consider though. We haven't even thought of Pops or the cats.'

'I talked to Pops. He would prefer to stay at home. Unfortunately, he doesn't want to look after the cats.

She smiles and gives Tony a hug. 'I've been thinking about the cats.'

Oliver gives me nudge. At last we'll find out what we're waiting to hear. We sit up and listen.

'The cottage is huge. My sister took her three cats there with them last year. She said it turned out well with no problems. Perhaps we can take Bella and Oliver with us.'

'That is an excellent idea, as long as we plan ahead,' Tony says.

Oliver butts my head. They might take us with them on holiday. What a dreadful idea. I'm not happy about leaving my territory and neither is Oliver. If we must leave our home why don't they take us back to that luxury cattery? At least we will know where we're going.

We are huddled over the heating vent. Karen is up early, wearing her thickest gown that makes her look enormous. She is sitting at her desk writing lists. She scratches her head as her list grows longer and longer.

'I'll have so much to do if we go away – all my clients to see and possibly to refer elsewhere. And things to do at home too,' she says to Tony.

'No "ifs or buts", we're going! You need a rest!'

Oliver and I look at each other. We have our final answer.

Amelia is here with her mother. She smiles at Karen and greets me with a gentle pat on my head. She stands erect and her green eyes shine with happiness.

'Thank you, thank you Karen and Bella for visiting my school. Everyone adored Bella. They say I'm special because my hair and eyes are like Bella's.'

'It's amazing, Amelia has suddenly become popular and there hasn't been a single bullying incident,' her mother says. 'She is looking forward to school now.'

'I showed my paintings to my teacher,' Amelia says. 'She says they are incredible. She wants to show them to the rest of the school. I said okay, but thinking about it makes me nervous.'

'You are a talented artist, Amelia, and should feel proud.' Karen says.

'I guess so.'

While Karen and Amelia's mother talk, I creep up to Amelia's chest to cuddle, where I can hear her strong heartbeat. I am about to curl up for an essential sleep, when

Karen tells Amelia and her mother that she has decided to stop work and take a holiday break before her baby arrives.

Amelia looks sad and starts to cry. 'I will miss you and Bella.'

'Don't be sad, you're well now and strong like Bella.'

'I'll take a photo of you and Bella,' her mother suggests.

'That's a great idea mum.' She puts her head next to mine and a light flashes.

They check the photo and seem satisfied.

'I'll have you with me now,' Amelia says, wiping away her tears.

Before they leave Amelia, gives me a few last gentle strokes and kisses my head.

'Oliver, where are you?' Karen calls.

He wakes from his sleep and though he hears her calling, he does not move. Eventually he stretches and walks over to her.

'Come on, Oliver, we have some important work to do. We are all going away together on holiday and it will be easier for you and us if you learn to walk with a harness and lead. Bella learned and now it's your turn.'

He is alarmed by the words "harness and lead". His tail drops and his eyes show his fear. When he sees the harness and lead, he races to the kitchen. With a powerful jump, he is on the table. From there he leaps to the space above the fridge. Karen calls him and tries to tempt him down with his favourite food, prawns, but nothing shifts him. She is tired, the baby inside is heavy and she has lost her patient voice.

'Enough, Oliver! This is too hard. Tony can teach you to walk with a lead.'

Tony frowns. 'Karen, you need to relax before we go away.'

'I have to see people in hospital before we leave. Once the baby comes I won't be going back.'

'Promise me you'll take it slowly.'

She nods and give him a kiss.

We are back the hospital and Karen is looking for Benjy. The nurse says that Benjy is home for a few days.

'I'll tell him that you and Bella came to see him,' she says.

Karen leaves the ward and carries me through the corridor.

'Let's find Heather now.'

Heather is sitting in a comfortable chair looking at her phone. She puts her phone down when she notices us. 'Hi, so good to see you both. This must be my lucky day.'

I am out of my box and on Heather's bed in seconds. Apart from smelling the same, she is barely recognisable. Her blue eyes seem larger than before, dominating her gaunt face.

'I've almost completed this round of chemo. I don't know if it's working or not.' She rubs her bald head. 'It's made me so tired, but, if it helps, it's worth it.'

Heather needs comfort, and I allow her to hug me and kiss my head. While Karen and Heather talk, I snuggle up to her and purr loudly. I close my eyes, breathe deeply and send her my healing energy.

'You make me feel so calm, Bella,' she whispers. 'I wish you could stay.'

Heather struggles to hide her disappointment when Karen tells her that this will be our last visit.

'Of course, your baby will be here soon, but I will miss you terribly.'

'I can give you the name of a friend who I think you'd like to talk to while I'm away.'

'I'll be okay.' She gives Karen a brave smile.

Oliver is sulking and refuses to go to Tony. His pride has been wounded by the harness and lead episode. Tony is not pleased either and has stopped calling Oliver to sit on his lap. This morning, Oliver expressed his distress with a pile of vomit on the new carpet in the sitting room.

Tony mutters to himself as he cleans up the mess, 'I don't know why we are bothering to take you on holiday with us, Oliver. You're the most uncooperative, ungrateful cat.'

Humans can be more like cats than I imagined. This tiny storm in cat's bowl will pass. I wish it would hurry.

Oliver

All visitors must be approved by me.

I have not come down from my position above the fridge. It is safe high up here, but I am hungry. Eventually I will be forced to jump down. Right now, I hate Karen for showing me the lead and harness. I can understand now why Bella disliked wearing these instruments of oppression. Vigilantly, I watch for the slightest sign of harassment. That's exactly what it is, bullying us to wear that constricting contraption. I refuse to have it touch my fur.

Tony is talking to me in his kindest voice. He is trying to persuade me to wear the harness. He doesn't know how obstinate I can be. He will find out when I will refuse to comply by yowling as loudly as my lungs allow. I yowl and he puts his hands over his ears.

'Stop it Oliver! You're impossible.'

I don't stop. Not yet. Cooperate, why should I? He is not pleased with me and tries to bribe me with prawn meat. How disgusting! He should've realised by now that I have no intention of giving in. I am a proud, Siamese cat. We do not roll over and subjugate ourselves when our owners try to bully us. I will remember this episode and resent his behaviour.

Today he frowns and his voice has a stern tone. He is determined to force me to do as he wishes. I wriggle and hiss as he attempts to force to me to wear the harness. I hope he will get the message, or I will be forced to bite him. That I will only do if I am desperate and feel under attack. I have just shown him how distressed I am by collapsing onto my side and pretending he is choking me. Anything to stop him!

'Perhaps this harness is too hard for your fine coat, Oliver. I'll find a softer one,' he says, trying to stroke me. I wriggle from his grasp and turn my back on him. He must understand that I am not a dog. Dogs wear harnesses and leads. I know Bella has been forced against her will to wear a harness and be dragged along by a lead. But she is a therapy cat and visits sick people in hospitals. She cannot do her job unless she is trussed up in a harness. How she copes, I don't know.

Tony won't give up either. We are in the garden and once more he tries to persuade me to wear the harness. I dig my claws into the grass and refuse to move. Doesn't he know that restraining a cat in a harness and dragging him on a lead to follow his owner is an insult to a grown cat? It is against natural cat law.

'Okay, okay, Oliver. You've made your point,' he says, as he lifts me into his arms and carries me indoors. A further insult. I loathe being carried.

Later, I hear him complaining to Karen. 'Oliver is impossible. He refuses to wear a harness and he even hissed at me. I'm giving up. We can take Bella with us and Oliver will have to go to the cattery.'

How can Tony consider taking Bells and leave me at the cattery? I must've gone too far this time. I won't be left out. Of course, I can learn to walk with a harness and lead, and within a few days.

Tony is home early. I go to him, lie on his slippered feet and purr.

'What do you want? You're an impossible cat.'

I roll over and expose my tummy, indicating my submission.

'So, you're telling me that you are giving in after that five-star performance. You do understand that you'll stay at home if you refuse to cooperate.'

I *meow* and look up at him with my most pleading expression.

'Okay Oliver, one more chance at wearing the harness and lead.'

I wince inwardly without uttering a sound, as he places the dreadful harness around me. It feels tight and uncomfortable. Seething inside, I oblige for a short while.

'It's incredible what Oliver can if he wants to,' he says to Karen.

'He'll have to hurry up and learn to walk on a lead. There isn't much time before we leave,' Karen replies.

'He'll learn fast.'

Today, Tony walks towards me carrying the harness and lead. I want to run away and hide, but I know that he expects me to try harder. I wriggle, as I do not want him to believe he has won too quickly. When I wear the harness and lead without complaint, Bella gives me an appreciative lick and I walk a bit further. He is back later to torment me. His eyes beg me to oblige. To encourage me he offers me sardines, another favourite. The compelling aroma is a bribe that works. I try harder, but not too hard.

He sighs with relief. 'Well done Oliver.'

Though I walk in an uncoordinated fashion, he is pleased with my efforts. He strokes me and tickles me behind my ears. Now I am committed to walking with this abominable thing. When he tugs the lead I am expected to walk. How humiliating, like a dog on a lead.

He smiles at Karen. 'Success at last! He is incredibly obstinate and self-opinionated.'

She laughs. 'Oliver is your cat.'

'I'll take him out in the garden now for a trial.'

Of course, he knows I like being outdoors. I show him once again that being pulled on a lead to follow him is an insult to a grown cat. I dig my claws into the grass and refuse to move. That will teach him. But, my resistance doesn't work. Eventually, I submit to his demands with another tasty inducement. He walks in the garden and I follow.

He is satisfied and strokes me lavishly. There must be a next step. What can it be?

Here it comes. This morning, Bella and I are both wearing our harnesses and leads. Karen holds Bella's lead and Tony holds mine. They make clicking noises and call us to follow them into the large garden. I hold my ground, but a swift kick from Bella's back leg makes me follow Karen. We are like two dogs on leads. I have seen them walking with their masters and mistresses through the large window in the front of the house.

'Come on, you two,' Tony orders

He tugs my lead and makes clicking noises with his tongue. Karen tugs Bella's lead and makes the same nose. How comical. Bella looks at me, and I look at her. We walk with our Humans responding to their tugs and clicks.

Karen and Tony look at each other, nod and smile.

Karen claps her hands. 'Wonderful! Well done Bella and Oliver.'

I sense our misery is over for a while. We have passed their tests this time. Food follows. As I fall asleep, I wonder what Karen and Tony are planning. Why are we all walking outside?

 # Bella

I am tried of running after balls. Why don't they fetch them?

'Wake up Bella, we're visiting Mrs Lorimer today for the last time. We haven't seen her for a few weeks and she must think we've forgotten her.'

The drive is short and I remember the smell of the ground and trees as Karen carries me to the entrance. It's a long walk through dark passages until Karen finds Mrs Lorimer. She is watching the television with a group of old people. They notice me in my carry box. Calls of, 'a cat is visiting', 'what's her name?' and 'can we see the cat?,' fill the room.

Karen explains to the group that we are visiting Mrs Lorimer. She promises to bring me back to spend some time with them later. A nurse helps Mrs Lorimer out of her chair and leads her to a contraption with wheels almost like a half bicycle. Mrs Lorimer holds onto it as she walks down the passage. We follow to her room. Once Mrs Lorimer is comfortable in her armchair, I hop out and jump onto her lap.

'Oh, it's so good to see you both again, I hoped you were coming back,' she says, as she strokes me.

I purr loudly and snuggle into her warm jumper while they talk. Within minutes, I'm asleep. When I wake, Mrs Lorimer smiles and pats my head. 'I'm glad you had a little sleep, Bella.'

Later, Karen stands. 'I promised to visit the others in the lounge before we go. They all want to see Bella.'

'I hope all goes well with the birth of your baby, and enjoy your holiday. Perhaps I will see you some time later.'

Mrs. Lorimer gives Karen a hug and we leave. Back in the television lounge, the nurse allows each person about five minutes with me. I don't mind their clumsy fingers and tight squeezes. I know how much they need cuddles and purrs.

When Karen returns from shopping, she struggles to carry heavy packages into the kitchen. Out of the packages pours human and cat food, plastic cups and plates, a large sunhat, summer clothing and sandals. Why has she bought light clothing? The summer has passed. Perhaps we are going somewhere warm? I cannot imagine how that could happen.

She is lying on the couch now, relaxing and sipping tea, the mystery liquid she uses to revive herself when she is tired and needs calming. She picks up her list and sighs. Surely it's time for her to stop, to slow down like cats do, and have a nap. Presently she is like a cat racing to catch her tail.

Today, we are in a hospital with many passages to visit Grant. He's had a setback after an operation and asked Karen to visit him before her holiday.

I sniff. Dog odour.

Karen whispers, 'Keep calm, Bella,' as a large therapy dog passes us. All I can see through the holes in my box is staring eyes in a large head. It smells my cage and it turns it's his head away. At least it is well trained and doesn't growl at me. I am relieved when it passes us.

A nurse stops us to ask the usual question – why is Karen bringing a cat into the ward? Karen hands her a letter confirming my appointment as a therapy cat. After reading it, the nurse says that therapy dogs have visited the ward before, but not a therapy cat. She apologises and leads us to Grant. I am not allowed to jump onto his bed as he is recovering from an operation. Any infection could set him back.

'Hi Karen and Bella. How great to see you both.' He tries to sit up and collapses onto his pillows. 'After I saw you last month, I was discharged, but my wounds from the accident hadn't healed. The doctors decided that I needed an operation plus a further stay in hospital, so I'm still stuck in here,' he says, attempting to smile. 'I'm grateful to the doctors, they've done a wonderful job.'

'I'm sorry you've been going through all this, but despite your troubles you seem more optimistic.'

'I have some positive news to tell you. I listened to your advice and I've been more open with my wife, Jacqui. We're talking a lot now and her support has made all the difference. With the help of a friend, I've been offered a new job as soon as I am well enough.' He smiles. 'So things have improved, apart from my health.'

Cats can be miserable too when life turns against them, but in general we are resilient creatures provided we find food and a warm, safe place to stay. I am surprised to find that Humans are not that different. Support and care promotes their Humanness and recovery.

We are visiting a hospital for the last time before we go on holiday. We walk along the twisting corridor that leads to the teenage cancer ward. Near the door to the ward I hear sounds.

'Shush, they're coming,' voices whisper.

As we walk through the door, joyous shouts of "surprise" greet us. Pink and blue balloons fly in the air. In the centre of the ward is a table topped with cakes, sandwiches and packages in pink and blue. It takes me a few moments to realise that the teenagers, who are all fond of Karen, have made a celebration for her baby, and to wish her a happy holiday.

Pink and blue? Is the baby going to be pink or blue? More extremely weird, ritualistic, human behaviour.

'Wow! All this for me?' Karen says, surprised.

'And we have something for darling Bella too,' one says.

'How could we forget Bella?' another comments.

'How exciting! But you shouldn't have,' Karen says.

'Come on, Karen, take Bella out of her cage, open your presents and then we can all have cake and sandwiches.'

Once I'm out of my carry box I chase a balloon. It's too slippery to catch immediately. *Wowmeow!* I've got it in my paws. My claw zaps it and it breaks. I discover it is plastic and I can't even eat it.

Karen stands at the table heaped with presents and starts to open them.

'Oh, the cutest booties! Who knitted these?'

'Me! I like knitting.' A teen wearing glasses waves her hand.

'And the most gorgeous little hat.' Karen looks around to locate the knitter.

'I knitted the hat,' a young teen says, 'I've made lots of them for my nephews and thought you'd like one.'

'Oh, how lovely! Some handmade bibs. So pretty...and very welcome!'

'They're from me,' an older teen waves her hand.

A rattle and two wooden toy ducks are from the boys. The nurses give Karen a parcel tied in ribbons. Inside is cot quilt for the baby.

'Oh my! This feels so soft, and the little flowers on it are adorable.

Thank you all for your gifts, what a lovely surprise.'

'The surprise isn't over.' I recognise Heather's voice. She looks healthier and has grown some spikes of new hair. 'This is from Benjy and me.'

'Oh, goodness, thank you both,' Karen says, fumbling as she opens the parcel. 'How adorable. Two little baby grows ... so useful.'

They are like the baby suits that George wore all the time when he was little.

'Thank you, Karen for all your help, and Bella's too,' Benjy says.

'We made Bella a big cuddly blanket for cold nights, and hope it keeps her warm,' Heather says, placing a blanket large enough for two cats on the table, 'Keep warm, beautiful princess.'

'Thank you, on Bella's behalf,' Karen says. 'She'll enjoy sharing it with our other cat, Oliver.'

After all the excitement, Karen sits in one of the big padded chairs drinking tea and eating a huge slice of chocolate cake. I am with Benjy and Heather eating the fish they have for me. It is delicious and gone soon.

There are hugs and good wishes from all.

Karen wipes away happy tears and stands, 'We'll have to go. So, goodbye, and a big thank you to all for the presents and the cakes – such a lovely surprise.'

A nurse helps us to collect all the gifts and carry them to the car.

Since Karen stopped her therapy work, she is like a wild cat, collecting towels, sheets, pillows and doonas and stuffing them into huge floppy bags. She stretches and pulls suitcases from the top of the tall cupboard. A suitcase falls to the floor and it just misses her head. She sits on the bed to recover, and then pulls down another case. Suitcases make me scared. All the hairs on my back stand up in fright. I can't help connecting suitcases with being left in a cattery. There are no good catteries. Even the luxurious cattery took us away from our home and our territory. I try to think like a cat with cat logic, but I am too afraid.

Karen notices I am upset. 'Cool it, Sweetie. We are going away together. You and Oliver are coming with us to the beach. It will be new for you, an amazing experience.' She bends to stroke my head above my eyes, behind my ears and her hand travels all the way down my body.

We will be going with them to "the beach". She wants us to be pleased, but she doesn't realise that our territory is of utmost importance to us. Where is this place she is taking us? Will there be place for cats at "the beach"?

Oliver

We prefer fresh fish and meat to tins, or last night's left overs.

Flecks of pink light under the curtain curl over the floorboards and wake me. My body tells me that I have not been asleep for as long as usual. I poke my nose through the net curtain to watch the sun turning the world gold. Bella is still asleep oblivious of the early sunlight. The clock in the big bedroom buzzes, waking Tony. Quickly he kills the noise, and then wakes Karen. Reluctantly she rolls onto her back and gradually moves her huge body out of the bed.

'Time to wake up. We're going away today and there's a lot to do before we leave,' Tony says.

I shiver in fright. It's happening. Shortly, they will take us from our home to this "beach" place. Bella opens her green eyes, sees my distress, and realises that we will be leaving home soon. George complains noisily about being woken early, but Karen ignores his complaints, dresses and feeds him. Karen and Tony eat a small breakfast and give us food.

Karen hands Pops a piece of paper. 'This is a list of our phone numbers at the cottage and some other emergency numbers as well. Jodi will be here every day, so don't hesitate to ask her to buy you extra food or to help you.'

Tony puts his arm around his grandfather. 'Are you sure you have everything you need? Anyway, I'll call you every night to check you're okay.'

'Shush, shush you two. Stop fussing,' Pops says. 'You seem to forget that before I came to live here I was on my own for ten years. Having Jodi visit will be lovely she's a darling.' Pops pats Tony's shoulder and gives George a kiss. 'Go now, or you'll never get there. Have a wonderful holiday and have a rest, Karen!'

Tony and Karen rush from room to room collecting forgotten items. Once Tony has packed all they need for the holiday into the car, he turns to us. He is not in the mood for refusals and virtually pushes us into our carry boxes. He finds place for us on the back seat. We're in a narrow space packed like mice in a drainpipe. We can hardly see a thing. Oliver meows loudly and I join in.

'Oh no, a cat's chorus to start our holiday,' Karen says.

'Ignore them. They'll tire of complaining soon,' Tony adds.

Tony checks that all is in place, waves to Pops and starts the car engine.

I dislike the motion of the car and meow. George is unhappy too and cries. Tony mutters about the noise and turns on the radio. The sun is awake by now, making it hot in our tiny space. Sleep is impossible during the endless journey. Karen tries to soothe George whose cries of discontent develop into sobs.

'He needs a break. We all need a break,' Tony says, as he slows the car down.

About time too, my paws are stiff from lying in a tiny space. We are ignored while Tony takes George to pee behind the bushes. Then he spreads a blanket under a tall tree to arrange the food Karen prepared before leaving.

Karen attends to us before eating. 'We haven't forgotten about you two. Out you come, cats.'

I look about, check the grassy ground before me, the trees and wild flowers. No threats in sight. The smell of this strange place is unusual. I am afraid of unfamiliar places and step out of the box cautiously. Bella's ears are back as she jumps from the cage onto the grass to join me. Neither of us are comfortable in this strange environment, but lying in our boxes in a cramped position for a long period makes us desperate to move around. We have no choice other than to allow Karen to attach a harness to each of us. She is gentle and pats us encouragingly. Then she clips a lead onto each harness.

'First, food for hungry cats,' she says, as she offers us our pellets and water in little bowls. I drink but don't eat. The journey has made me nauseous. Bella is fine and eats her food as well as mine. Karen tries to feed George with a spoon, but he hardly eats.

'I'm starving,' Karen says, as she takes a bite from a sandwich. Tony eats faster than Karen and more. He breaks a sandwich into tiny pieces for George to tempt him to eat.

One taste and George spits it out. 'Yuck!' he says.

Karen's voice is angry. 'Don't ever say "yuck" to food, George!'

Then Tony's loud voice calls, 'Come cats, let's walk!' He takes our leads and makes the familiar clicking sound with his tongue to instruct us to follow him. We begin to follow him, when suddenly he stops to break off a bough from the tree. It must be protection against any stray dogs around. We both welcome the opportunity to walk in the long grass. Tony expects us to follow his wide strides, but we stop occasionally, waylaid by smells and sounds. A long worm makes its way towards me. My claw shoots out and "gotcha". Bella catches her own small prey and is eating it. I nibble my worm but I'm not hungry, and leave it in the grass. Tony calls us sharply and we keep walking.

The wild grasses remind me of my escape from the captivity of the house last year. I enjoyed the experience, and in many ways, would like to be free to roam, climb tall trees and hide in dark places. I sniff the grass and identify dogs and other animals. Then I see them, huge, dark, fat, four- legged creatures eating grass. They appear to be passive, but their size is terrifying. Near them there are the largest, fattest poos I've seen. I avoid them. Tony laughs loudly.

After our walk, we lie on the blanket and sleep in the shade. Tony wakes us to remove our harnesses and places us in our carry boxes. The journey continues and we sleep until Tony stops again.

Sounds of cars and Humans surround us. The smells of food waft through the air and I notice that it is pleasantly warm. We wait in the car in our carry boxes, while our Humans go to pee and buy food. Tony lifts us from our boxes, and on go our harness and leads. Karen and Tony eat and give us more pellets in bowls and water. This time I eat a little. Once again, we walk with him controlling our leads. Walking on the short, lush grass is pleasurable. A sniff tells me that many Humans and dogs have walked across it. Large, brightly coloured flowers bloom and the trees have shiny leaves. I am grateful for the exercise, though I would like to run. Bella is satisfied with a short walk. But then, she is easier to please.

We don't linger during the stop and resume the interminable journey. George is restless and whimpers like a kitten. He has had more than enough of this endless journey too. Karen kisses him and strokes his head. We are both extremely uncomfortable by now and long to be freed from our boxes.

'It won't be long, my angel,' she says to George, 'Look, a supermarket, a bank and other shops,' she says, pointing them out to him.

I have no idea what shops are and why Humans require

them. Karen goes shopping a few times a week. She seems to like shops.

'There's the vet, the doctor for animals,' she says to him.

I growl softly at the word "vet" and shiver. I hope we don't have to visit this Human while we are away from our home.

 # Bella

We like what we know and loathe change.

The car finally stops with a loud groan. The journey must be over. There are sounds of young, rushing feet and piercing yells of joy to greet us. They hug, kiss and talk loudly. What is it with Humans? Most undignified! We are left in the car while they inspect their accommodation. I am near a window and all I can see through the holes in my box is the sky. No clouds - a positive sign.

Satisfied, they unload the suitcases and packages. They then carry us into the cottage. We are freed into an area large enough to run in. It has one high and dirty window that hardly admits light, so we have no way of seeing outside. The walls are made of wood with cracks that allow fresh air into the room. Two broken couches, a table, and tattered chair stand on the cold floor. Compared to our home, this is a prison. Before I upset myself at the starkness of our accommodation, Tony brings us our baskets and a large strip of carpet. Karen carries in our separate water, food bowls, and litterboxes with a new type of litter. Anything unusual is worthy of suspicion and neither of us like the finer litter we are forced to use. It is a primitive arrangement with food, warmth and shelter, and we are safe. As apprehensive as we are, we have no choice but to accept this dungeon as our temporary home. As a cat rescued from near a garbage can, I shouldn't complain. I have become accustomed to a luxurious life and time doesn't move backwards, even for cats.

We look at each other as we listen to the insistent sound outside. It is like a roaring beast with a salty smell. It is unlike anything we've heard or smelled before. Being cats, our ritual sniffing and checking begins. Cats and dogs have lived in this place, rats and mice have made it their home too. Systematically, we rub our scent on all the corners, over the floor and old furniture. Oliver chases rats in the hope of frightening them away. We will ignore the mice unless we are hungry. Our work is done for now. Our temporary home is safe and cat-liveable. Exhausted, we curl up in our baskets for a nap with the constant growling sounds outside.

Tony wakes us when he stomps in to check if we are settled. He grunts when he notices the filthy window.

'That won't do at all,' he mutters as he leaves. Later, he returns with a pail of soapy water and long brush on a stick. 'This should bring in some light and warmth,' he says, as he works away at the window until the sun's last rays. He leaves and closes the heavy door, effectively locking us into our new prison.

The sky is navy when Karen arrives. 'There you both are.' She bends to stroke us in turn. 'I hope you've done you rubbing and scratching and are happy.' She notices our ears twitching. 'You're listening to the power of nature, to the sea.'

We look at her, but don't understand her words.

'Come,' she says. After long stretches we follow her cautiously through the door and into the passage, stopping to sniff here and there. The passage, with the scent of foreign creatures will need a great deal of our rubbing attention as well. She leads us into a large room with two wide, soft couches and padded chairs. The open windows are barred to the night. At least, Oliver won't think of trying to escape. I notice that our friend the moon is growing fat again, and that the glittering lights in the sky are brighter here than at home. The room is packed with talking Humans. Karen's father, they call Dad, sits next to her on one side of the couch and Tony sits on the other. Dad is a lean, older man, slightly younger than Pops and still energetic. His crinkled skin is tanned, the few strands of hair left on his head are almost white and his beard is as bushy as my tail. Fortunately, he is fond of cats and nothing like Karen's mother, Liz, an awful human. I can understand why he left her long ago. Karen's older sister, Nicole, sits on the other couch with her husband James. Their three teenage children, Jeremy 16, Marcie 14 and Kate 12, are huddled on the other couch like prawns in a tin. They behave like strangers as they do not visit Karen and Tony often. I watch them carefully. Jeremy is slim and muscular like his father and speaks quietly. He is not the leader. Marcie, already rounded like a woman, speaks decisively and loudly, ignoring her brother and controlling her younger sister. They all appear to like cats and fuss over us. With so many Humans in the house, it is just as well Karen's brother and younger sister and their families are not here.

We do the rounds from one Human to another for strokes and cuddles. Then we go to our owners. George is on one side of Karen's tummy and I am on the other. Oliver is on Tony's lap. What Bliss! Karen sighs with tiredness and rubs her tummy.

'The baby inside is growing big,' she says to George. She takes his hand and allows him to feel her tummy. 'Can you feel it moving?'

He nods. 'Is it a boy like me, or a girl?'

'We don't know yet. I can only tell you that it will be your brother or sister. Isn't that wonderful?'

'Will it be able to play with me?'

'Not when it is born. It will be like a tiny kitten. You've seen newborn kittens. It will play with you when it is older.'

He looks at Karen and nods. 'It will be tiny and sucking mama's milk.'

'Yes. Do you remember sucking my milk too?'

He nods again and touches her breast.

'When the baby arrives there will be a lot of changes for you, George. You will have to share more, but never forget that you are our first born, darling boy, and that we love you. No new baby will ever take your place or be more loved than you. We decided to have another baby so that you won't be lonely any longer.'

He snuggles up to his mother and smiles.

'When the baby is little I will have to spend a lot of time caring for it. I'll need you to be my big boy and help me.'

Though George looks at her while she tells him about the new baby, I don't think he grasps the impact it will have on his life.

The bored, young ones leave for their rooms to play with their phones and small computers. Tony and James are friends as well as brothers-in-law and even look alike. They sit next to each other chatting and drinking red liquid. Nicole and Karen giggle like two joyful birds chirping on a tree. Nicole drinks red liquid and Karen has water. As I watch Karen and her sister together, I understand how much they miss each other when they're apart. I think of mama often, but I don't miss my brothers and sisters, all pushy and greedy for mama's milk.

George is already asleep in his room. The others yawn and talk of sleep. We follow Karen to our prison room. The door bangs shut. Throughout the night, the wild creature outside booms and crashes, but whatever it is, we are safe. That is, until loud noises outside our window alert us. Large paws pound, growl and bark. Dogs. And they can smell us. Oliver slips into my basket and we huddle together in fear. Dogs, especially large ones, are our enemy, and like other small mammals, we are their prey. Their sense of smell is even more powerful than ours. They are fast animals – a serious challenge. My memory of being a tiny helpless kitten, sniffed and pawed at by a dog remains sharp, and I am afraid.

When the dogs realise that they can't reach us, they run off. We sleep together in my basket until the early morning light wakes us. The roar is still outside when Karen and the youngest child, Kate, arrives with our food, fresh water and clean litter. Karen notices we are lying together.

'You two must've been scared last night. I heard the dogs howling. Don't worry, you're safe inside with us,' she says, giving us both a pat.

We eat and wait for Karen to return.

At last, we hear the prison door grind open. 'Come and join us, cats.'

My only thought is to find out more about where we are and the strange sounds and smells. In the large room, I jump from the couch onto the window ledge. Oliver is next me. Then we see it. An immense whiteness leading to endless, pounding water. This must be the roaring creature. Terrified, we hide under the couch. Tony and George arrive and spot us under the couch.

'Poor cats! We thought there wouldn't be dogs here, but there's a pack of them.' He shakes his head. 'It won't be safe taking them onto the beach as we'd hoped.'

'I want the cats to come to the beach with us,' George says with a stamp of his foot.

'Darling, they're safest inside. While we're out they can have the run of the place,' Karen says. 'You can play with them later.'

George glares at his mother and doesn't reply. She has been too short-tempered lately for him to dare argue with her.

'I'll ask about a safe, dog free area to take them for a run.'

The other Humans arrive for breakfast and the sound of their talking rises. They are wearing hardly any clothing and their bare skins shine in the light. Karen dresses George in a shirt over his bathing pants and smears him with cream. Before they leave, they all put cream on their bodies and rush around collecting towels and hats.

Karen stops to stroke our heads. 'Bye my sweeties, enjoy the quiet cottage. We'll be back later.'

I can't help wishing they hadn't brought us to this weird place. I suppose being with them is preferable to the luxury cattery. We'll cope. Catness teaches us to adapt, wherever we live, or if the climate changes.

Oliver claims the large soft armchair and is soon asleep. I sit at the window and watch the activity on the beach. The beach spreads as far as I can see, but most Humans are close to our house. They are small but I can see them. Some walk near the water, others are swimming and the young ones amuse themselves with games. I can just about make out our Humans sitting on their towels on the sand. Bored by the scene, I find a cosy spot on the couch and sleep.

Shrieking outside wakes us. Through the window, we see enormous, white birds with large wings and black markings on their heads flying together like a pack of stray dogs. They are nothing like our duck, or the small birds in our garden. They circle around the Humans waiting to pick up bits of food. A group breaks free and flies near the cottage. They spot us at the window and try to attack. One even hits his head on the glass window. Initially it is stunned and then flies away.

Oliver shudders with fear. These are bird predators. We

are safest inside, away from them and the dogs. I cuddle up to him until he relaxes and sleeps. Then I return to my position at the window. The sea animal must be gigantic. It has crawled up the beach and is frothing and licking the pale sand.

Our Humans return to the cottage to eat. The young ones feed us scraps from their plates even though Karen tells them not to. After their meal, a heated discussion about plans for the afternoon drives us back into our room. Oliver goes to his food bowl for a nibble of dry food and finds it empty. My bowl is empty too. We are both hungry. I begin to meow and Oliver joins me until our cries turn to yowls.

Finally, Karen enters the room. 'Shush, shush cats. What's upsetting you?' she says, as she looks about.

Our noses point to our empty bowls.

'The rats must've had a good feed,' she says, staring at our bowls. 'With so many about, you two will have to eat quickly.'

Karen astounds me. She understands immediately. My earlier thoughts are confirmed. She must've been a cat in a past life.

This morning, the young ones are ready early, partially covered in new, coloured, patches of material. At least, now I will be able to spot them easily on the beach. They play on their phones while they wait for their parents to feed them. I wonder what they see on their tiny phones and why they are so attached to them. They take the small things with them wherever they go, push buttons and stare at them. Karen and Nicole make breakfast and they all eat. We have learned to eat quickly to prevent rats touching our food.

The white birds squawk as they fly over the cottage to the beach. George looks up at the sky with a scared expression. 'Horrible, big birds.'

'Try not to worry about them and don't give them food,' Karen says, patting his head affectionately.

Once the Humans have left, the cottage is ours. We both watch the beach scene through the window. Tony is holding George's hand as they enter the froth and waves. George breaks free and runs back to the beach. Later, he paddles with Tony next to him. Our teenage Humans are sitting together away from the adults, laughing and playing on their phones. By now, I am no longer interested in watching them and sleep until Oliver wakes me with a paw jab. He calls me to the window and nods in the direction of the sand. Four big, young humans stand in front of our teenagers looking like aggressive tomcats ready to pounce. They are horrid bullies pointing and waving their hands. Marcie, our middle teenager laces her arms around the backs of her brother and sister. She talks to them softly, and then they all turn their backs on the bullies. Slowly, with a toss of their heads, they walk away. We purr excitedly. That's the way to fight off bullies, like cats! Oliver tells me about his experiences with cat bullies and I share mine. We have so much to talk about that we are still engrossed in our memories when our Humans return from the beach.

The young Humans pat our heads absentmindedly. We leave them and sit with Dad who enjoys long cuddles. This afternoon, while the others are out, Dad relaxes on the couch and we snuggle close to him. He tells us in whispers about Terry, a cat that lives with him, and his elderly sister. He says Terry resembles Oliver. He is just as smart, but whiter, rounder and lazier.

The cottage is alive early this morning and they all leave to walk on the pale sand. Oliver looks longingly through the window at the sunlit world. Restless and bored, he runs around the big sitting room jumping on and off couches and onto the tallest ledge. Still full of energy, he races through the rooms. I forget about him and sleep until I hear banging sounds. Two dead rats lie on the floor and he's chasing another. He pounces! Now, it dangles from his mouth. He shakes it and tears it apart with his claws until it is dead.

Later, when they return, Tony sees the dead rats near his slippers and yells, 'What on earth, Oliver?'

'He is giving you his killing of dead rats as a gift,' Karen explains. George looks at the rats and turns up his nose.

'Stinky rats,' he says.

'I wish Oliver wouldn't do this, but I suppose it's a show of affection.' He sighs. 'Where are you Oliver? Thank you, you're my good boy. I'm sorry that I will have to throw the rats in the bin.'

Oliver is far more than a magnificent Siamese. Like all cats he is a predator. With his athletic ability and speed, he is a highly skilled killer. Most Humans don't understand how powerful the predator is within us. It is part of our Catness, and our survival.

George is growing into a strong Human. He talks a lot, runs and climbs. Oliver says he will be a smart Human, because he is already able to tell stories and work out puzzles. Oliver remembers how long it took for George to arrive. He has used that knowledge to calculate that Karen's baby will come out soon.

'Come, cats, we have found a safe place where you can walk. You both need some fresh air and exercise,' Karen calls. She leaves George with her sister and kisses him goodbye. He tries to hold on to his mother and cries. She frees herself and blows a kiss to him.

'Since the start of the holiday he's been clingy. Perhaps he senses the baby will be here soon and things will change for him.

'He wasn't like this at home,' she says to Nicole.

Tony arrives with our carry boxes and we jump into them. We haven't been outside for two days and miss the feel of the sun, earth and wind. After a short drive, the car stops. Tony opens our boxes and quickly snaps on our harnesses and leads. The smell of salt and grass greats us.

'Come, cats,' he says, making the clicking noise with his tongue that tells us to follow him.

Before us is the pale, beach sand with clusters of long grass, spiked weeds and small bushes. The sand is hot and burns my pads. It is soft, but heavy and as I try to walk, I feel I am sinking into it. I try to grasp it with my claws, but it is too slippery. Walking on the sand is slow and tiring. There are strange plants that pop out and unusually shaped rocks dotted about. They look as if they have fallen from the sky.

Karen sits on a rock to rest while Tony takes our leads. The holiday has made him patient enough to allow us to stop to smell the grasses as we walk. I catch a bug and he laughs. Oliver tries to catch one too, but it is too quick for him and his lead is too short. When we come across a rock pool, Tony steers us away from it.

'Perhaps we can swim here another day,' he says, as he waves to Karen in the distance.

The days of the holiday merge like mud puddles. I can't tell how long we have been away from our home. We eat and sleep, walk in the afternoons and sit with the Humans at night. We can't complain, we receive more than enough pats and strokes. The pounding ocean is familiar now. We feel safe in the cottage and are no longer bothered by the birds, rats, or dogs that prowl at night.

This morning, clouds gather and the dark sea crashes

angrily on the beach. Our Humans rush out before the storm breaks. After our breakfast, as most mornings, we watch the activity on the beach through our window. With the threat of a storm there are hardly any people on the beach today. We are about to move to sunnier, sleeping spots, when we notice the four mean boys who tried to bully our teenagers. The bullies laugh as they parade on the water's edge with long strides. A small boy tries to pass them. They move close together to prevent him from passing. The boy looks afraid and hangs his head. One of the bigger boys chases him into the water. We can't hear any of it, but even from a distance, we can tell that they are insisting he swims. Just in time, a tall Human lifts the small boy from the water. He takes the boy's hand as they walk along the sand together.

I am upset for the young boy and Oliver is too. We agree that he was rescued just in time. Unfortunately, he's had a nasty experience. After watching Human bullies on the beach, I know that they are as horrid and dangerous as cat bullies. Humans are supposed to be highly evolved creatures. They walk on two legs, talk and think in more complex ways than cats, but are just as aggressive. Perhaps dogs have their bullies too. I find all of this too hard and distressing. I am going to sleep.

Oliver

Sunlight and indoor heating charge our batteries.

We are waiting with Tony and his brother-in-law, James, while Karen and Nicole wait in the car. The sun has warmed the earth and the slight breeze through the tall grasses is pleasant. Tony and James chat cheerfully. When we reach the rock pool Tony stops.

'Maybe we should let the cats swim in the pool today. Oliver likes swimming and Bella can go in if she wants to. What do you think, James?'

'With both of us here it should be fine,' James says.

Tony kicks off his sandals and steps into the pool. 'We'll start with Oliver,' he says as removes my harness and lead. Bella watches as I follow Tony to the edge of the pool. My paw touches the sticky mud and I hesitate. He lifts me into the shallow water. The cool water smells and feels different to the pool at home and there are stones and plants beneath my feet. I look at Tony and he smiles.

'Swim Oliver,' he says. He is close to me as my paws strike out and I find a rhythm. I avoid the rocks and keep swimming. Glorious and seductive! I can't remember such ecstasy. Once again, I am the wild cat I dream about, that swims in rivers and pools.

In the background, I hear James talking to Tony. 'Bella doesn't seem keen on swimming,' he says. 'She's missing out, but that's her choice.'

The swim is over. I scramble over the rocks and shake myself dry in the last of the sunlight. On goes the dreaded harness and we are back in the car heading for the cottage.

That night I dream of wild cats swimming.

The afternoon is warm, and Karen and Tony bring George along when we visit the rock pool again. I can't wait to swim and strain on the lead in the direction of the pool. Bella is not at all interested in swimming in this strange place and won't even put her paw into the water.

'Okay, okay Oliver. You'll swim soon,' Tony reassures me.

I swim, avoiding the plants and rocks until a creature bumps into me. It is not a sea mouse, nor like any creature I have seen before.

Tony laughs. 'It's a fish, Oliver. Catch it.'

It's gone before my paw can strike it. Then I see a smaller fish and chase it. I have it in my mouth and I carry it to Tony. It is silvery and glints in the light.

'Good boy! Smart cat!' He says, calling Karen, 'Look what Oliver caught.'

Bella is watching but doesn't move any closer to the water.

Karen smiles as she shows George my catch. 'Fish,' she says to him slowly.

'Eat the fish, cats, and enjoy it,' Tony says to me and Bella.

Bella sniffs the fish and doesn't touch it. I bite a bit. I'm not used to eating raw fish and leave it too. It smells nothing like the cooked fish we like, or fish in tins.

The walk back to the car in sudden swirling wind is cool and unpleasant. Karen shivers and puts a cardigan around her shoulders.

'Let's get moving and head for home before it's dark,' she says.

That suits me. I've had my swim and the sooner we

return to the cottage the better. Unfortunately, there are no heating vents at the cottage. Tony and James will light a fire tonight. The flames are as fascinating to watch as they are warming. I am convinced that Humans are unaware of how important heat is to us cats. We need a certain amount of heat as fuel for our bodies and to maintain our fur coats. Retaining heat allows us to stay cosy and warm when we sleep, and we sleep a lot.

Despite the cold night, the morning sun burns with surprising intensity, and the Humans leave early for the beach. I watch Karen struggling to walk in the sand with her weighty body and worry that she is tiring herself. Tony and James erect umbrellas and she lies in the shade. The birds circle the cottage and then move to the water's edge hunting for food. At least the dogs haven't been about this morning. We sleep until the Humans return.

Karen is the kitchen with her sister preparing lunch, when she cries out, 'Tony, Tony, come quickly.'

He rushes to her.

'My water's broken. It's so early!'

We both run to kitchen. Karen is standing in a puddle of liquid. I know that she must be about to give birth to her baby. When I ran away from home last year, I saw wild cats giving birth. Their water was tinged with blood before they began to push their kittens out. Karen's baby wants to come out much earlier than expected.

'Tony, the hospital is further away than we thought. I don't know if we'll make it in time,' she says.

Tony goes to the phone to ask for help. After two conversations, he calls out to Karen. 'There's a professional midwife nearby who can be here in fifteen minutes.'

'Yes, tell her to come.'

I look at Bella and she looks back. A midwife?

Nicole hovers around Karen looking worried. Then

there's a knock on the door. It's the midwife carrying two bags. She is older than Karen and younger than her mother, Liz, with fuzzy brown hair and quick eyes. She moves fast, setting up a special bed for Karen covered with towels and pillows to make her comfortable. Then she gives instructions to everyone. She closes the door and only allows Tony to enter. At first, there is quiet, until Karen begins to moan. Day turns to night. It takes ages for Karen's moans to become louder and more guttural, like an animal calling. Through the door, we can hear the midwife and Tony's voices. Nicole and James' faces are long with worry.

George does not understand any of it. When he hears his mama's moans, he begins to sob. Nicole tries to calm him, but it has no effect. Marcie is only 12 and already a knowing woman. She takes George's hand and leads him to a quieter part of the cottage. She plays games with him and sings the songs he likes. For a while, he forgets about his Mama and the baby. How strange it is that Marcie has taken over Jodie's role as George's carer so easily. Perhaps it is her kind nature that draws him to her.

We all wait as Karen's increasing pain continues into the early hours of the morning. The smiling sun brings the new baby. What joy, a girl. I am relived she is out of Karen's tummy.

Tony shouts with joy, 'We have a darling, little girl who came early.'

'I'm calling the ambulance. She might need hospital care for a while,' the midwife says.

From a distance, I hear a wailing sound. The noise persists as a white van drives up the path to the cottage. Two big Humans rush inside. They carry Karen and the baby out and place her securely in the white van. The noise returns as the van drives away at top speed. Tony carries Karen's small suitcase and rushes to his car. He follows the white van with the midwife beside him. Nicole and James take George with them and leave for the hospital too.

I am tired of having to be a brave cat when so many things scare me. The birth of a fragile, baby is concerning. I'm sure Karen will stay in the hospital with it for some time. What will happen to us if Karen is away? She is the controller at home and here at the cottage. Will we be fed regularly if she is away? Will anyone care about us when so much is happening? A worrying situation indeed. Bella wouldn't guess how much I worry, and that I have a kitten's heart inside. I hate to admit it, Bella is the stronger cat. She adapts well and has a huge capacity for love.

Bella

There is no time of day or night that a cat can't be fed.

Bastet's statue is not in the cottage, but I believe she is everywhere protecting cats. I close my eyes, see her in my cat mind, and ask her to watch over Karen and her baby. I think of Karen, purr loudly, and send her and the baby white healing. Karen is the most important Human in my life.

Oliver tries to show how brave he is, with an attitude of indifference, but I've noticed him pacing through the house, his belly close to the ground with anxiety. I try to help him with purrs and cuddles. Usually he pushes me away, though this time he moves closer to me.

We wait for Tony to return with news of Karen and the baby. It seems like hours before we hear his car.

'The baby is a little too small and too weak to come home yet. They are looking after her in the hospital and Karen is with her until she is stronger,' he announces

'Will we be staying or going home, Dad?' Jeremy asks James.

'We'll stay in the cottage with Tony and George until the baby is well enough to travel.'

Disappointed, Jeremy and Kate look down. They would prefer to go home. Marcie smiles. 'I want to stay with George until Karen is able to care for him.'

When Karen comes back to the cottage she will have a

small, crying creature with her who is always hungry. Just as well George is growing up and is more independent. We cats will experience huge change. Karen and Tony will be so busy with the little ones that they will have hardly any time for each other. We will have to fend for ourselves. If they remember to feed us we'll cope. We cats are resilient and survivors. So much is happening at once. It is all positive and there is no need for concern. Marcie has turned into a true cat mama a lot like Karen and even kinder than Jodie. With Karen away, I want to be with Marcie all the time and Oliver does too. We follow her around the cottage and sit on her lap or next to her on the couch. George is there too and because he is a Human, and our owner's child, we allow him to choose where he sits.

Karen remains in the hospital until Tony brings her home without the baby.

'The doctor wants me to leave the baby at the hospital and visit her during the day. I will provide enough food for her,' she tells her family. 'Thank goodness she is growing stronger. It won't be long until I can bring her home.'

'Wonderful,' Nicole says, giving Karen a hug.

'Great news,' James says. 'Have you both decided on a name for her yet?'

'Yes, her name is Lily, I love it.'

They all murmur about the pretty name.

'Come on, let's drink to Lily,' James says, as he heads for the kitchen to find wine and glasses.

Tony fills small glasses with wine for the adults. Karen and the young one's drink lemonade. They all lift their glass and clink them together. How weird! I've stopped commenting on strange Human rituals. There are so many.

Karen and Tony travel back and forth to the hospital until one afternoon Karen carries Lily into the cottage.

'Hello everyone, we're home with Lily!' She shouts excitedly.

The following day, Nicole, James and their family leave. Marcie kisses my head before she climbs into the car. I will miss her.

Karen feeds the baby. Between feeds she eats and rests. She hasn't time for George or us and we try not to bother her.

George peers at Lily's tiny face and is disappointed. 'She's tiny and pink.' He has forgotten what his mother told him about taking a back step for a while. He is not receiving the attention he expects from her and sulks. I place my paw on his knee to calm him, but it doesn't help.

He whispers to me. 'Bell-Bell, I don't like Lily. She makes smelly vomits and poos and so much noise that I can't sleep. Mama doesn't love me since she came.'

When he sees his mother sitting on the couch feeding Lily, he remembers her feeding him and looks sad. With a stamp of his foot he turns away from his mother and sister. This is cat-like jealousy from a Human child! I watch him wondering what he will do next. I don't have to wait long. He runs to his room and opens his cupboard. He finds a jumper and struggles to put it on. In the kitchen he grabs a handful of biscuits from the tall cupboard and some chocolate. He places his stash in a plastic bag. Not quite satisfied, he runs back to his room to fetch the soft dog that has joined the bears on his bed.

'Bell-Bell, I'm very cross with Mama. I'm leaving and taking my doggie with me.'

George is jealous of Lily and he wants to show his family how upset he is. Where could a small Human like George go? He is too little to leave home and can't even look after himself? What about nasty Humans, dangerous dogs and vicious birds?

He walks towards the front door and stands on the tip of his toes to open it. I try to prevent him from leaving by blocking his path. He pushes past me.

'Bye, Bell-Bell,' he says. I am not allowed outside, so I don't follow him. I find Tony and begin to meow loudly. He takes no notice. I cry louder and louder but he shuts the door so that he can't hear me. In frustration, I scratch on the door, but he yells, "go away." I have done all I can. When Karen calls George for lunch there is no answer. She searches for him and can't find him. Then she calls Tony and they search together. I run back and forth from George's room to the front door. Karen understands my message.

'Bella is trying to tell me that he left through the front door.'

'Oh no! I think she tried earlier to tell me he'd gone. She was bothering me, so I sent her away.'

Karen glares at Tony.

'I'm going outside to look for him,' he says, 'Surely his tiny legs can't take him far.'

When Oliver discovers that George has gone, he hides under the bed. Too much has been happening, coming to the cottage, the sea, dogs, birds, the birth of the baby and now George's disappearance. It is like a final bee sting and it unsettles him.

I wait at the front door for Tony's return. He runs inside panting, but George is not with him.

He looks upset. 'I've searched everywhere, down the road and among the trees and I can't find him.'

'Poor, little Georgie.' Karen wipes tears from her eyes. 'He must've been jealous of Lily and decided to run away. I don't even want to think of the awful things that could've happened to him.'

'I'm calling for help, now,' Tony says, as he picks up his phone.

Three Humans in dark uniforms arrive. Police. They listen carefully to Karen and Tony.

'Try not to worry, we'll find him.'

Tony joins them and they drive off. I pace the floors of the cottage. Karen feeds Lily but is unable to rest. By the time I hear Tony's car in the garage, the sun has almost disappeared. He is carrying George who is sobbing. Karen rushes to take George in her arms, kisses and hugs him.

'We've been so worried, my darling. We love you so much.'

George hugs his mama.

'Thank goodness you're safe! Why did you leave us, my boy?' Tony asks.

'I was very, very cross with Lily.' He looks at the floor and begins a new round of sobbing. He looks back at the door. 'And I lost Harry, my doggie.'

'That must be the soft toy he sleeps with. Lately he prefers it to his bears,' Tony says to Karen.

'We'll look for Harry tomorrow, darling,' Karen says, stroking George's head. 'You've cut yourself, ... nothing serious. Mama will fix it for you.' She attends to his cut and cleans his hands. 'Now for something nice to eat and drink. Georgie my love, you can always tell me or dad if you're angry, upset or feel left out. We love you and understand. No more running away.'

He nestles close to her and then drinks his cocoa.

 The crisis is averted, for now. Perhaps he will learn to love his little sister. His job is to help his mother and to protect his sister. She is a tiny, weak Human and he is the big brother. Karen will have to spend more time encouraging him to look after her.

Unfortunately, we cats don't protect our young well. Our territory is of key important to us, and any other cat becomes a competitor, even one from the same litter. Fights can break out and younger or weaker cats can be attacked.

George is in bed asleep, smelling fresher. Karen and Tony discuss what to do about his jealousy.

I wake when the first signs of pink tint the sky. While Lily and George are still asleep, Tony tidies the cottage. Satisfied that the surfaces and floors are clean, he collects the suitcases. Suitcases always indicate a move. *Meeeyay!* We must be going home. About time too! I have had enough of this holiday. They pack their clothes, then the sheets and towels. Tony makes several journeys to the car.

Karen calls us and wakes George. She feeds Lily before making a quick breakfast. We eat our pebbles while they eat cereal and coffee. George has recovered after a long sleep and drinks his milk without complaint. Tony checks the house for anything left behind and carries our baskets to the car. With Lily, we will have an extra passenger on the home journey. There will be hardly any space for us.

Tony mutters as he packs the car, 'It will be a tight squeeze driving home.'

George is in his carry seat in a cramped spot next to the window and grumbles. Karen sits in the front next to Tony with Lily on her lap wrapped in soft blankets. A large bag with everything Karen requires for Lily is under her feet. She must be uncomfortable in the small space. Into the back of our car we go in our carry boxes. We are squeezed between boxes, hats and other odds and ends. All we can see is the back of Tony's head. We dare not protest.

Tony starts the car and we are on our way home. Though Oliver is meowing like a kitten, I ignore him and sleep. After what seems a very long period, we stop suddenly. I smell food as Karen opens packages. Once Lilly and George are fed, and the Humans have eaten, they pay attention to us. The back door of the car opens, and we are in a field.

Tony releases us from our boxes and snaps our harness and leads in place. Karen fills our bowls. We eat hungrily and drink.

'This is safe spot with no dogs, where we can walk,' Tony says.

I shiver. Here the air is cool and the breeze ruffles my fur. The ground is hard, the grass dry, and the trees are without leaves. We walk quickly over a flat area until Tony holds up his hand.

'Enough, cats, back to the car.'

We don't stop again though Karen complains about feeding Lily in such a small area. It is dark and cold when the car finally stops.

Tony sighs. 'Phew, that was a long drive.'

'I'm pleased to be home,' Karen says as she lifts Lily from the car. As they unlock the front door, the whiff of home greets us. Once our carry boxes are open, we run through the house to confirm our territory is untouched. All is well and safe.

Pops greets us with hugs. He peeks at Lilly who is asleep. 'How adorable! She's a beauty like you Karen. I'm blessed to have lovely grandchildren.'

Oliver

Why do Humans enjoy leaving their territory so often?

We are back in the cold, but at least the house is heated and Pops has cooked a meal of fish and chips. The Humans eat hungrily and we are given bits of delicious, soft of fish. Tony tells Pops about the holiday, Lily's birth and George leaving home. Pops listens amazed.

How unexpectedly bright my house and everything in it seems after a period away. It is as if I am looking at my territory with fresh eyes. I am delighted to be home. I settle slowly, appreciating my freedom after the long journey. There are many tasks awaiting my attention. First, I wash thoroughly, removing the cottage smell and any beach sand from my silky coat. Smelling fresh again is of utmost importance. My next chore is to secure our house. Bella has already made her territorial marks. Now it is my turn with my slower more thorough style of rubbing my chin and cheeks on the carpets and furniture. I do not forget to leave my scratch marks on the front and back doors of the house and next to my favourite sleeping spot. Once my huge job is done, I rest.

As I fall asleep, I think of the time spent away from home. What was the point of the holiday? It was trying for us, and for them. Poor Karen gave birth to Lily in an unfamiliar place far from home. I'm sure this was not what she or Tony had planned. I can't imagine why they left their home when the birth of the baby was near. As far as I am concerned, there was hardly anything about the inside of the cottage that I liked. We were harassed by the white birds, dogs and rats. But, I must say that swimming in the rock pool was glorious. I will hold the memory forever. If only they would take me to rock pools closer to home.

I wake to a watery sun and the irritating sounds of Lily crying. George is running about wildly with his hands over his ears to drown her out. Karen and Tony certainly have a tremendous job with the two of them to care for. It isn't fun for us either. I realise that in the same way kittens' meow for food, babies cry for food when they are hungry, and loudly too. Irrespective of the cold, we are both spending more time in our peaceful garden away from Lily and George.

Today George is seeking Karen's attention by stomping through the house making loud noises.

'Stop it immediately!' Karen yells at George. 'I've had enough of your carrying on.'

I've not seen her shout like that before, and especially at George. I run and hide under the big bed. I don't want her to vent her temper on me next.

The noise has woken Pops. He rushes from his room. 'What's going on, Karen?'

'George wants attention and I lost my temper with him. I was up with Lily during the night and I'm exhausted.'

When George understands that he was a baby only a while ago, and that he cried too, things might improve.

'It's time Jodi came back to help you. The young children are too much for you to cope with on your own, ' Tony says.

'I should've phoned her as soon as we came home. I'll call her now.'

After her phone call, Karen smiles with relief. 'Jodi is coming to help tomorrow. Not a moment too soon.'

 # Bella

We will continue to go out of our way to
annoy Humans who dislike cats.

The house is quieter and life is pleasant. I appreciate being home in my own territory again. Karen has been involved with caring for Lily, who isn't sleeping well. There is less time for me or Oliver. Since Jodi began to look after George he is calmer. Tony is helping Karen with the children and as a result, we cats see less of him. It has been positive for us as we have become closer and rely on each other now.

The two children are not alike in appearance or behaviour. Little Lily is more delicate than George. She has light brown hair and pale colouring, while George is darker skinned with his father's almost black hair. Her features are finer and she has a smaller frame. She cries more than George did, and wakes immediately if the phone rings. I wonder how she will develop. I hope she will like cats.

George is excited that Jodi has promised to take him for a walk and an ice-cream. On the way home, they intend to visit her friend whose dog has had a litter of puppies and George wants to see them. I can't understand why he wants to see the puppies. After all, he already has us two devoted cats.

Jodi rushes past me into the house with George running

after her. She is carrying something curly and black in her arms. As she passes me, I sniff the air. I smell dog.

'Karen, where are you? I need your help,' she calls.

Karen comes out of her room, 'What's the matter Jodi?'

Jodi begins to tell her a long story. Her friend's dog had six puppies, the mother accepted and fed five of the pups, but rejected the smallest one and left it to die. As it is, her friend is struggling to look after the healthy pups. This tiny one is struggling and needs special attention.

'The poor little thing. George was upset about the puppy and refused to leave it. So, I brought it home with us.'

Karen looks at the puppy. I look at it too. It is exhausted and starving. It might even be sick. Animals reject their young if they are ill or too small to survive.

'As much as I'd like to, I can't care for it, Jodi.' She searches in her bag and hands Jodi the car keys. 'Take my car and drive it to the vet. After he's examined her, he'll tell you what to do.'

For a moment I see the puppy's tiny black, fluffy head wrapped in a towel, and then Jodi drives off. We hear Jodi park in the garage. She enters the house carrying a box, a bottle of special milk and dry food, 'The vet says the puppy is a "he" and is a Maltese Poodle Shih Tzu mix, a mouthful. He is undernourished, but otherwise healthy. He must be kept warm and eat special puppy food to build him up. I have all the information about how to feed him.'

George doesn't stop talking about the tiny puppy whose mama doesn't want it. Oliver looks distressed and I am not pleased either. A puppy will ruin our lives. Lily and George are enough for us to cope with. We sit together fearing the worst.

Jodi places the box containing the puppy on the floor. Oliver sniffs it tentatively. His tail is down and his tummy close to the floor as usual when he is upset. He runs to hide and I jump onto the tall dresser to observe. No one notices us cats, and that's the trouble. All the love and attention will go to this smelly, little dog. Why didn't Jodi find someone else to care for it?

'Please mum, please, let's keep him and make him well. His mama didn't want him, but I want him.'

Jodi runs her hands through her hair in distress. 'He's adorable and I wish I could take him. Right now, I'm sharing with a person who doesn't like animals.'

'I have so much to do already, how can I take him?' Karen says. 'He's a darling, and once he's fatter he'll be a lovely little dog. But, the cats will hate him, and it's unfair on them.' She throws he hands in the air. 'I don't know what to do.'

Jodi mixes the puppy's food, places a small amount on the floor for him and strokes his head. Slowly he begins to eat.

Pops is in the kitchen watching. 'The poor little thing, I wish I could look after him.'

Karen looks down and doesn't speaker for a while. 'We'll wait for your dad to come home and let him decide.'

By the time Tony arrives, the puppy is in the laundry asleep in his box. Newspapers cover the floor for him to pee and poo on. After Tony hears the whole story and listens to George's pleas, he puts his hands over his ears.

'Enough George, I give in. You can keep he puppy, but only if you help me to look after him. Puppies aren't like cats. He will make a big mess all over the newspaper at first, and then he will have to learn to go outside.'

George jumps up and down with joy and gives his dad a kiss.

'What will you call him, George?' Tony asks.

'Simon, like the dog I saw on television.'

Karen whispers to Tony, 'George has wanted a dog for a

long time. Perhaps having this puppy to care for will help him to grow up.'

Cats can feel down. We are both upset and neither of us have eaten or slept much. We are taking it turns to guard the laundry door in case Simon comes bounding out. Why call him Simon, anyway? Simon is a cat's name, and far too grand for a dog.

Though Tony doesn't complain, looking after Simon is a lot of work. George is helping his father by giving Simon food and water. Yesterday, Karen went out to buy him a dog litter box. It is larger than our litterboxes and has a cover.

'The litter box is there for him if he can't make it outside and he needs "to go" in a hurry,' Karen says.

It smells dreadful. He dare not come near our litter. Our lives have changed for the worse. George doesn't even notice us, or give either of us a pat. He adored us before Simon turned up. Karen doesn't have the energy or time for us. Tony is helping her to look after George, doing some of her chores to ease her load and cleaning up after Simon. We are forgotten cats and when Simon develops into an adult dog our lives will probably be intolerable.

Just as well Simon is with Pops during the day, confined to the back of the house. We hear his whines and howls, but have almost nothing to do with him. They must be feeding him well. He is almost twice the size he was when he arrived. As expected, he is still messing on paper, hasn't learned to go outside and rarely uses his litter box. He can't be smart if he is taking so long to learn something so basic.

Listening to Simon whimpering and barking is painful to sensitive cat's ears. What a pathetic creature, so dependent on Pops and George for affection. Worse, he is robbing us of the attention we are entitled to receive. We resent this and will turn our backs on our owners when they remember us. They need to be taught a lesson.

Pops is calling us. I'm not responding. He hasn't bothered with us since Simon arrived. Oliver doesn't go to him either.

'Where are you Bella, Oliver?'

He walks slowly searching for us. 'I should've known I'd find you both near the heating vent.'

He walks away and returns carrying Simon. The puppy tumbles out of his arms and sits at the other end of the carpet staring at us. We stare back.

'The time has come for the three of you to get to know each other.'

Simon jumps up and barks.

Neither of us are interested in this small dog. Playing with Honey is quite different, as she doesn't live with us. I pull myself up to my full height, puff out my body, make my tail like a brush in the cupboard and hiss at Simon. Oliver's long body is puffed and arched scarily. We stand our ground and wait. This is our house and he is the intruder. Simon looks at us with his head to the side as if trying to fathom our messages. There will be no further messages from me. I am ignoring him.

He whines and runs away. Pops calls him back. He doesn't come.

'Well, that's it for the day,' Pops says.

Simon is obviously terrified of us and doesn't even growl at us. Good. He'll keep out of our way.

Oliver

*Humans seem to enjoy playing with us more
than we enjoy playing with them.*

The little dog is an intrusion into cat life as we know it. Like Bella, I will ignore him. Pops brings him into the main part of the house, hoping we will accept and like him. We know exactly what Pops is up to and his plan is not working. Simon doesn't like us, and we like him less.

'I don't know what to do,' Pops says to Tony. 'The cats and Simon don't like each other and they aren't interested in becoming friends or sharing the house.'

'I haven't the time to bother with it now,' Tony says.

'He should be outdoors. You know what the cats are like, they won't allow him to share their garden,' Pops replies.

'There is space for him. I haven't the time to create a special area for him. Meanwhile, he can play in the main garden if you or Jodi watch him carefully. The danger is that he is tiny enough to squeeze through the railings around the pool.'

Simon is in the front garden with Jodi. He must feel unwelcome and doesn't even glance at either of us. I have been nasty to him, even nastier than Bella. He will have to prove himself as cat friendly before I ease up and accept him.

Honey arrives to play with Simon. Through the window I watch the two dogs playing. Honey is a tiny dog, though larger than Simon. She understands he still a puppy and is gentle with him. They run, roll and chase each other. I'm lonely here in our bare garden and wish Bella would come out to play. Unfortunately, she dislikes the harsh wind and prefers to sleep near the vents.

So far, Simon has been smart enough to keep away from us and avoid our chairs and baskets. The only form of dog aggression he has shown has been a soft growl. Eventually I will find living with him less of a problem. He's a small dog, not a true predator, and will only be slightly taller than me when grown. I should be able to control him without much effort.

Jodi talks on her phone while watching Simon in the garden. He stops to pats the earth with his paw. Then dirt flies as he digs frantically. He is too tiny to use power in his digging, but he persists.

'Hey Simon, stop it...silly dog!' Jodie yells. He ignores her and digs determinedly. A bone emerges and he battles to hold his treasure in his small jaw. His tail wags furiously. He must feel like a grown dog doing his job now. His pride is short-lived, as Jodi takes the bone from him and throws it into the garbage.

'Silly doggie,' she says again.

He barks at her in an indignant tone. She has ruined his day.

 # Bella

Do not under any circumstance allow a
Human to think he or she owns you.

Simon is behaving himself and trying to be friendly, as friendly as any dog can be. I can't say that I like him, nevertheless I accept his existence. One positive thing about him is that he doesn't have a powerful "doggie" smell. Jodi washes him often and his coat is more like Karen's woolly jumper than Honey's fur. Oliver pretends to ignore Simon, but when he doesn't know I'm watching, I've seen him chase Simon playfully. Pops is pleased that we are friendlier towards each other and starting to get along like "happy, good animals".

Pops' loud grumbles wake me. There is no time for a lazy stretch before leaving my basket. I run directly to the source of the noise. Pops is cleaning up an enormous heap of vomit. Cats vomit regularly so I've seen a lot of it, but nothing like this. Though the smell is revolting, I force myself to investigate. It is dog vomit with dark chunks of meat in it. Oliver wakes from the noise and arrives. He sniffs the air and steps back. His sensitive, Siamese nose twitches with disgust.

'Naughty, Simon!' Pops says, waggling his finger at the puppy who is cringing in a corner. 'You've been eating the cat's food. You like the extra meat they eat. They need it, you don't.' Pops cleans the mess away and sprays the air to clear the dreadful smell. He is hurrying so that the kitchen will be clean before Karen and Tony wake.

So, he has been eating our left overs. How greedy! Oliver turns his back on the puppy and goes back to sleep. Perhaps we accepted him too soon. Obviously, he is not to be trusted. The proof is in the vomit.

Oh no! Simon is shuddering and heaving. I hope he's not going to mess on the clean floor again. The poor dog is sick, and I'm sorry about it. He has brought it on himself and will have to learn the hard way. Do dogs learn as quickly as cats? I wonder.

Pops scoops Simon into his arms and puts him in the laundry. He covers the floor thickly with newspaper and places the puppy's basket on it. All he gives Simon is a bowl of water.

'No food for you. All you're having today is water, then we'll see.'

Whimpering, the puppy slinks into his basket.

When the family wake, Pops tells them quickly that Simon is sick and that they should avoid the laundry all day. He explains that our food must be moved to a higher spot in future. Karen is too busy to bother and is only half-listening.

'I'll put it up here.' He points to a shelf, 'The cats can jump up and eat in peace but Simon won't be able to reach it.'

'Good idea, Pops. I'm sorry I don't have time to check on Simon. I know you're looking after him.'

There are no sounds from the laundry apart from an infrequent whimper. Pops visits the laundry every few hours and seems satisfied that Simon is recovering. George is worried about his puppy and opens the laundry door. Pops sees him trying to stroke his sick puppy. 'Leave him alone George,' Pops says. 'He needs to sleep to recover.'

'I want to...'

'No, George. He will be fine if he sleeps.'

That evening, Simon is allowed out of the laundry.

Pops makes an announcement. 'Simon is not well. No food or treats for him or he'll be sick again,' he says loudly so that all can hear. He repeats his message to George.

Karen mixes Simon special, soft food. He looks at the food and hardly eats. He does not move from his basket. His dull eyes tell me he is still sick. Oliver shows no interest in him and walks away. I walk away too.

In the background, I hear Simon whine. He is sick and lonely. Suddenly I am overwhelmed with guilt. I am a therapy cat after all, and I have treated this puppy appallingly. Of all cats, I should know better. I must do something to help this little creature. I creep into his basket and cuddle close to warm him. He grunts and gives me a nudge of appreciation. Oliver edges forward and watches me warm the puppy. During the night, when the temperature drops, he creeps into Simon's basket. He indicates that it his turn to warm Simon. It is not comfortable lying next to Simon, but keeping him warm and encouraging him to sleep so that he recovers is more important. Oliver is maturing and being more caring. I can't imagine him helping a dog a year ago.

I wake early after my turn of warming Simon. His eyes are open. He is alert, though weak. He sees me next to him and gives my coat a "thank you" lick. A dog's lick is too much for me to handle and I jump out of the basket. I watch him. Will he jump out too, feel hungry and eat? He moves slowly to the kitchen searching for food. Pops has left dry dog biscuits in his bowl. The noise wakes Oliver and he finds us in the kitchen. Simon goes to Oliver and gives him lick too. Oliver flinches and covers the lick with a few fast licks of his own. After eating a little, Simon is back in his basket. He yawns a doggie yawn that could swallow a mouse, and he goes back to sleep. I'm relieved, he is almost well.

There is no going back now. We have shown that we care about this little woolly creature, and he cares about us. We will have to share our house with him. Soon he will learn that cats never share completely. We will demand respect for our territory and that he follows our rules. He is annoyingly active, constantly wanting to play. He'll have to learn that play is another matter that we decide. We play after our sleep and when we are in the mood for exercise. Just as well he hasn't tried to go through our cat door into our private cat garden. He will not be welcome there.

Oliver

Cats are never undecided. They are busy planning.

Simon is turning from a puppy into a dog, with sturdy legs and firm muscles. It is about time he outgrew his rolls of puppy fat. Within a few months he will be full size, slightly taller and broader than a cat. He is passive now, respectful enough towards us and gentle with George. He is aware that the house is ours and that we allow him to live in it on our terms. When he's fully grown he is likely to challenge us. I don't look forward to that. I dislike having to admit that he is quite intelligent, for a dog, that is. The one thing I dislike about him is his whimpering and yapping. He barks persistently, whether he is bored, lonely, or if he hears a noise outside. I am learning to distinguish between his different barks, as he is learning about our many meows. Though he is small, every creature needs to be taken seriously. Perhaps that is why he yapps a lot more than bigger dogs. In his own way he is as territorial as a cat and he growls and barks if he hears a noise or has any cause to protect the area we all share. He lifts his back leg to pee on things he owns or are part of his territory. We don't need his extra markings, but at least stray dogs will keep away.

Honey is waiting for Simon at the fence again. She has been showing more interest in him than usual. He prefers to sniff her than to play. Recently, he has been restless, staring at the door and wanting to go out. Honey is on his mind. Karen is too busy to notice the change in him.

She is making a big mistake by allowing Honey into the garden to play with Simon. I am keeping away from the two dogs. Pops must be more aware of the changes in Simon than I thought. He has decided that Simon is now old enough to be "trained". This will be interesting. What will his training involve? He poos and pees outside as expected and knows his name. What is next?

I've been thinking about Simon too much. Sleep is what I need. Once I find a comfortable spot, I'm asleep in seconds.

I wake from a dream about being chased by a dog in a past life and surviving. I have learned a lot about dogs from my dreams. They are powerful animals that hunt in packs, and their survival depends on following the pack leader for direction. They are more dependent on Humans than cats, and consequently, bond and cooperate with their Human owners for their survival. I understand all of this, as strange as it seems to me. Training is important for them to make Human directions clear and easily understandable. As a result of their training, Humans have a dog's obedience, and dogs know that their owner is the leader of the pack. How awfully restrictive!

Cats, on the other hand, like to socialise with other cats. Unlike dogs, we hunt independently. And unlike smelly dogs, we keep ourselves meticulously clean, so that no odours will warn our prey. As much as we like Humans and cooperate with them, our survival doesn't depend on them. We don't need to follow Humans or other cats to hunt. We can survive on mice and rats but not as pleasantly. And we like to do as we please unless Humans or other creatures interfere. It is clear to me that attempting to train cats is both unnecessary and ridiculous. Of course, it is possible to train us, but why bother. We will only comply if we want to, if we see a reason or benefit. We were "trained" to wear a harness and lead. I suppose this was necessary while we were on holiday. Simon's training is progressing. I'm surprised how trusting he is, and that he doesn't challenge Pops. He does as he is told, "sit", "stay", "go" or "down". A small reward of food helps him to learn. Most of the time he responds eagerly. If he refuses to obey commands or barks excessively, he is given "time out" in the laundry. This is severe punishment for him. He needs company more than we do and howls pathetically.

The latest – Tony is training Simon to perform tricks by offering him food rewards if he is obedient, and he's learning. He brings Tony his slippers every night after dinner and lifts his paw for him. No cat would resort to that for any Human. Has the creature no pride? This is a step too far! We like to be petted, cuddled and have our tummies rubbed by our Humans, when it suits us. Simon is so thirsty for attention that he is allowing himself to be treated like another baby in the house. He will turn into a spoilt brat if they aren't more careful. We cats enjoy playing and we can amuse ourselves. Dogs like to be played with. Simon enjoys being taken for a walk or fetching a ball in the garden.

I mustn't forget to mention some of Simon's most irritating habits. Apart from yapping, his digging is hard to understand. Cats instinctively bury or cover their poo and uneaten food to avoid attracting any predators to their area. We are not scavengers who bury food to consume later, while Simon digs holes in the garden and even in the pot plants to bury toys and bones to chew later. Often, he digs and buries nothing, or he digs a hole as big as himself to lie in, another aspect of illogical dog behaviour. Pops was furious with him when he dug up a dry plant that had a round blob like a potato beneath it. Pops said that it would've turned into a magnificent flower in spring. The filth on Simon's coat after digging is another matter. Dogs don't clean themselves. All they do is shake their coats, hoping it will do. Their odour must be important to them.

Licking is another bothersome issue. Not only does he lick Humans all over, but he likes to lick us too. He tried to lick my face this morning and I flicked my tail at him. When he wouldn't give up, I growled and bit his ear. I hope he stops this disgusting habit.

Tony has suggested that it is time Simon was neutered. Karen, Pops and Jodi agree. Poor Simon doesn't understand what they are saying. He will be a different dog when the vet has finished with him. Perhaps that awful operation will stop him peeing over our shared territory. I hope it does as it is smelly.

Recently, he has been obsessed with female dogs. Not only Honey, but the dog on the other side of the house. Neutering will probably stop it. Karen and Tony have asked Pops to decide when to have Simon neutered. He has been putting it off. Yesterday, Simon squeezed through the garden fence to chase Honey again. He refused to return when Jodi called him, or when Pops whistled for him. Jodi went into the next-door garden to retrieve him yapping and kicking. We won't know the result of the time he spent with the neighbour's dog until later. Perhaps, a few tiny puppies with woolly hair will arrive. Pops thought Simon was still a puppy and didn't realise that he had matured sexually.

This morning, Pops made a quick decision. Jodi put Simon in the car and drove him to the vet. Lately it seems as if we are constantly waiting for something to happen. I hope his neutering will be less unpleasant than mine, and that he recovers well. Not that I should care all that much about a dog.

The vet is satisfied with the result of the operation. But, Simon returns looking sick, refusing to eat and moaning in his sleep. The operation has made him tired and it takes another few days for him do more than nibble his food and go outside or to his doggie litter box.

Today, he is recovering and guzzling a bowl of his favourite food. No cat would touch it – meat with foul-smelling vegetable mush. Karen has been putting our food bowls on a ledge in the kitchen where he can't reach it, as Pops suggested. It is working well.

Simon is has changed since his operation. He will always be a barker, but he has become friendlier to us and to our Humans. At least, he no longer stands at the fence waiting for females or tries to follow them. That part of his life is over. We wait. Will the active dog next door have his puppies?

Karen is out with George and Lily. Pops is asleep, and we are not interested in playing with Simon. He sits at the door whining as he waits for our Humans to return. How pathetic. Karen says he has signs of separation anxiety, whatever that is. And that babies and toddlers have it too when their mother leaves them. This confirms my thoughts about the way they treat him, – like a human baby. They should know better!

Mid Winter

 # Bella

Most dogs disgust us, but we accept their existence.

The sky is pale, a weak sun peeks from behind the clouds and winds howl around tress shaking their bare branches. I shiver as cold bites through my winter coat like a wild cat. While Oliver still visits our garden, I prefer to stay indoors, eat more than I do in summer to build up my warmth and sleep next to the heating vents.

This morning, I stand at the window and watch white flakes fall from the sky. Soon, all is white outside. Last year, I stepped into the whiteness, felt its icy, slimy wetness that bit my paws and made my coat slushy. Then I scurried back inside. I shudder at the memory. Once and never again, if I can help it. *Meeyuk!* Oliver rushes out and heads for the half tree, glistening in the pale light. He battles to find footholds as he climbs. He succeeds and reaches the tallest branch to sit like a white statue surveying all before him.

George calls Karen, 'Look at Ollie high up in the tree.'

'He's a strong cat to climb in the snow, and he looks incredible.'

'Please...can I go out too,' he nags.

'It's very cold out there. Bella is sensible and stays inside.'

'Please!' George persists.

Karen takes George's hand and they walk to his bedroom. He emerges dressed in a warm coat, scarf, gloves and a hat. Karen is warmly dressed too. As they open the door, an icy blast sweeps into our house. George runs out shrieking with joy and throwing snow in the air. Karen makes balls with the snow and throws them. He copies her and they laugh. Then she scoops up snow and builds a weird Human. She goes inside again and rummages in the fridge and hall cupboard. Back in the snow, she works on the white creature placing a carrot in the middle of its face for a nose, tiny potatoes for eyes and half a red apple for a mouth. After adding one of Tony's old hats, a torn scarf and piece of wood for a pipe, it looks almost Human.

Tony is home, and he and George play in the snow. George sits on a wooden sliding thing and Tony pushes him down a slope for a short ride. George enjoys himself and asks to ride again and again. When heavy snow falls they hurry back inside.

I wake to a dark sky and chill. While Oliver is still asleep, I intend to visit Bastet. I creep though the house to the lounge room, but Bastet is no longer in her usual place. After searching, I find that Karen has moved her to a high shelf in the television room. Moving her is not a good idea. It upsets the order of things and, there will be consequences. As I walk through the house and, I find snow creeping under the door and onto the floor. I knew something like this would happen. The white stuff is so high that it almost reaches the windows. What in cold Catland is happening now? I run to Lily's room to check that she is breathing and check on George. They are both well and asleep.

Karen wakes to find melted snow in the house. She calls Tony and together they shovel up the snow, dry the wet and block the doors with towels.

'I bet the car is stuck in the snow. The driveway is covered in it. I won't be able to dig my way out. I'd better phone the office and stay home,' he mutters.

What gloomy weather! Tony spends the morning in his study and Karen is with Lily and George.

Oliver's is behaving in a puzzling way. Before Simon joined us, Oliver was Pops' and Tony's special cat. Simon is a demanding creature, hungry for human strokes and has snatched Oliver's place, or that's what Oliver says. Oliver is a proud and independent cat. I wouldn't have thought he'd care about our Humans. Obviously, he cares more than I imagined. He is collecting their dirty underwear and socks – smelly things, and hiding them under a low bookcase. Of all things to collect or steal. Tony has noticed his underwear is missing and Karen has complained about her lost panties. Even George is missing things. They have guessed that Oliver is the thief because he has stolen items before. If they search well, they will find their possessions.

I am involved in a tedious, but thorough wash of every part of me, especially my sensitive pink bits. Every day, my head and cheek rubs mark the furniture and carpets as part of my territory. It is a huge job in a big house like this one. My Humans are not forgotten either. I mark them too as mine with head rubs. They provide me with food, shelter and affection and I am aware of their location all day, making sure that they are well and able to care for me. Oliver has a superior attitude to our cleaning rituals. He thinks he does a better job. I doubt it, he simply takes more time over identical tasks.

George has grown taller and is more muscular, has gained weight and looks like a boy Human. He enjoys building with pieces of plastic and blocks, kicking and catching balls. Karen says he is going through a troublesome stage. That would explain his destructive mood, kicking his toys and pulling my tail, something he hasn't done before. He wants to do things himself even if he can't, and argues with Karen and Tony about nearly everything, from dressing to eating. I've noticed that his favourite word is "no." Karen has incredible patience. I doubt that any cat mama would put up with a kitten like George. She'd give him a fast, paw swipe. Karen doesn't demand that George follows her orders. She gives him hugs and lets him choose simple things, like what he wants to wear each day, or if he prefers peas or beans with carrots. He is a lucky, little Human.

I remember being the only cat in the house until Oliver arrived. He is so handsome and smart that I was jealous of him. So, I understand George's jealousy of Lily. It is interesting to observe the differences between the two children as they develop. Lily has settled down to be a quieter baby and only cries if she is hungry or wet. She has a gentle nature and is more sensitive than George. Her early smiles delight Karen and Tony. Karen has stopped feeding her. She is making milk for her in bottles from powder. I ask Bastet to ensure that Lily will grow up to be a healthy, true cat lover like Karen.

When George was younger I had an intense connection with him. He sensed what I was thinking then and I could understand him too. Now he appears to prefer dogs to cats and he has bonded with Simon. It is obvious that Simon is attached to George, the smallest male closest to him in size. He follows George everywhere and watches him with his ears cocked, waiting for a word or a pat. I find it disgusting that Simon is learning a new trick for George, rolling over to "play dead." He is fickle and doesn't know his master. He learned tricks for Tony and now he is learning for George.

George and Simon are both as active as kittens wanting to run and play. Jodi deals with both of their demands for action by taking them to the park every day. I have no idea how they play at the park, but they return tired and sleep afterwards, a positive thing for us, as the house is peaceful.

Jodi tells Karen that she is concerned about George. 'He sees the same children daily, but he doesn't make friends.'

Karen nods. 'George hasn't played with many children.'

'Two of the children are bullies and try to pick on George if I am not watching,' Jodi says. 'Maybe George is afraid of other children due to the bullies.'

Karen rubs her forehead in concern. 'It's a pity about the bullies. I wonder if their parents know how badly their children are behaving.'

'Their father is with them. He laughs and seems to like seeing his children dominating others and being mean.'

Karen sighs and shrugs. 'George is young and hasn't learned how to get along with other children. Bullies scare him.'

In spite of their muscles, height and bigger brains, little Humans must be cared for and watched. Anything could happen to them if they aren't supervised. George thinks he is strong enough to climb walls, trees and jump over puddles. If he falls, and he does fall, he cries like a baby. We are tougher, we cope with bullies, fight with them if we are strong enough, or hide. I am sorry for Karen. She will have to watch and look after her children for a long time, from their birth until they are big enough and sensible enough, to manage alone.

George needs an eye kept on him almost all the time. I don't know how Karen would cope with Lily as well as George if Jodi wasn't helping her. For the first time I understand why most Humans have families of only two to four children. Cats have many kittens in a litter – four, five or more that grow up quickly, or their Mama wouldn't manage.

Today while Jodi is caring for George, she is talking on her phone and distracted. When her gaze leaves him, he slips away. Impulsively, he attempts to push through the cat door into our cat garden. By now, he is too big and is wedged in the door. His head and arms are through the door and his bottom is stuck He wrestles and cries. Though Jodi battles to free him, she can't. His cries turn to piercing screams.

Jodi holds her head in her hands. 'Shush, George, I'm trying to work out how to free you.' She pulls off his socks, shoes and shorts. 'Stay calm, Georgie. I will go around to the cat's garden and try to ease you through.'

He begins to whine.

'Try to concentrate. Wiggle your bottom now, and I'll ease you out.'

He wriggles and she tugs until he is lying on the grass in our garden.

'I'm not going there again,' he says.

'You'd better not!'

What a disappointment! With George's body developing. I thought he was becoming more reasonable. Just when I think I am gathering further understanding of Humans, I find that I know almost nothing about them.

Simon has been enjoying running freely in the main garden, that is until he began to eat leaves and flowers. Tony makes excuses for him, 'It's his puppy energy. He'll calm down soon enough.' When Tony notices that Simon dug up the roots of an entire garden bed, he is furious. He carries Simon to the destroyed flowerbed and yells at him waggling his finger. Simon's punishment is a soaking spraying and a long spell in the laundry. Sadly, Simon doesn't learn. This week he is digging in the garden again. Tony's face turns red with fury and Simon is back in the laundry howling. If there is one thing Simon dislikes most it is being alone in the laundry that smells of soap and dirty clothes. Tony sits in the television room mumbling to himself while drinking. After three bottles of brown liquid, he phones his mate Jules to ask for help.

Jules arrives, and the two men gather tools from the garage and head for our cat garden. The snow has melted and the earth is soft and wet, making work in the garden easier. Despite the cold they keep working. They are enlarging our garden for Simon to have space to run and play. From the window we watch Jules and Tony move rocks, cut down bushes and remove part of our fence. Once they have measured the ground, they begin to erect a new fence. The new garden will be almost twice its original size.

'You're losing a slice of your own garden for your pets,' Jules says.

'Our garden is big enough. I don't care if we lose a bit, but Simon, the little devil, is not going to dig up any more plants. He will have his own area next to the cats. He'll have to behave himself and keep away from their part of the garden, or they'll sort him out,' Tony says.

Oliver looks at me and I at him. We're going to have to share our garden with Simon.

When the sun creeps into the clouds and darkness falls, the new garden is ready. That night, we hear running, drumming sounds outside. Rats and mice that once lived under rocks that were moved, are leaving the garden for a new home with their friends in our ceiling.

The following morning, Tony notices a trail of tiny black droppings. 'Damn rats,' he says. 'They must all be in our roof by now.'

He cleans the droppings and collects dry plants and pieces of wire lying about. Next, he yanks out the special cat door that leads to our garden. He makes an awful noise hacking the wall with a hammer until the hole is bigger. After much groaning and using ugly words that are banned in front of George, he opens a large box with a knife. We watch him place the contents of the box into the hole and secure it with nails. It is a larger door that serves as both a dog and cat door leading into the extended garden.

'I'm exhausted,' he says as he collects his tools, and then spreads himself out on the couch.

'Go on, Oliver, Bella and Simon, enjoy your new garden.'

He drinks brown liquid and falls asleep.

Karen's shrieks of delight wake him. 'You've done a fantastic job, Tony. Now the three of them will have to sort out their territories.'

Simon is the first through the new door and bounds into the garden. His large feet stomp over our grass and flatten the flowers. He isn't even aware of the damage to our carefully maintained territory. When he pees on our rocks, my anger rises, my fur bristles. I am about to pounce when he yelps. I chase him into his own area and growl at him. Oliver is behind me and his growl is more threatening. There is no mistaking our message, "keep off our turf."

Karen arrives with gifts of meat for us and a bone for Simon. What a dumb dog! He is stupidly protective of it. Doesn't he grasp the fact that we don't want his bone? We can't hold it and our smaller jaws can't bite it. We enjoy the meat Karen has cuts from the bone for us. He chews his bone and then buries it.

He is beginning to learn a routine of keeping to his part

of the garden, but with Simon learning is slow. I expect trouble.

Oliver

Exercise is necessary, but only when we want it.

It is early morning and our Humans are still asleep. I wish we were out in the sunshine. The weather is so unpredictable that we must grab the sun's warmth when possible and store it. Bella is pawing me, restless and wanting to play. We don't growl or hiss at each other. We know the rules of play fight. Her ears are back in the position of an angry cat. When she pounces her claws are sheathed and can do no harm. I want to play too. I pounce and bite gently. She bites back and runs. I chase her until I catch her. Then it's her turn to chase and catch me. Or, I ought to say, I allow her to catch me. Simon watches us from a distance. He knows better than to interfere with our play.

Our running through the house wakes Karen. 'Heavens, it's Sunday and all the noise woke me. I'll open the door to your garden and go back to sleep.'

We both rush out and check our territory. Simon follows and does his own checking. Dog checking is less thorough – just a few sniffs. Then he establishes ownership of his garden with a long pee. He has reluctantly accepted that his area starts at the tall, black rock half-way down the garden and ends at the new wire fence. Learning for him has been the hard way, with paw swipes and hisses if he pees on our rocks and plants or eats them. Rolling on our grass is out too. He has plenty of his own. The half tree is virtually sacred. He is not allowed near it. Naturally we keep out of his garden. He is a dirty animal, as all dogs are, and his part of the garden smells disgusting. Just as well Tony washes him regularly, hoses the rocks and grass and picks up poos too, as dogs don't bury them like we do.

Simon wants his turn to play. We are both tired and ignore him. When he sees Honey at the fence he barks insistently. His barking continues until Karen opens the side gate. Honey bounds in and we sniff the air. Honey is dirtier than Simon. What an odour! I forget their smell and find watching them play entertaining. We've seen them play before and know that they have their own rules for each game. Their bodies are low, eyes narrowed, and they growl softly as they begin their mock fight. Watching their bottoms wiggles is best. They play chase like we do in a rough way and bite each other. Their favourite game is grabbing each other's faces. They roll over, stop and start playing, stare and pounce as they have fun. Suddenly, the fun stops. Simon has grown and is the same size as Honey and he has become more of a threat than he was as a puppy. Honey's eyes flash. She snarls showing her teeth, and a real fight is about to take place. Fortunately, Karen makes loud banging noises to stops them and chases Honey home through the gate. Simon hasn't faced an attack before and he crouches in fear with his tail between his legs.

'Both you and George are babies, and must toughen up', she says stroking Simon's head.

Bella has left the garden for the warm heating vents. The quiet is delightful and I can do as I wish. The bare area is like a racetrack and I run around it to keep warm and fit. There is nothing worth chasing apart from rats on their way to the warmth of the house. I patrol the fences on both sides of our garden and notice a sleek, green-eyed, cat beauty at the opposite fence. We greet each other with loud purrs. Only a few month ago, she paced the fence and called to me in seductive meows. Unable to resist her intense perfume, I crawled under the fence to visit her. I was a virile, entire cat then. Now that I'm neutered, that terrible word, a vital part of my male life is gone, but not forgotten. I miss chasing female cats and often dream of responding to them. Anyway, Tony has closed the hole under the fence. All I can do is dream about her.

She leaves, and I am about to run inside, when a soft, human voice calls, 'Hello, lovely Kitty.'

A small Human wearing a coat, scarf and hat obscuring most of her face stands at the fence. I move closer and watch her. She appears to be shy.

'You're a beautiful kitty and with such pretty, blue eyes.'

I keep away from most children other than George. They are unpredictable, pull our ears or tails and put their fingers in our eyes.

She starts to cry. 'Mamma is busy and she left me with my sister. She's horrid and says nasty things.'

I am not like Bella who brims with empathy for Humans, but somehow, this child's distress concerns me. I move closer to the fence, close enough for her to touch me with her tiny fingers. When she hears her sister calling, she runs inside.

On clear days, she waits at the fence for me. We are becoming friends and I look forward to seeing her. Today, she is at the fence while her mother puts her washing on the line.

'Hello my beautiful friend,' she says. Her mother watches and smiles.

I purr for her and let her touch me through the wire for longer.

'I have a surprise, a pressie for you, Kitty,' she whispers.

Her tiny hand opens and she passes some chicken through the wire. Chicken is always welcome and I eat it quickly.

'Maybe I can steal more for you tomorrow, Kitty,' she says, before running off.

Days of rain keep the child away. When the sun returns she is not at the fence. I forget about her until her mother knocks on our front door. Karen greets her and invites her inside. They drink tea and chat, while I listen from a corner of the room.

'Maya has been a sickly child. Her health improved this year so she was able to go to school. Sadly, she's had a relapse and is back in bed. The doctor says she must rest.'

'Oh, I'm sorry. Poor Maya. Can I help?'

'Well, yes, she talks about your cat all the time ... the lovely Siamese. Before her relapse she insisted on waiting to see him every morning at the fence. Now she's asking to see him again.'

'I didn't know about Maya and Oliver. He is usually afraid of strange children and avoids them. Certainly I can bring him to visit her.'

The mother thanks Karen and leaves.

Karen is brushing me. The brush stokes are invigorating and sensually pleasing. I purr loudly.

'You are visiting Maya, your friend next door. Let's make you look your handsome best.' She dangles something in her hand. 'I think this new blue collar with these little jewels will suit your eyes perfectly.'

She changes my collar and then forces me into the oppressive harness and lead. At the front door she calls me to follow her. I am not accustomed to going out through the front of the house and I obstinately refuse to go out. After several attempts to urge me to follow her she gives up. She carries me the short distance next door in her arms.

Maya's mother greets us warmly. 'She'll be thrilled that

you're here. I hope your cat can perk up her mood. She's hardly eating and sleeping poorly.'

I smell the carpets and furniture in the house. A cat lived here many cat moons ago. After allowing me a quick rub of my scent, Karen pulls on my lead. I follow the two Humans to Maya's bedroom.

She claps her hands. 'Hello, you've come, beautiful kitty! I'm so happy!'

'My kitty's name is Oliver and he is a Siamese cat,' Karen says stroking me.

'Oliver is a lovely name. It suits him,' Maya says.

Her room smells of Maya and her gentleness.

'Please take that off him.' She points to my harness and lead. 'He doesn't need it here.' Maya pats her be and I realise she wants me to jump up onto it. I hesitate before joining her.

'I'll leave Oliver here with Maya and come back for him later. I brought a small litter tray for him, some of his food for Maya to feed him and he'll need some water too.'

I am on the bed with everything I need. Karen is a Human who cares about our needs. Now I understand why Bella thinks of her as her Human mother. Karen strokes me and whispers cat sounds. Then she waves and is gone. My tummy lurches and I am scared. I am alone with this sick child and I don't know what to do. I am not a therapy cat. If only Bella was here to help me. As hard as I try to remember what Bella has told me about her work, my cat mind is as blank as an empty food bowl. All I know is that Bella shows children her affection by cuddling close to them and purring. My inner cat would prefer to sit on the end of the bed, wash myself, and then sleep. I am here with a job to perform and I must try my best.

Maya strokes my fur and I move closer and purr. I have a loud purr like all Siamese cats.

'Come to me beautiful, Oliver,' she says. She places her head next to mine. At first, I recoil. Strange Humans so close make me uneasy. I suppress my urge to move away as her gentle fingers relax me until cuddling comes naturally. I snuggle up to her. She is happy and I am too. It was easier than I thought.

We both sleep until Maya's mother opens the door. 'Food for Maya and for you, Oliver. A bowl of food is on the floor.'

Maya eats and her mother smiles. I realise how hungry I am. After eating a few of my cat biscuits, Maya's mother places a small bowl of strong-smelling fish in the bowl for me.

'Sardines, Oliver. My cat Tammie, bless her, loved them.'

Delicious! I eat with relish.

'I feel a bit better, Mum. I want to sit in the chair and play with Oliver.'

'That's a good idea, I'll find some toys.'

Maya climbs out of bed slowly and takes a few tentative steps towards the chair.

'I've put a small ball, string and some other bits and pieces in this box. Cats like boxes,' her mother says. 'Play together.'

Though the toys look uninteresting, I try to please Maya. She throws the ball down the passage for me. I run after it and return it to her.

'You are such a clever kitty, Oliver.'

She throws it again. I have had enough of the ball and lie on the carpet.

'Enough ball, let's play with this.' She produces a shiny thing at the end of a string. When she dangles it, it becomes a creature that I can't resist. I chase it across the carpet and behind the sofa. What fun! I hear her giggle with pleasure.

Karen arrives to take me home. I run to Maya and rub her ankles. I like her and she is mine now.

'Oliver was wonderful with Maya. She had a little to eat and was up playing with him. I hope he can visit again,' her mother says.

When we arrive home, Karen places me on the sofa. 'I didn't realise I had two therapy cats. Oliver, you were great with Maya,' she says, stroking me from the tender spot on my head to the tip of my tail. Bella is too curious about my visit next door to wait. She stands before me demanding to know all the details. I take cat time, embellishing the scene and my actions. Even if she guesses I am embroidering details, she shows her delight with purrs and head butts. She is proud of me.

I look forward to visiting Maya. I think of her gentleness often during the day and wonder what she is doing. She must be an exceptional young Human to involve me in this way, as I haven't felt warmth and caring for Humans other than for Tony, Karen, Jodi and Pops.

Throughout the winter, Karen or Jodi take me to visit Maya. We cuddle, eat together and play. Her health is gradually improving and she can walk around the house. On sunny days we play on the patio.

This is a new, valuable experience. Now I understand Bella's job helping sad and sick Humans. I am pleased with myself. I have proved that there is more to me than my handsome appearance. Though I doubt that I could be a therapy cat like Bella and shower strange Humans in hospitals with the same affection I give to Maya. At least I am not just a superficial show cat.

The sun appears more often and shoots of green pop up from the dull earth. Maya is not at the fence or in the garden.

I guess she is sick again. I wait for her mother's phone call asking me to visit. The call comes and Karen takes me to Maya.

She's asleep in her bed and her hair covers most of her face.

'Let Oliver wake her, she'll like that,' her mother says.

Karen places me on the bed. I touch Maya's arm gently with my paw and she wakes.

'Oh, what a lovely surprise. Hello Oliver!'

She sits, propping herself up against her pillows. The paleness of her skin and her shallow breathing tells me she is not well.

'Poor Maya has had another relapse. Her doctor gave her medication and I'm hoping it will help her.'

Karen and the mother talk, while Maya strokes me from head to paw. What Bliss!

I am almost asleep next to Maya, when her mother says, 'We've decided to buy Maya a kitten. As much as she loves Oliver, she needs her own cat to care for. It will help her recovery.'

Shock grabs me like the claw of a huge tomcat. I take a few moments to absorb what Maya's mother has just said. She will have her own kitten and no longer need me. I sit up and move away from Maya. I look at her pale face and jump onto the floor. When I stand at the door meowing, Karen realises I want to go.

'I'd better take Oliver home now. I hope Maya recovers soon and that she has lots of joy with her new kitten.'

Karen answers her phone. She is talking to Maya's mother. 'So, you've bought twin kittens for Maya ... and they look like Oliver. How lovely!'

I run to my basket and hide. She has two kittens to replace me.

'Simon, Bella, where are you?' Karen calls. 'Maya is better and playing in the garden with her kittens. She is missing you, Oliver, and wants to show you her kittens.' She pushes Lily in a contraption with wheels that she calls a pram and George stumbles after her. We take our time to follow her to the fence. Maya is sitting on the grass waiting for us, playing with her two identical kittens, both cream with brown tipped ears and paws. Bella pushes me aside and moves as close to the fence as possible. She meows softly to call the kittens and rubs her head against the wire. Then I have a turn and see the tiny kittens that have taken my place in Maya's heart. They are Siamese kittens and probably look something like me. I turn my back on Maya and the kittens.

George puts his fingers through the wire and tries to touch them. 'Pretty kitties, cute kitties,' he says.

Karen shows Lily the kittens and the little one chuckles and smiles.

Maya calls out to me, 'Oliver, I will miss you lots, but you belong to George and Lily and can't be with me all the time. Thank you for helping me to recover, and please come and visit me. You will always be my favourite.'

I run off. I will miss spending time with Maya, but I'm not good at taking second place and won't visit her. I tried my best to help her and learned about being cat therapist.

 # Bella

We do yoga many times a day.

I am relaxing in a warm spot sheltered from the wind. Simon is barking and his tail is wagging, signalling that he wants to play again. Oliver has had his fill of exercise and ignores Simon.

Just as I begin my cleaning routine, I hear scratching at the fence. Oliver's ears quiver. Simon growls and I sniff a strange, unpleasant odour. Catland is under attack! Three feral rabbits have tunnelled under the wire into our garden to eat our flowers and leaves. They are nothing like the tame, white, pet rabbits, that escaped a from their hutch and found their way into our garden a few months ago. They were gentle rabbits that made clucking and purring sounds while nibbling grass. The feral rabbits smell foul and are aggressive. Even though cats and dogs are rabbit's predators, they stand up to the three of us thumping their paws, snorting, grunting and hissing. Simon is too young to think of consequences. He pushes us back with his hind leg, and uttering guttural growls, lurches at the intruders. The rabbits realise his strength and grunting, scurry back under the fence.

Karen, who has been watching this minor drama from the kitchen window, giggles so much that I hope she won't burst.

She calls Jodi, 'Look at Simon attacking the rabbits. It's too funny.'

I feel a warmth towards our dog. He made sure we were out of the way before attacking the feral intruders. Simon's loyalty and protectiveness amazes us both. Cats can fend for themselves, but the little dog's instinctive reaction is touching. He has taken on the role of our protector. We are a bonded family now. Two cats and their dog.

We take our turns on Pop's bed. He is kind and tells each one of us, 'you're my favourite.' I will never know if he prefers cats to dogs, or which one of us he likes best.

He is giving me a total body massage that is pure delight. His stiff hands move slowly as they caress one tender spot and then another. I move closer and snuggle into his warmth, aware of his unusual, sweet smell. As he sleeps, I lie next to him. I wake and stretch.

'Don't go yet, Bella, my beauty, I like having you with me. I'm staying in bed, feeling so tired and dizzy...can't even read the newspaper.' He stretches for the third glass of water that morning.

I'm certain he's not well, but doesn't realise it. What do I do? It can be tough being a cat and unable to communicate with my owners. When Karen pops in to find out why Pops is still in bed, he smiles and tells her he's tired. I run to her meow loudly and point to Pops with my nose.

'What are you trying to tell me, Precious?'

I repeat the meowing and pointing.

'You're telling me that Pops has a problem.' She sits on his bed and takes his hand. 'Are you sure you're okay?' She asks him.

'I'm very tired and my eyes are blurry. I'm old and I guess it's to be expected.'

As he talks, she is aware of his sweet breath. Her forehead crinkles in worry, 'I think you need to see the doctor.'

'I'm fine, I don't need a doctor. I'm old, that's all.'

Karen has her determined look. She gives Pops a kiss, 'How about your favourite, grilled cheese and tomato sandwiches with a green salad for lunch?'

'Thanks, you're an angel.'

I follow Karen into the kitchen. 'It's you, my Bella, who is the angel. You knew Pops was sick and found a way to tell me,' she says, as she strokes my coat tenderly. She places some cheese on a plate for me. I lick my lips and eat the treat quickly.

Tony arrives early from work and goes to see his grandfather. I sit at the door and listen. 'I know you don't like doctors, but you're not well. Please let Dr Morano check you out...You like him.'

Pops sighs deeply. 'Okay, I give in. I'll shower and dress.'

Oliver looks worried. He's noticed that Pops isn't well too. Simon hasn't known Pops for long and doesn't seem to be aware of any changes.

We three animals wait at the window for Tony's car to return. Karen looks concerned and waits too. When they arrive, Pops is grumbling.

'What did Dr Morano say Pops?' Karen asks.

Pops sighs and looks at the floor, 'He wants me to go into hospital for tests. I hate hospitals.'

'I'll help you to pack a small case and we'll both take you,' Karen says as she gives Pops a hug. 'Try not to worry, your doctor is being careful, making sure about what's wrong before giving you any medication.'

Pops has been in hospital for five days and everyone misses him. George doesn't understand why his Pops isn't there. I avoid walking past his empty room as it makes me worried that he won't come back.

This morning, a big, white van stops outside the house. A Human helps Pops into the house.

'Home at last. I'm rattling with pills that I don't like to admit make me feel better.'

'We'll have to make some big changes in your food. No sugars and careful with the potato crisps and biscuits,' Karen says.

He nods. 'I don't know where my diabetes came from, but I'll have to deal with it. Thank you for looking after me, Karen and Tony.'

We watch as he goes to his room. Karen holds up her hand to stop us following him. 'He needs to rest now.'

Spring

Oliver

*We protect our Humans. After all, they provide
us with food, security and affection.*

Our garden is alive again. Birds are signing and buildings
nests, the trees have leaves and their mass of blossoms
greet the sunshine.

Buds open to perfume the air, grass covers the earth
and our pots of catnip are full. We are happy cats! We sleep
less and enjoy being outdoors where there are mice, rats,
lizards and bugs of all sorts to chase.

A family of feral rabbits are living in Simon's part of
the garden. If he approaches them with a growl, they hide
in one of their burrows. They are too comfortable for my
liking. Simon barks with joy at the seasonal changes in his
garden, running back and forth and rolling in the fresh
grass. There is no stopping him digging up roots and eating
new leaves with relish. This is his first taste of the warmer
weather and he chases butterflies, but he is too slow and
clumsy to catch them.

Karen is tired of his large paw prints on the floor and
carpets and has resorted to washing and drying his muddy
paws before allowing him inside. We are more careful
about messing. He dislikes the cleaning routine, pulls away
from her and is off to his basket to sulk. I am surprised that
he sleeps almost as much as we do.

Today his sleep is woken by the buzz of mosquitos. He

shakes his head and tries to ignore the high-pitched sounds. When he is bitten, he rubs his nose and growls. Awake now, he chases the mosquitos. As Karen opens the door to collect the post, the mosquitos fly out and Simon shoves past her following them. He runs out to explore. Karen calls him, but he takes no notice. Enjoying his freedom, he races up the driveway and disappears. Karen runs after him calling but returns without him. She takes the car to search for him and again returns without him. When Tony comes home, he visits all the neighbour's houses to look for Simon but cannot find him.

He sighs loudly. 'This is happening again. First George runs out and leads us a dance finding him, now it's Simon.'

'Where's Simon? I want Simon!' George cries.

Karen tries to reassure him that Simon will be back. Her words don't soothe George, who continues to cry.

'I hope he hasn't been stolen. He's a friendly dog and would go with anyone who is kind to him,' Karen says.

Tony looks concerned. 'He's small and therefore vulnerable. I hope he hasn't been bitten by other dogs.'

When they go to bed, they leave food outside the front and back doors hoping he will be hungry and return. Early sunspots dot the floor when I hear him scratching and whining at the front door. I wake Oliver and together we run to the big bedroom and jump on the bed to wake Karen and Tony. Karen turns over still asleep and ignores us. Tony opens his eyes and sits up. By now Simon is barking loudly.

'Okay, okay, I'm coming to let you in,' he shouts.

As the door opens, Tony has one look at Simon and calls Karen,

'Come quickly. Simon is covered in filth. Heaven knows what he's been up to.'

Karen laughs and shakes her head and laughs. 'Glad

you've decided to come home, Simon, but you won't enjoy all the cleaning.'

First, she uses a tiny comb to free all the muck from Simon's coat. Then she brushes him. He wriggles and whines. Two washes and several rinses in the tub follow. The process isn't finished yet. Once Simon is dry, she checks for tiny bleeding spots and applies ointment. Poor Simon was bitten.

She pats his head, 'Off you go, but don't do that again.'

We look at each other and hide in case Karen decides to bath us too.

He is a black, curly bundle huddled in his basket. We are relieved he is back and lie next to him. The following day we leave his basket and ignore him as before.

Simon is not yet accustomed to the idea that life is not perfect, that something big or small can occur to cause discomfort or disruption at any time. His complaints are about minor changes in routine, or if his food isn't exactly to his liking. This is where an ability to adapt is of key importance. We can't expect too much of him. He is a dog.

The house has it challenges. Lily is growing teeth and makes an intolerable noise that upsets our sensitive, feline ears and interferes with our sleep. She vomits, pees and poos endlessly. Poor Karen cleans and changes her often. I can't wait for her to become more independent and turn into a little Human like George. With caring for Lily and George's demands, Karen hardly has any time for us cats.

Today the delightful warmth has disappeared and cold rain drums on the roof. The weather changes every day and winds swirl. My stomach aches, my blocked throat throbs, and I cough from the mass of hair that moults from my coat at this time of year. Simon is coughing loudly too, and his teary eyes are burning. I vomit on the carpet to rid myself of another fur ball and Simon vomits on a different spot of the carpet.

When Karen sees the vomit, she shrugs. 'You, Bella have fur balls and I think Simon has hay fever,' she says, as she scrubs the carpet. 'I can't complain of having nothing to do.' Pops remains in his room. Either he sleeps or relaxes in filtered sunlight on his lazy chair. He is like an old cat who lies in his basket and comes out only for meals. We take turns in visiting him so that one of us is with him almost all day. Spending time with Maya taught me how to make Humans feel more at ease and I'm using my knowledge with Pops, snuggling up higher on his chest to keep him warm, purring loudly and giving him head butts so that he knows I care. I'm enjoying giving him affection and he seems to know it.

'Oliver, you're a handsome cat and you've matured. You're a cat with a lot of heart.'

He stokes the pleasure spot on my head and whispers, 'I want you here with me every day.' I know now that he prefers cats to dogs, so Simon comes last. I will never know if he prefers Bella to me. It doesn't matter, if he finds pleasure in being with us both and is able to recover.

Pops has his meal and complains that it lacks taste without fat, sugar and salt, but he eats most of it. He opens a small tin of tuna for me. It's a new make with a light sauce and I can't eat it fast enough. I lick my lips and purr. Life is wonderful. I am being fed scrumptious food and helping Pops. Being useful makes me happy.

Pops is growing stronger, and today for the first time, he takes a brief walk in the garden to admire the spring blossoms and flowers. He is exhausted after his exercise and collapses on his bed.

'I will persevere Oliver. I must, or I'll end up in a wheelchair.'

I jump onto the bed and snuggle up to him. I hope that he will improve by summer.

Karen is talking on her phone. I listen to the conversation about the birth of puppies.

'So, you think that our Simon could be the father? Six puppies, all small, black and white and woolly. How wonderful! I'll come and see them later.'

I keep the information I overheard secret and wait until Karen has seen the puppies. She is excited when she returns from visiting our neighbour.

'Wow! What adorable puppies. Where are you Simon? You made five adorable puppies with Honey,' she says. 'They are small with floppy ears and fluffy coats.'

He barks and goes to her.

'I'll take you to see them.'

'I want to see the puppies too,' George says, jumping up and down.

I look up at Karen and meow. 'Yes, Oliver. You and Bella will see them too.'

Karen calls Simon. Wearing a harness and lead has been part of his training, and unlike us cats, he wears the harness without complaint.

'Come, Daddy Simon,' she says with a laugh, as she clips on his lead. Simon follows her out the door wagging his tail. Perhaps he understands that he is visiting his puppies. He might be smarter than I thought.

After his visit, he rushes inside wagging his tail frenetically.

'I think Simon recognised his puppies. He barked a happy bark and licked them all,' Karen says. 'This is Honey's first and last litter of puppies. Her owner is not pleased with so many to look after.'

Today, the neighbour brings the puppies to the fence so that George can see them. We follow. The three black puppies and two mixed black and white, woolly creatures look much like kittens. They are agitated without their Mama, and the neighbour carries them back inside.

'Aren't you lucky to have their daddy!' Karen says to George.

Whenever Maya is in the garden, she calls Simon, but he ignores her. I can tell by the way his nose quivers that she has upset him. This morning Maya calls Oliver to the fence again. He turns his back on her and twists his head away.

'Come on, Oliver, you know I love you best. You're the cat who helped me when I was sick.'

Finally, he turns towards her. She thrusts a tiny tin of jellied prawns through the fence wire. 'There, a pressie for you, my very special cat, Oliver.'

He eats quickly, emptying the tin and licks his lips.

Bella

Each day in a cat's life is special.

The sun's glow is weak, but at least I am relaxing in a spot sheltered from the wind and falling blossoms. I hear scratching at the fence. Oliver's ears quiver. Simon growls and I sniff a recognisable odour. Wild rabbits. A large group of them have tunnelled under the wire into our garden to join the rabbit family already established in Simon's part of the garden. All the rabbits appear from their tunnels to greet the newcomers. There is now a mass of them. The biggest ones are standing up aggressively hissing, grunting and growling. I feel no fear as a throbbing juice flows through me. Simon appears and barks his warning bark. Oliver and I look at each other. We know what to do. We will attack the feral intruders daring to enter our territory. Oliver arches his back and I form a bristling ball. We hiss loudly.

Karen appears holding Lily in her arms. 'Oh, my goodness! We have a war in the garden.'

She puts Lily down and reappears with a long broom in her hands.

'Scat, rabbits! Get going!' she shouts, lunging at them with the broom.

Some of the rabbits move back, others scurry away and the largest ones hiss at her and hold their ground.

'Come, Simon, Oliver, Bella, inside. Now!'

When Karen is that insistent, we obey her and follow

her into the house. She locks the small door that leads into our garden and mutters, 'You're all to stay indoors now.'

She talks to Tony on the phone, 'I'm going to do something about the rabbits immediately,' she says.

Later a tall Human in dark clothing stomps into our garden. He talks to Karen and moves his hands about pointing to the rabbit burrows. He starts work and Karen comes inside.

'We have to get rid of the rabbits. So, cats, you'll be staying inside the house for a few days. And Simon, you will be inside most of the time too. We'll let you out into the big garden for short periods.'

We have no choice, we are all inside but we understand, the rabbits must go.

Days pass until the Human says it is safe for us to return to our garden. What a mess it is! Earth is overturned where deep tunnels must've been. Our flowers have been stomped on and are shrivelled. As most of the rabbits were in Simon's part of the garden, it's now mostly earth and stones. He looks at the mess and howls.

'At least the rabbits have gone,' Karen says in her kindest voice. 'Tony has promised to fix it as best as he can over the weekend.'

The love I feel for Karen now extends to Tony. He works in our garden over the whole weekend. It isn't the same as it was, but we have a new garden now, with flowers that will bloom soon and grass that will grow. Our half-tree is still here and the pots are filled with catnip.

I thank Bastet for freeing us from the stinking rabbits and helping Tony to repair our garden. We are lucky cats indeed.

We sit on the patio in the dappled light. I am next to Karen. Oliver is on Tony's lap and Simon is at George's feet. Pops is asleep in his chair and little Lily is on Karen's lap. She smiles and her mouth makes little bubbles. When my eyes are half-closed, I see a white, glowing light around her. It is a light of goodness, even brighter and purer than the light that shines around Karen. Lily looks at me and I feel her warmth and love. There is much to look forward to in Catland.

Acknowledgements

My cats and dogs over a lifetime have been a great source of love and joy and I have learned so much from them. When I decided to write about cats and their interaction with dogs, I drew on my own experiences with my pets plus much research.

My thanks for help with writing "Bella – an Ordinary cat with an Extraordinary gift ", and this book, "Dawn in Catland", go to firstly to my Husband Hymie who has given me months of support, his invaluable suggestions and his observations about our cats. Sylvie Blair from BookPod has provided me with her friendly, patient support with my writing and illustrations, as well as her own suggestions and expertise in formatting the book. My friends who have cats of their own have shown their interest in both my books about cats and added some of their own experiences that have been incorporated in my writing.

About the Author

Joan has spent most of her working life as a counsellor, but now devotes her time to writing. She lives in Melbourne with her husband and their new cat, Lily. Though she has written non-fiction books and novels she is now writing about cats, her life- long interest and passion. "Dawn in Catland" follows her first novel about cats, "Bella-an ordinary cat with an extraordinary gift."